The Lost Secret of Ireland

BOOKS BY SUSANNE O'LEARY

STARLIGHT COTTAGES SERIES
The Lost Girls of Ireland

THE SANDY COVE SERIES
Secrets of Willow House
Sisters of Willow House
Dreams of Willow House
Daughters of Wild Rose Bay
Memories of Wild Rose Bay
Miracles in Wild Rose Bay

The Road Trip
A Holiday to Remember

Susanne O'Leary

The Lost Secret of Ireland

Bookouture

Published by Bookouture in 2021

An imprint of Storyfire Ltd.
Carmelite House
50 Victoria Embankment
London EC4Y 0DZ

www.bookouture.com

ISBN: 978-1-80019-918-7
eBook ISBN: 978-1-80019-917-0

For Eoghan, Peter, Grace, Louis, Oscar and Daniel,
the best grandchildren in the world.

Chapter One

Eight weeks after the accident, Ella's life took an interesting turn. It all started with a phone call from Lucille, her late mother's best friend.

Ella was still recovering from a fracture. She had fallen from a ladder while putting the final touches to an eight-foot mural in one of Killarney's biggest hotels. It was a huge seascape with many details, especially of birds and clouds that were tricky to paint. She had concentrated so hard on getting it right that she hadn't paid attention, even when the rickety ladder started to wobble. Before she could do anything to save herself, she had crashed to the ground and been unable to move until the ambulance arrived taking her to hospital. That had been two months ago. Now she was sitting on the terrace of her cottage in Sandy Cove, looking out over the ocean, the early morning sun casting a golden glow on the glittering sea. She could see a small fishing boat with a red hull approaching the harbour and wondered what kind of catch they were bringing in. Had the nets been full of hake and cod, ready for the market? Or maybe they had caught some monkfish as well, which might be on the menu at the little seafood restaurant in the village that evening. She thought longingly of a night out there with friends when her phone rang.

Startled out of her musings, she picked it up. 'Hello?' she said, her voice a little faint.

'Hello, Ella,' Lucille said. 'How are you?'

The familiar voice made Ella sit up. Lucille called Ella occasionally but they hadn't been in touch much lately. 'Hello, Lucille,' she said. 'How nice to hear from you.'

'Sorry for not calling sooner,' Lucille said. 'But I've been a little busy. And I didn't want to disturb you while you were recovering. But I hope you're beginning to feel better by now?'

'Yes. I'm making fairly good progress,' Ella said. 'I'll be off the crutches in a week or two. How about you? Are you well?'

'No. Getting worse,' Lucille said darkly. 'I can't hack this living on my own much longer. It's very boring.'

'I know,' Ella said, feeling sorry for Lucille. She and Ella's mother Rose had lived together in Lucille's huge Georgian mansion in Tipperary for over five years. When Rose had sadly passed away two years ago she'd left Lucille to live on her own. It had to be very hard to get used to being all alone after so long. 'You must miss Mum very much.'

'Yes, I do. Terribly. Nobody to argue with and no more giggles.'

'You and Mum were such close friends,' Ella said. 'Closer than anyone I know. It doesn't surprise me that it's taking some getting used to.'

'Yes.' Lucille sighed. 'That's why I'm calling you. Just for a little chat, really. And a suggestion. Do you have time to listen?'

'Of course,' Ella said. 'Go ahead,' she continued, her heart going out to Lucille as she heard the sadness in her voice.

Poor thing, she must be so sad and lonely, Ella thought. Lucille and Rose had both been widows when they'd moved in together. They had been friends since childhood but had lost touch when they both graduated. But they had met up again at a class reunion over five years ago and had rekindled their friendship. Lucille had lost her husband fifteen years earlier and Rose had just become a widow after the death of Manfred, Ella's father, and was trying to cope with her loss.

Fed up with living alone, Lucille had suggested that Rose move in with her, which had been a huge relief to Ella, who, as an only child, was the sole carer for her mother at the time. With Lucille as companion, Rose was no longer on her own and the two women cared for and supported each other, which gave Ella the freedom she craved as an artist. She had moved into the cottage in Kerry she had just bought, where she was inspired by the stunning scenery of the sea and mountains. It also allowed her to travel to Paris when she wanted, where her paintings were often exhibited and sold to lovers of dramatic seascapes. Her other career as the illustrator of children's books also took off as the little village and its surroundings gave her the peace she needed for her work. It was the perfect guilt-free resolution for her, to see her mother living with Lucille.

Lucille and Rose were happy together for around five years and rural life in Tipperary seemed to suit Rose, who loved animals and gardening. They had three dogs, two cats and a flock of hens. Ella would visit and would always be pleased to see her mother enjoying life again after the death of her husband. It all seemed so perfect and peaceful that Ella began to believe this would last, if not forever, for a long time to come anyway. But then, just as Ella was about to travel to Paris for an exhibition of her paintings, she got the news that Rose had died suddenly.

'Heart attack,' Lucille had told Ella on the phone through tears. 'So sorry, darling.'

'Oh no,' Ella whispered, her eyes welling up with tears.

'She didn't suffer,' Lucille said in a soothing tone. 'And you know, at our age, that's a blessing.'

'It's not a blessing for me,' Ella said and started to cry. 'I can't believe she's gone, Lucille. Oh God, this is such a shock.' Unable to say anything else, Ella had hung up. She had cried uncontrollably as it sank in that she would never see her mother again, never hear her voice or feel her arms around her. This was a terrible grief on top of everything else that had happened to her. Ella knew she would always miss her mother no matter how much time had passed. But deep down, she knew Lucille was right. Her mother would have hated to be a burden on anyone.

In the days that followed the news, Ella had remembered a saying of her mother's: 'I don't mind dying, but I don't want to be half-dead.' She knew her mother didn't want to be frail and dependent, that she'd want Ella to look on the bright side, as she always had. And when she spoke to Lucille about the funeral, Lucille agreed.

'She's in a better place now,' Lucille said. 'A much happier place, with your dad.'

'That's a nice thought, of course,' Ella said. 'But I hoped she might hang around a little longer.'

'She hadn't been that well lately,' Lucille said. 'She was very tired and our doctor thought she should go to see a specialist. But it was too late.' Lucille sighed. 'I'm rather cross with her, to tell you the truth. She left just like that, without saying goodbye.'

'I'm so sorry for you,' Ella said, holding back her tears, realising that Lucille was just as devastated to lose her friend.

'There's nobody like Rose,' Lucille said with feeling.

'But you have a family,' Ella said, trying to console Lucille despite her own grief.

'I suppose,' Lucille said, sounding as if her family wouldn't offer her much comfort.

Ella had often seen the two sons when she was at the house for weekend visits, and she hadn't taken to the older one at all. But Rory, the younger of the two, had been more her type, despite his hot temper. He had always been ready to argue with Ella on any topic under the sun, which she had secretly enjoyed as their repartee was often just for fun. But she forgot about them while she and Lucille planned Rose's funeral, which, with Lucille's help, was beautiful but incredibly sad.

Now two years had passed, and Ella was recovering from something very different.

She'd fallen quite suddenly, and had been lucky that her injuries weren't worse. After a week in hospital, she had spent two months in bed, as her doctor had ordered complete bed rest so, with the help of friends and neighbours, managed to survive the first horrible weeks. She had improved physically but not mentally. The memory of hitting the tiled floor in the hotel where she was painting the mural was still fresh in her mind, giving her nightmares and flashes of anxiety.

'So you're getting around now?' Lucille asked.

'On crutches, but yes, I'm feeling nearly human. I'm still quite weak, though, which is frustrating.'

'You're having physiotherapy?' Lucille asked.

'Yes, and it's excruciating. But my physio says that two months in bed has atrophied my muscles and I need to work hard to get my strength back. You have no idea how broken I've felt.'

'Is anyone looking after you at home?' Lucille wanted to know.

'Nobody is living here, but there's a whole gang of friends in the village taking turns to help out. My lovely Dutch neighbour is on standby if I should take a turn during the night. It's like having an army of nurses at my beck and call.'

'Is that good or bad?' Lucille asked.

'Uh… a bit of both, to be honest,' Ella said, amused by how astute Lucille was. 'There's always someone walking into the house looking at me as if I'm completely helpless.' Ella looked at her breakfast of bacon, eggs, soda bread, a bowl of chopped fruit and another with porridge. 'And they're feeding me like a battery hen. I'll be as big as a house if I eat everything they give me. Honestly,' Ella muttered into the phone, 'it's getting on my nerves not to be able to manage on my own.'

'How annoying,' Lucille declared. 'Especially for someone as independent as you. I know how you love your own space and being as free as a bird.'

Ella sighed. 'Exactly. Everyone hovering around like this is hard for me. I know they mean well, and I should be grateful, but…'

'I know,' Lucille said, her voice full of sympathy. 'But you know what? I think you need someone to actually live with you. Someone you're not afraid to tell off, who will do what you want but leaves you alone at the same time.'

'Sounds great,' Ella said with a wishful sigh. 'But where will I find such a person?'

'Right here,' Lucille stated. 'I'm coming down to Kerry to look after you.'

'What?' Ella asked, alarmed. Although she loved Lucille dearly, she was also rather eccentric – always up to something. 'When?'

'Right now,' Lucille said. 'I'll be there tomorrow, so then you can call off the troops.'

'But I…' Ella protested. 'I mean, I don't think…'

'No ifs or buts,' Lucille said sternly. 'I'm already packing. I know you have a guest room, and I'll make my own bed and so on. I do have a little trouble getting upstairs, but I'll manage.'

'There's a stairlift,' Ella said, despite wanting to put Lucille off. 'The one I put in for Mum. It came in handy after the accident but I was going to have it dismantled when I get back to normal.'

'Perfect,' Lucille chanted. 'See you tomorrow, then,' she said and hung up before Ella had a chance to say anything else.

Ella groaned and put her phone on the table.

'What's wrong?' someone said behind her.

Ella turned and discovered her neighbour Saskia standing in the doorway with a teapot. 'Nothing much, except I seem to have a new nurse coming to look after me. My mother's friend Lucille.'

Saskia put the teapot on the table and sat down on the chair next to Ella. 'But isn't that great?'

'It would be if it weren't an arthritic eighty-five-year-old woman with attitude.'

'Oh,' Saskia said. 'That could be tricky.'

'To put it mildly. She's already busy packing her things, whatever those are.'

'How is she getting here?' Saskia asked, sweeping her mane of black hair out of her eyes.

'She's driving, God help us,' Ella said with an exasperated sigh. 'She has this old Volvo estate that she drives all over the country to visit people. Don't know how she manages to pass the medical tests, but she does.'

'She must be in good nick then,' Saskia remarked, lifting the teapot. 'More tea?'

'No thanks,' Ella said, pushing away her plate. 'And thanks for the huge breakfast, but it was a little too much for me.'

'Yes, it would be for someone whose breakfast usually consists of black coffee and a croissant,' Saskia said with a touch of scorn in her voice. 'You picked up some bad habits in France.'

'Oh, I know. But at least I don't smoke a Gauloises first thing, like my ex-husband,' Ella said, with a pang of nostalgia as she remembered those three tempestuous years of marriage in Paris with Jean-Paul. 'But I liked the smell of them, I have to admit. Even now if ever anyone smokes one of those, it takes me right back to Paris, if you know what I mean.'

Saskia nodded. 'I know what you mean about certain smells. It can be like a time machine. If I smell pickled herring, I'm back in Holland eating *maatjes* in springtime when I was young. My ex used to love them. But that was a long time ago.'

'Do you think you might start dating again if you meet someone you fancy?' Ella asked.

Saskia waved her hand. 'No, I don't think I will. I like my peaceful life.'

'I don't,' Ella said with an impatient sigh. 'I can't wait to be mobile again so I can get back to painting. And I wouldn't mind meeting a dishy man with whom I can be desperately unhappy.'

'You have to try to find someone who's nice,' Saskia remarked.

'Nice men are less interesting.'

'But more loyal. Why don't you try to eat more?'

Ella looked apologetically at Saskia. 'I managed to finish the porridge, but the eggs and bacon were too much for me. Sorcha doesn't give me such a big breakfast.'

'I got the morning shift today,' Saskia said as if she had drawn the shortest straw.

Ella let out a laugh. 'You two took this on as some kind of mission. With Brian as a backup.'

'Brian is a nice man,' Saskia remarked. 'And single,' she added, waggling her black eyebrows.

'I wouldn't inflict myself on him. I'm sure our local vet has more important concerns than looking after me. You have all been so amazingly kind,' Ella added. 'This way I can recuperate at home and don't need to be in a hospital, which would have been awful.'

'Well, this is what we do around here,' Saskia stated. 'I have to say I like it. In my country, you would still have been in hospital. Dutch people aren't as helpful and kind as in this part of the world.'

'It's unique to this village,' Ella agreed.

'That's true,' Saskia said. 'I hope my new neighbours will be as helpful.'

'You have new neighbours?' Ella asked, sitting up.

Saskia nodded. 'Yes. Jason is letting his house for the summer. He and Lydia are moving in together now that Lydia's daughter has finished school and is going abroad for a gap year before she starts university.'

'Oh. I missed this news. I'm glad Jason and Lydia are finally going to live together. They were dithering about it long enough.' It was true. Jason and Lydia's love story was well known in the village. Lydia had arrived at the little coastguard station and moved into the cottage she had inherited from her great aunt two years ago after the death of her husband. Jason had helped and supported her through the first hard year and they had fallen in love but had been living in separate houses until now.

'Oh yes, me too. They seem very happy to be together at last.'

'Who's the new neighbour then?'

'I haven't met them yet. But I plan to knock on their door once they're settled and introduce myself,' Saskia declared. 'And once you're a bit more mobile, I'll do a coffee morning for them or something and we'll all get to know each other.'

'I'll be more mobile very soon,' Ella promised. 'I know it's been hard work to look after me. Especially the first few weeks.'

'It hasn't been too bad,' Saskia said. 'Except that you've been a little bit cranky at times. Understandable but from this end, it can be irritating.'

'I know,' Ella said, feeling a dart of guilt. 'I'm sorry about that.'

'Oh, that's okay,' Saskia soothed. 'Now that your mother's friend is coming, we can relax a bit.'

'I wouldn't be too sure,' Ella muttered. 'She might cause more trouble than we think.'

'At her age? Would she have the energy?'

'You don't know Lucille,' Ella said.

Saskia laughed and started to clear the table. 'I'm dying to meet her.'

'You won't have to wait long,' Ella said, thinking of the conversation with Lucille. She suddenly felt puzzled at Lucille's sudden decision to take off from the house that she loved so much. Was it simply loneliness? Or something to do with her two sons? Some kind of family row? Ella thought of the sons and how they hadn't been very supportive about her mother moving in. Martin, the elder, had been stiffly polite to her on many occasions. He seemed suspicious of both her and her mother, and Ella had wondered if it had to do with the size of Lucille's house with several hundred acres attached and possibly quite a lot of money in the bank. And what about Rory? Good-looking, but moody, she had thought when they first met. There was a touch of resentment behind his teasing Ella all the time. Or maybe he was jealous? Ella had been quite puzzled by his behaviour towards her when they often clashed and sniped at each other. And now Lucille was coming here to look after Ella. What would her sons think of that?

'I'll put these in the dishwasher before I leave,' Saskia said as she started to walk into the house with the remains of Ella's breakfast.

'Thanks,' Ella said and heaved herself up with the help of the crutches. 'I'll go and do my physio exercises and then I'll do some sketching for the new children's book I've been commissioned to illustrate. Lovely story about a little girl who meets a lost bear in the forest and she helps him find his way home. There are a lot of wild animals in the forest that the little girl makes friends with. And then she discovers how climate change is threatening their habitat. It's meant to teach kids how they can do little things to contribute to saving the planet. Beautifully told, I have to say.'

'Sounds lovely,' Saskia agreed over her shoulder and then disappeared indoors.

'Yes,' Ella said to herself when she was alone again. 'It's a lovely story. But how will I draw it so it appeals to children?'

Ella adored children and the fact that she hadn't been able to have any was the greatest sorrow of her life. She had always dreamed of having a family, but that dream had been dashed when during her marriage she'd endured several miscarriages. The road she had taken to try to build a family had been painful and eventually she had given up. It was all just too hard on her. And her marriage, which had been a last-ditch attempt at building a family. She and Jean-Paul had finally divorced as a result of their failure to conceive. That was five years ago, which seemed like only yesterday sometimes.

After the divorce, she had directed all of her energy into her art and her illustrations. Painting had been her first love and she had carved out a successful career in France as her paintings sold well there. Illustration had been just a sideline until now, when she found herself unable to stand at an easel for long. The children's books she had worked on before had been easy, requiring quite traditional artwork, but this one was special as it would convey an important message and teach children about the importance of protecting the environment. It was quite a challenge and one she wasn't sure she could meet in her weakened state.

Ella had found that her mental energy had suffered as a result of her accident and she didn't feel the usual enthusiasm for her commission. But she had to try; her contract demanded it and she needed the income as her painting work had stalled – she wouldn't be paid for the mural in the hotel in Killarney until she finished it. But how could she? The thought of getting on that ladder again made her feel sick with fear. The trauma of the accident, the pain and the horrible sensation of her body being broken were still so vivid. She would probably never recover from that. Someone else would have to finish the mural, someone with more courage than her, and perhaps better balance.

Ella decided to forget about the mural and her painting for the moment and concentrate on her recovery and the project she had just embarked on. And now Lucille... Would her arrival bring fresh problems? Ella felt a shiver of premonition as she gazed towards the horizon and a mass of dark clouds approaching. It looked as if stormy weather was heading her way. But she was used to that. Stormy weather – in one way or another – had always been looming in Ella's life from a very young age.

Chapter Two

After a restless night, Ella woke just before sunrise. She had dreamed about going to a concert, but now she was still hearing music. Was she still dreaming? No, she could hear it clearly and it was coming from the open window. Beautiful, gentle piano music. She sat up and grabbed her crutches and limped to the window, leaning out. The sky was still dark in the west, but there was a strip of pink over the mountains in the east. A lone star shone over the bay and a soft breeze brought with it a salty tang from the sea. The piano music continued, and Ella realised it came from the house next door to Saskia's, where the French doors of the sunroom were wide open. She listened intently to the beautiful melody that made her think of the sun rippling on water on a summer's day, or a gentle breeze in the mountains.

Who was playing this heavenly music? Did it come from someone's radio? Or from Saskia's new neighbours? But there was no piano in Jason's house. Maybe it had come from somewhere else? But all the windows of the other houses in the coastguard station were closed, the curtains drawn. The music ended on a low note, the sound still resonating in the air as if riding on the first rays of the rising sun. Ella stood there, wondering if it had been a figment of her imagination in the wisps of the dream that still echoed softly through her mind. If it was a dream, she wanted it to continue.

Ella closed the window and went back to bed, yawning. The music had made her feel so relaxed and she felt like going back to sleep. She got back into bed and pulled the duvet over her. She needed to rest if she was to cope with the whirlwind that Lucille's arrival would cause. She had an eerie feeling that this quiet time was coming to an end.

But had her life ever really been quiet? The only daughter of a German professor of economics and an Irish teacher of history and English – who both worked at various European universities – Ella had grown up living in several different countries. She had had to change schools often, which hadn't been easy for a girl with a rebellious nature who didn't adapt easily to change. It had eventually resulted in her parents sending her to boarding school in both Ireland and England, ending with a short, disastrous stint at a finishing school in Switzerland, where she was supposed to become 'more polished and accomplished', as her grandmother had put it. Ella wasn't the academic type, much to the chagrin of her parents, turning instead to art in all its forms. When her parents finally gave in and agreed for her to go to the École des Beaux-Arts in Paris, Ella was over the moon. Once there, she knew she had found what she was meant to do, painting in oil being her favourite among all the different courses. She truly thrived in this world of art and completed her degree with flying colours.

If only she could have had the same luck in love, she often mused, as one relationship after another crashed and burned. Was it her fault? she often wondered and later came to the conclusion that it was her attraction to difficult, contrary men that was the source of the problem. Several disastrous relationships and a failed marriage later, she was, at the age of forty-six, now nearly resigned to a life on her own, which was perhaps lonely but a lot less stressful. Maybe, one day, she would find a mild-mannered, kind man to grow old with. But it didn't seem very likely.

Despite the lack of romance in her life, Ella was happy in the house she had bought, just after the divorce. It was at the end of a row of four cottages, which had been the coastguard station in the early nineteenth century. They all had the same layout: a porch and hall leading into a spacious kitchen that overlooked the front of the house with a view of the mountains. Then the staircase to the upper floor and a short corridor that led to the living-dining room at the back, and a sunroom that opened up to a small back garden that had breathtaking views of the bay and the ocean beyond.

Ella had been wowed by the view and not worried too much about the derelict state of the house, which she had quickly renovated. The walls had been replastered and painted, hardwood floors had been laid throughout and the two bedrooms upstairs redecorated. The wall of the tiny bathroom had been knocked down to incorporate the small boxroom, which resulted in a spa-like place with both a power shower and a jacuzzi bath. Ella had been overjoyed with the result, even though it had cost most of her savings. But, after her divorce, she was eager to turn the page and start a new life on her own in this little village on the south-west coast of Ireland.

When, shortly after her arrival, the other cottages in the row had been sold and done up, she found herself with three new neighbours, all artists who had been equally inspired by the beautiful setting of the old coastguard station. Her new life had got off to a good start.

As she sat up in bed, looking out at the window, the music having stopped, she felt at peace, despite the ache in her lower back.

*

The feeling of peace stayed with her all through the morning. Until she heard the tooting outside.

Ella, who had made her way to the front door on her crutches, peered out. 'Lucille,' she exclaimed. 'You're here already! You must have got up very early.'

Lucille, dressed in a blue silk tunic, white trousers and pink trainers, kissed Ella on both cheeks. Her white curls were blowing in the wind. 'Not at all, darling,' she replied. 'I was up at eight, which is late for me. And then I got going from Tipperary at around ten or so. I stopped in Adare on the way for a loo break and a cup of coffee at the Manor and then continued on. Nice trip, but the roads are in a shocking state in some places. Must complain to the County Council when I get a chance.' She stopped and looked at Ella. 'How are you? You look a little peaky, I have to say. Horrible accident, wasn't it?'

'Yes,' Ella agreed. 'Awful. But I'll be off these things soon if I work hard. It's a bit of a nuisance having to ask people for help all the time.' She couldn't help smiling at Lucille, who looked amazingly elegant, her white hair cut in a chin-length layered style and her face discreetly made up. Her peachy complexion only had a few wrinkles, mostly around her blue eyes, more like laughter lines.

There was just a hint of Chanel No. 5 wafting from her clothes, which added to her polished appearance.

'But now I'm here, so you don't have to ask anyone for help,' Lucille announced. 'I'm so happy to see you.'

'Me too. You look wonderful.' Ella smiled and backed into the hall, still slightly shell-shocked. Lucille's arrival felt like being hit by an avalanche. How was she going to cope with Lucille's energy? But seeing her again also brought back fond memories of Ella's mother, which was a huge comfort to her in her weakened state. 'Come in,' Ella said. 'Do you want to unload the car now or wait for a while and have some lunch?'

'I'll do it in stages,' Lucille said and grabbed her Dior handbag from the front seat. 'I'll come in and look around for a bit. Maybe try the stairlift and see the bedroom too.'

'That's fine. You can go up there now, if you want and then we can eat. One of my lovely neighbours made a salad and laid the table on the terrace, as the weather is still so nice.'

'Perfect,' Lucille cooed, continuing to the bottom of the stairs and sitting down on the seat of the stairlift. 'This is nice. I should have put one into my house in Tipp. How does it work?'

'You push the button that says "start",' Ella replied. 'But put on the seatbelt first in case you get a little wobbly.'

'No need,' Lucille said and pushed the start button. The seat moved slowly along the rail and up the stairs. Lucille laughed as she was going up. 'This is great,' she shouted down at Ella. 'Better than the funfair in Tramore.' The stairlift stopped and Ella could hear Lucille walk on the upstairs landing. 'The bathroom is a bit small,' she shouted. 'And this shower looks dangerous.'

'It's a power shower,' Ella shouted back. 'Great for relaxing my muscles. Takes a bit of getting used to, though.'

'Okay,' Lucille said as she seemed to walk back onto the landing, opening doors as she went. 'The front bedroom would be mine, is that it?'

'Yes,' Ella called. 'Hope you like it. My friend Saskia made the bed.'

'I could have done that myself,' Lucille said. 'The bed looks comfortable, but the wardrobe is a bit small for all my things. I'll try to squeeze it all in somehow.'

'How much did you bring?' Ella asked, trying not to laugh, wondering how long Lucille had planned to stay.

'Everything important,' Lucille said from above. 'Coming down again,' she announced and before Ella knew what to say, Lucille glided down to the hall and came to a stop, smiling broadly. 'Whoa, I think I'll like this way of travelling.'

'I'm looking forward to being able to run up the stairs like I used to,' Ella replied.

Lucille got up from the seat. 'Ah, but you're young. Your body will repair itself. Mine is in a permanent decline. Old age is not for sissies, as Bette Davis used to say.'

'Who?'

'An old movie star from the Forties. When they were real stars and not ordinary like now.' Lucille walked into the living room.

'Ordinary?' Ella followed Lucille on her crutches. 'I don't think Scarlett Johansson or Charlize Theron are what one would describe as ordinary.'

Lucille looked around the large living room. 'Of course they are,' she said, gazing absentmindedly at a painting on the wall.

'We know all about their private lives. In the old days, stars had a certain mystery. That's all gone now. Even royalty share the details of their private lives in the media. It's so disappointing to find that they're just like anyone else.' She pointed at the painting. 'I like that. One of yours?'

'Yes,' Ella said, looking up at the abstract consisting of elliptical shapes in strong colours against a pale blue background. 'I did that one when I had just arrived here. After the divorce and Mum moving in with you. Everything was a bit confused then for me. Feelings, memories, all mixed up together.'

'Excellent,' Lucille said. 'It looks like all the anger and sadness floating up into the universe.'

'Exactly. You're very astute.'

'Why wouldn't I be?' Lucille said. 'I've lived a very long time. Seen and done so much all through the years. And now I want to put all that behind me and have fun.'

'Sounds great,' Ella said with a laugh. Lucille's take on life had always delighted her. She began to realise that Lucille's motives for moving in had a lot to do with her own loneliness as well as wanting to look after Ella. 'Let's have lunch,' she suggested. 'Go through to the sunroom and try not to trip over anything. It's my studio, so it's in a bit of disarray. I haven't been able to tidy up or do any painting since the accident.'

'You'll get back to it very soon,' Lucille declared and walked ahead into the sunroom, glancing around at the stacks of canvases against the wall, the large unfinished seascape on the easel, the table littered with tubes of paint and brushes, and the paint stains on the floor. 'I'll sort this out,' she muttered before she opened the glass door and stepped out into the sunshine on the terrace, where Saskia had laid out lunch on the table under the large striped umbrella. 'How glorious,' Lucille exclaimed, taking in the amazing views of the coastline and the deep blue ocean. 'You'd think we were in the South of France.'

'Until it starts to rain,' Ella added, sitting down on the chair Lucille pulled out for her. 'And it's hot now, but the evenings can be chilly, even in the middle of summer.'

'Oh well, you can't have everything,' Lucille said as she settled on the chair opposite Ella. She pushed the salad bowl across the table. 'Go on. Get some food into that skinny body.' She picked a slice of soda bread from the basket and spread a generous amount of butter on it and handed it to Ella.

'Thanks.' Ella helped herself to the salad and then took a few slices of ham and cold chicken from a selection of cold meats on a platter. 'I haven't had much of an appetite since the accident, but I'm suddenly hungry.'

'It's the fresh air,' Lucille said as she served herself cold chicken and salad. 'And the company. And not having anyone breathing down your neck, I'd say.'

'Maybe,' Ella said, smiling. 'So what did you do with the house? Did you let it?'

'No. I'm going to sell it,' Lucille declared. 'I've had enough of that place.'

'What? But you've been living there over fifty years.' Ella was surprised by Lucille's news.

'Well, isn't that long enough?' Lucille asked. 'I loved it when my husband was alive and when we had a family. But now he's been gone over fifteen years, my children have grown up and left, and most of my friends are dead. Your mum made that place special and I realise I don't want to be there without her. Rose left us two years ago, but it feels like yesterday. The house is so empty without her. I don't want to live in a mausoleum for the rest of my life. I want to do something fun and different, live somewhere with a bit of a buzz.'

'Oh,' Ella said, startled by the passion in Lucille's voice, her pink cheeks and the spark in her eyes. This woman was eighty-five years old but still wanted to live, to experience new things, to have fun and meet people. 'Amazing,' she said. Ella was only now coming to terms with her own grief and had managed to put it behind her, but Lucille was still sad. That old house held so many memories – it wasn't so strange she would want to leave.

'What's amazing?' Lucille asked, looking sternly at Ella. 'That I haven't given up on life? That I'm not sitting in a rocking chair knitting sweaters for my grandchildren? I don't even know how to knit and my grandchildren wear strange clothes called hoodies and jeans with holes in them. You know, Ella, growing old is only physical. I'm still the same woman who kicked her legs in those numbers in the dance company I was in. I might not be able to kick as high, but I do remember the steps.' She drew breath and drank some water, looking defiantly at Ella. 'I need to keep my brain alive and moving and changing my environment is a good way to keep the mind active.'

'I love that fire in your eyes,' Ella said after a moment's silence. 'I'd love to paint you looking just like that.'

'You're just trying to humour me,' Lucille said. 'You looked a little frightened there.'

Ella laughed. 'Yeah, it was a bit scary to see you looking like someone on a mission. But I agree with you. I think people tend to be very ageist and just see a number rather than the person.'

Lucille nodded and sighed while she speared a lettuce leaf onto her fork. 'They do. But it's true that many older people have health problems and maybe even dementia. I'm very lucky, really. I have normal blood pressure without any medication. But then I also work very hard to stay healthy and active. It all works except for my knees, which are a bit creaky and painful at times. So that's why I was so happy to find the stairlift.'

'I'm glad you find it useful.'

'It's great.' Lucille ate her lettuce and then concentrated on the rest of the food on her plate.

'So tell me,' Ella urged, when she had finished her salad. 'What is the real reason you came here? I can't imagine it's because you want to look after me.'

'I do,' Lucille argued. 'But that's just part of my plan. I wanted to come to Kerry because my family had connections with this area and I want to see if I can find out more about them. I needed to get away from my children for a bit as well and told them a little fib so they'd leave me alone for the summer.'

'What did you tell them?'

'I said I was going on a cruise in the Mediterranean.'

'What did they say?'

Lucille snorted a laugh. 'They believed me. At least Martin and his rather boring wife did. Rory was more difficult to convince. He knows I'd rather stick pins into my eyes than go on one of those things, but I told him I've changed my mind and decided to try it.

Said I can always go home if I didn't like it. He asked me to keep in touch and let him know how I was getting on, so I have to fake it somehow.'

'How?' Ella asked.

Lucille shrugged. 'I can always download some cruise photos from the internet and send them to him. I haven't decided yet. I might just text him to say I'm so busy playing deck games and flirting with the captain that I haven't time to take photos.'

'And he's going to believe that?'

'No idea,' Lucille said. 'But what can he do? He won't be able to find me here, will he? And then, in a little while, I'll be selling the house. I'll look for something smaller around here and before they can protest, it'll be done and they won't be able to stop me.'

'Why would they?' Ella asked, wondering what was going on with Lucille's two sons. Were they worried she would spend their inheritance? It certainly sounded as if they were.

'They think I should just descend into old age and keep living in that old house and not spend any money until I die. Especially Martin. I think it's his wife who's behind that. Rory is different. He tries to understand me, and sometimes he even succeeds.'

'He's your favourite?' Ella asked. She had always thought so but she'd never asked Lucille directly.

'Yes.' Lucille smiled. 'My baby boy. He isn't married and has never really settled down. You'd think that at his age, he'd have a wife and a few children like his brother, but he never found anyone he liked enough to marry. He's had a series of girlfriends, all lovely, but none of them stayed.'

'How old is Rory?' Ella asked, trying to remember.

'Forty-eight. A year or two older than you but still a little boy at heart. He's a lawyer by trade but now he's working for the government. Department of Justice. At least that's a good solid job with a pension.'

'He'll probably find someone one day,' Ella suggested. 'Some men take a long time to mature.'

'Some men never mature at all,' Lucille said. 'But never mind them. I'll have a lovely break here with you and then I'll contact them and tell them I'm all right. When I've found my dream home that I'll want to stay in for the rest of my life.'

'Oh.' Ella looked at Lucille and wondered how long it would take for her to find her dream home. 'So you think you'll want to live here? In the village somewhere?'

Lucille nodded and drained her glass of water. 'Yes. I heard you talk about this place when you came to visit Rose. And then…' She stopped for a moment. 'Like I told you, I found out that my family has roots here. But I don't want to go into that right now.'

'Why not?' Ella asked. 'It sounds really interesting.'

'I'll tell you when I know more. I'm doing some research right now.'

'I see,' Ella said. 'So what's your plan, then? What kind of place do you think you'd like?'

'I think a small house would be lovely. Right in the middle of the action, so to speak.'

'Action?' Ella said, laughing. 'I don't think there is much here. This village is quite lively now, in the summer with all the visitors. But in the winter it's really quiet. I usually pop over to Paris for a while then.'

'Of course you do,' Lucille agreed. 'But at my age, just a trip to the shops followed by a coffee and a bun in some nice little café is enough excitement. And I'll see if there's a reading group at the library perhaps and maybe there are other groups, like gardening and some kind of walking group for people my age.' She leaned forward and looked earnestly at Ella. 'My big house in the country is in a remote area, as you know. It takes over half an hour to get to the nearest town for shopping and seeing my doctor or the dentist. Even though the countryside is very pretty, I was beginning to feel lonely now that Rose is gone. So I thought that if I could live in a village, near shops and all kinds of other services, and near people, I wouldn't have to drive anywhere. I'd have everything on my doorstep. And then, when the weather is bad, I have my laptop.'

'Your laptop?' Ella said, intrigued. 'What do you do with it?'

'Lots of things,' Lucille said, suddenly looking coy. 'There's a Facebook group or two I like to keep in touch with, and my Twitter and Instagram accounts. I have a lot of followers, you know,' she said proudly.

'How many?' Ella asked, highly amused. How incredible that this older woman was surfing the internet as well as everything else.

'Several hundred,' Lucille said proudly. 'And there are more every day.'

'Wow, that's amazing,' Ella said, impressed, picking up her phone. 'What name do you use?'

'Oh, you wouldn't find it very interesting,' Lucille replied. 'It's for old people like me who don't want to give up. Not for young things like you at all.'

'I wouldn't mind having a peek at what older people are saying,' Ella said. 'I find that very interesting, actually.'

Lucille shook her head and smiled. 'I don't think you would. We talk about the time before you were born. The good old days when we were all young and wild. I did have a life before Johnny, you know,' she added with a wink.

'So Mum told me,' Ella said. 'You were a dancer and you even acted in a movie, she said.'

'A tiny part,' Lucille said. 'I think I had three lines. Not something I could build a career on.' Lucille smiled wistfully. 'Those were the days, though. The Fifties and Sixties, I mean.'

'That was a wonderful era,' Ella agreed. 'I wasn't even born then, but I've seen photos and films. The music, the clothes, the fun you must have had. I wish I had been there.'

'If you had you'd be a lot older by now,' Ella said with a sigh. 'But I'm so glad I was young then. And that I met Johnny and that we were so happy together. We had more than forty years of marriage living in a wonderful house until he died.'

'So sad,' Ella said, remembering the story of Johnny's death. He was thrown off his horse and had died instantly.

Lucille nodded. 'Yes. Horrible thing to happen. I haven't even been near a horse since then, which didn't earn me any medals with the horsey set in Tipperary. But I didn't care. I had to make sure my children had at least one parent. It felt like risking my life to go anywhere near one!' Lucille stared out across the water. 'And now I want to live in the *now*, in this moment with you looking out over the Atlantic Ocean.'

'Yes,' Ella said. 'Me too.'

Lucille regarded Ella. 'Do you mind if I ask you to keep quiet about me being here? I mean, should my sons suspect that I'm not on a cruise after all.'

'You mean if they should contact me and ask?'

'Yes. Would you tell a lie for me?'

Ella looked at Lucille and saw the fear in her eyes. The fear of being caught out and treated like an old, vulnerable person instead of the strong, brave woman she still was. 'I would lie through my teeth for you,' she declared.

'Well, I simply meant to bend the truth a little,' Lucille said. 'Smoke and mirrors. That kind of thing.'

'Whatever it takes,' Ella said.

Lucille smiled fondly. 'That's my girl.'

Ella suddenly realised that, even though they weren't related by blood, there was still something that connected them – their free spirits and rebellious natures. But Lucille's sons were probably not as easy to fool as Lucille thought. What if they caught up with her? That could cause some problems and confrontations. But whatever happened, the summer stretching ahead seemed a lot more interesting now.

Chapter Three

Lucille's arrival turned Ella's convalescence into a more normal existence – if anything to do with Lucille could be called 'normal'. Ella's sedate routine of getting up, doing her exercises, resting, eating the lunch one of her kind friends had prepared, reading, more resting and some aimless wandering around the house, watching endless rom-coms on Netflix and finally going to bed came to an abrupt end.

The morning after her arrival, Lucille, dressed in black wide-legged trousers and a bright yellow top, burst into Ella's bedroom with a big mug of café au lait and a basket of rolls on a small tray. 'Good morning,' she chanted, putting the tray on the bedside table and opening the curtains. 'It's a lovely day. A little rain earlier but now the sun is chasing the clouds away and the birds are singing. Drink your coffee and then come downstairs. I'll make a light breakfast and then I'll lay out your mat for your exercises, followed by a little trip to the library in my car. How's that?'

'Uh,' Ella grunted, sitting up and rubbing her eyes. 'What time is it?'

'Eight o'clock. Or just after,' Lucille corrected herself. 'I just listened to the news on the radio. Nothing much has happened in

the world that we need to worry about. A little bit of bad weather in
the north and some kind of political row in Dublin. That's about it.'

'Oh, good.' Ella looked at the tray. 'Coffee!' she exclaimed.
'And bread rolls. Fabulous. How did you know that's exactly what
I wanted?'

'I have a good memory,' Lucille said proudly. 'I knew how much
you loved a French breakfast. There were no croissants in your
breadbin, but we can remedy that tomorrow. This was the best I
could do today. The apricot jam is delicious, I have to say.'

'It's all perfect. How did you manage to bring that up on the
stairlift?' Ella asked.

'Very carefully,' Lucille said. 'When there's a will there's a way,
I always say.'

'I suppose.' Ella took the mug and sipped some coffee before
she helped herself to a half a roll spread with apricot jam. 'Did you
say the library?' she asked. 'Why are you going there?'

'To get myself a library card and to take a look at what's going
on. Libraries always have very interesting notice boards. And you
need to get out of the house.' Lucille walked to the door. 'I take it
you can handle the shower by yourself? If not, I'm happy to help.'

'I can manage.'

'Good. See you downstairs in a minute then.'

Ella could hear the stairlift going down as she finished the bread
rolls and drank her coffee, shaking her head, not knowing whether to
laugh or cry. Lucille was like a whirlwind and there was no stopping
her when she had a plan of action. But Ella knew this was what she
needed. It had been easier to succumb to doing nothing and she
needed to pull herself up and start working on getting her body

back to its former health. The sorrow of losing her mother and the lingering pain of her divorce hadn't helped either, as the division of assets took a long time after the actual separation.

Ella got out of bed and made her way to the bathroom on her crutches, thinking about the divorce and the painful aftermath. How she wished she hadn't rushed into marriage. They could simply have moved in together and found out how badly matched they were without any legal issues. But she had thought she was in love, and this time it had seemed so perfect – until it ended in such a painful way after her miscarriages and she was left trying to recover both from the loss of her pregnancies and the subsequent divorce. Maybe they would have been happy if they'd had a family, she had thought at the time. But in hindsight, she realised that Jean-Paul's reaction to their plight proved he wasn't the right man for her.

Will I ever learn? she asked herself as she stepped into the shower and turned on the jets. The pressure from them massaged her back and legs to the point of pain – it hurt but it also helped revive her. Each time she stepped out of the shower her skin glowed and her muscles felt more flexible and supple. She rubbed herself with a large fluffy towel and went to dress and get ready for another day, another step towards recovery.

Lucille was on the terrace when Ella arrived, putting a bowl of fruit salad on the table. She smiled. 'You look so fresh. Must be the coffee and the shower-power or whatever it's called. It nearly blew me out of the bathroom this morning.'

Ella laughed and sat down at the table. 'Power shower. And you can adjust it. Should have shown you. Sorry about that. Hope it wasn't too much of a shock.'

'It shook me up a bit,' Lucille said as she joined Ella. 'It's a little too much for an old gal like me. But I'll learn how to work it. Coffee and croissants aren't enough for breakfast. You need something healthy too. So eat your fruit and then I suppose you'll want to do your exercises.'

'Yes. I should. This fruit salad is a good idea. I need the vitamins. Thanks for making it. And for not asking me to eat porridge and a full Irish as well.'

'That would be far too much. You need to build strength, not turn into a sumo wrestler,' Lucille remarked. 'And I like this kind of continental breakfast myself, so that's one thing we agree on.'

'That's a good start.' Ella chewed on a piece of apple and looked at Lucille. 'You know, I always feel a little tired after my exercises, so do you mind if I don't come to the library with you this time?'

'Well, I thought you might like to get out of the house for a bit. But we can take a little drive this afternoon instead. Maybe I'll just go and take a look when I've tidied up.'

'Good idea,' Ella said. 'Could you call into the grocery store and get something for dinner, if that's not too much trouble? I have an account there, so just tell them who you are and you won't have to pay.'

'That's a good idea,' Lucille said approvingly. 'What would you like?'

Ella waved her hand. 'Oh, get whatever you want. Surprise me.'

Lucille smiled and got up. 'I will indeed,' she said. 'See you later, then.'

When Lucille had left, Ella got her yoga mat from the living room and rolled it out on the terrace, deciding to do her physio workout in the fresh air under the blue skies and warm late spring sunshine. The exercises were quite tough and required a lot of work from weak muscles that often refused to cooperate, but Ella persisted, spending a torturous half hour going through every move. Finally finished, she lay down on the mat, her eyes closed, and tried to relax her aching body. With the warmth of the sun and the soothing sound of the waves, she managed to let herself go, feeling her body sink into the mat, her mind drifting. It was lovely to feel the strain of the exercises ease from her aching muscles and let the sun warm her whole body. She nearly drifted off, but after only a few minutes, was startled by a voice in her ear.

'Hello,' someone said above her. 'Are you sick or dead?'

Ella opened her eyes and peered at the shadow above her. She shaded her eyes with her hand and discovered a little girl, dressed in blue shorts and a white T-shirt standing on the terrace. 'Hello, there,' she said. 'I'm quite alive, thank you. Who are you?'

'I'm me,' the girl said. 'Amanda Bridget Louise Quinn. Who are you?'

'I'm Ella.'

'What else?'

'Ella Jane Caron,' Ella said, feeling her full name was required. She sat up. 'So where did you come from, Amanda?'

'Dublin. And my daddy calls me Mandy. You can too, if you like,' she said graciously.

'Oh, thank you,' Ella said laughing. 'How old are you, Mandy?'

'I'm five. How old are you?'

'I'm a little older than you.' Ella smiled at the girl, whose dark blonde curls tumbled down her back. Her bright blue eyes were fringed with dark lashes. 'You're very pretty.'

'So are you, but you look very tired,' the little girl said. 'I live over there,' she said, pointing to the left of the terrace. 'We just moved in. My daddy is trying to get the cooker to work and he told me to get out of the way so I did.'

So they were their new neighbours. Ella smiled at the little girl. 'Where's your mummy?'

'In heaven,' Mandy said in a matter-of-fact voice. 'She went up there when I was three.'

'Oh, I'm sorry,' Ella said with a dart of sadness, regretting having made an assumption. 'That's very sad.'

Mandy nodded, her face solemn. 'Yes it is. But Daddy says we must go on living and be happy that we had Mummy in our lives even if she's gone. And we must treasure her memory, but I don't really know how to do that. Do you?' Mandy drew breath and looked expectantly at Ella.

'Well… I suppose it means that you should remember the happy times,' Ella tried. 'All those nice things you did with your mummy. Stories she told, songs she sang, that sort of thing.'

'Oh,' Mandy said, looking thoughtful. 'I remember hugs. And the "Hush, Little Baby" song. And a smell like, like vanilla buns.'

'Those are very nice things, aren't they?' Ella said gently.

Mandy nodded her head, making her curls bounce. 'Yes.' She turned as a man's voice called in the distance. 'That's my daddy. I have to go home.'

'Okay,' Ella said. 'Bye for now, Mandy. Nice to meet you.'

'Bye, bye,' Mandy said and started to skip down the steps of the terrace as the figure of a man appeared from the house next-door-but-one along the terrace and started to walk towards them.

'Mandy!' he chided. 'There you are. Didn't I tell you to stay around the house?'

'No, you said to get out of your way,' Mandy replied. 'So I did and here I am. And I met her,' she added, pointing at Ella. 'She was sleeping on her mat.'

Ella shaded her eyes with her hand against the bright sunlight and peered up at the man, who was tall and blonde and not bad-looking, she was delighted to discover. 'Hi,' she said. 'I wasn't asleep. I was just relaxing after quite a strenuous exercise routine.'

'Yoga?' he asked.

'No, physio.' Ella scrambled slowly to her feet, ignoring his hand and grabbed the crutches. 'I'm recovering from an accident.'

'Oh. You broke your leg?' he enquired.

'No, my pelvis.'

'That's terrible,' he said. 'How did it happen?'

'I fell off a ladder while not paying attention. But I'm nearly all better.' Ella sat down on one of the chairs by the garden table and held out her hand. 'Sorry. I should introduce myself. I'm Ella Caron.'

'Ella Jane Caron,' Mandy corrected.

The man laughed and shook Ella's hand. 'Hello, Ella Jane Caron. I'm Thomas Quinn. I've just arrived in this gorgeous spot. I'm renting the cottage down there,' he said, making a sweeping gesture toward the end of the row of houses. 'Next door to a couple called Lydia and Jason.'

'Welcome to Starlight Cottages,' Ella said, smiling at him. 'Jason and Lydia have recently moved in together and they said they'd be letting Jason's house for the summer.'

He nodded. 'That's right. To me.'

'And me,' Mandy piped up and Ella smiled at her.

'It's a gorgeous place,' Thomas said, looking out over the ocean. 'But I have to say those cliffs look a little dangerous. I was happy to see the security fence and the locked gate to that steep path.'

Ella nodded. 'Yes, me too. We had it done last year as a precaution. We didn't want any accidents if anyone ventured to the little beach down there.'

'Jason gave me a key,' Thomas said. 'I don't think I'll want to go down there with Mandy, though. I might go on my own. It looks like a lovely spot.'

'It is. But sit down,' Ella said, gesturing at the chair beside her. 'I'm sorry I can't offer you anything. I'm still a little immobile.'

'I could make you a cup of coffee,' Thomas offered, sitting down on the chair and lifting Mandy onto his lap.

'I just had breakfast that my friend Lucille very kindly made for me, so I'm grand,' Ella said. 'Everyone has been amazing since my accident, but it gets a little too much sometimes.'

'I can imagine. We just had breakfast, too, so we're fine,' Thomas said. 'I'm having a little trouble with the cooker, so we had cornflakes and juice and toast. That induction thing is a bit tricky. I must ask

Jason to show me how to make it work when he comes back from his swim.'

'I hate those things,' Ella declared. 'Induction hobs, I mean. I have an old-fashioned gas cooker and it works for me. When I'm in my full health, of course,' she added.

'We have a piano,' Mandy said. 'You can play music on it.'

Thomas laughed. 'Yes, but it's lousy for making porridge.'

Ella laughed, delighted by his apparent sense of humour. She studied Thomas surreptitiously, taking in his blonde hair, blazing blue eyes and golden skin. She also noticed his beautiful hands with the long fingers of a pianist. 'I heard you playing early this morning.'

'Oh, I'm sorry,' Thomas said, looking contrite. 'I hope I didn't disturb you.'

'Not at all. It was heavenly. Are you a musician?' she asked.

'In a way,' he replied. 'I'm a composer.'

'Oh? What kind of music?'

'Pretty songs,' Mandy replied. 'Like "Loving You in the Moonlight". That's Daddy's song.'

'Really?' Ella said, intrigued. 'You wrote that? It was a huge hit a few years ago.'

'Yeah, well,' Thomas started, looking suddenly awkward. 'It's a bit of a jingle, really. Stuff that pays the bills. I'm working on a symphony right now. Classical music is really my first love.'

'I like all music,' Ella declared. 'I adored "Loving You in the Moonlight". I must have played it a thousand times.'

'"*Coffee, coffee, Bellamia coffee*,"' Mandy sang in her sweet voice. 'That's Daddy's song too.'

Ella laughed. 'I love that one too, and the coffee. So that's also one of yours?'

'Yeah,' Thomas admitted. 'Another one just to put food on the table.'

'Seems to be going well,' Ella remarked, noticing his polo shirt with the crocodile logo and the Docksider loafers.

'Not bad at all,' Thomas said, grinning. 'And now I can afford to take the whole summer off and create something unique.' He turned to the view over the ocean. 'This is so inspiring.'

'It certainly is.'

Thomas' gaze drifted to the sketchpad and the pencils on the table. 'You like to draw?'

Ella laughed. 'Yes. That's my way of paying bills. I'm an illustrator. And I also do a bit of painting,' she said, not wanting to mention her hugely successful career. He might think she was boasting.

Mandy grabbed the sketchpad. 'I like to draw too. Can I use this?'

'Of course,' Ella said and pushed the box of pastel crayons towards Mandy. 'You can use these too.'

'Thank you,' Mandy said and picked out a crayon from the box. 'I'll draw a picture for you.'

'That would be lovely,' Ella said as Mandy started to draw.

'Stay still,' Mandy ordered. 'I'm drawing you.'

Ella smiled at the little girl, who bent over the pad, her tongue sticking out, a picture of deep concentration. She lifted her head and looked at Ella for a moment and then pushed her hair off her face and went back to her work. 'It'll be ready in a minute,' she muttered.

As they waited for Mandy to finish her picture, Thomas looked around the terrace at the tubs full of flowers, the small hedge that surrounded the garden and the cabbage palm, its spiky leaves rustling in the breeze. 'You've done a great job with this garden.'

'Thank you. It's easy to care for. Except that flowerbed needs a little attention. But I'll get back to that when I'm more mobile.'

'You've been recovering on your own?'

'No, I've had an army of helpers. All from the village. The people here are amazing, which you will discover.'

'That's quite unusual these days.'

'True. I have a feeling they're getting a little fed up with me, though. But I have Lucille living with me now. Old friend of my late mother who's come to stay,' she explained.

'Oh. That's nice.'

Ella snorted a laugh. 'Nice? Of course the company will help. But she can be a bit of a handful. But fun at the same time. I'm a little conflicted here,' she confessed.

'I suppose you're not really ready for houseguests,' Thomas suggested.

'Not as such, but Lucille is more like a mother hen. She's already taking charge of my life. But she's good fun and she has a heart of gold. And she loves stirring people up. Nobody is bored in her company, that's for sure. Wait till you meet her.'

'I'm looking forward to it.' Thomas paused, glancing at Mandy, who was still working hard on her drawing. 'I hope Mandy will get to know some children her age while we're here.'

'I'm sure she will,' Ella said. 'Plenty of kids around here. Maybe you could enrol her in the children's craft group they run at the library? I think it starts next week. All the primary school children will be on holiday soon. Then there's the swimming classes at the pool in Waterville and the little playgroup they run on the beach when it's not raining. They seem to have lots of fun. That's what I've heard anyway.'

'You don't have kids?' Thomas asked.

'No, never been that lucky,' Ella replied with a touch of regret in her voice. 'And now I'm over forty so it's too late.'

'Oh, I'm sorry. We waited a little too long to give Mandy a sibling,' Thomas said with a hint of sorrow in his eyes.

Ella nodded. 'It's tough. You keep telling yourself you're not ready and then, when you feel you are, it's too late.'

'Finished!' Mandy declared, making them jump. She gave the drawing to Ella. 'This is you.'

Ella smiled as she looked at the drawing. 'You made me into a cat.'

'That's because of your eyes,' Mandy said. 'They go up at the sides, just like a cat's, and your face is… pointy.'

'Oh, yes, I see it now.' Ella kept looking at the picture, astonished that Mandy had captured her features so realistically. She had drawn a cat sitting with its tail wound around the legs, its face tilted up with Ella's dark, almond-shaped eyes, heart-shaped face and wide mouth realistic in its childish simplicity. 'You are a real artist, Mandy. This is gorgeous.'

'I was going to have you smiling to show that gap in your front teeth,' Mandy said. 'And your dark hair. But cats don't smile or have hair, so that would be wrong.'

'You're very observant,' Ella said. 'I'm going to put this on my fridge door. Thank you so much, Mandy.'

'You're welcome,' Mandy said graciously. She wriggled out of her father's grip and jumped onto the ground. 'Can we go and see if that playgroup on the beach you talked about has started now, Daddy?'

'I don't think it has yet,' Ella said gently. 'Next week, I think.'

'But we can go to the beach anyway,' Thomas cut in. 'I'm sure we'll meet some children there as it's such a lovely day.'

'That's a very good idea,' Ella agreed. 'I'd go myself if I could. But maybe later, when I can walk without crutches.'

'Then you have to do some more training,' Mandy remarked. She grabbed her father's hand and pulled at it. 'Come *on*, Daddy. We have to go to the beach. I want to wear my new swimsuit and the pink sandals Granny got me.'

Thomas smiled apologetically at Ella and got up. 'I'd better do as I'm told. Nice to meet you, Ella. Give me a shout if you need help with anything.'

'Thank you,' Ella said with a pang of regret that they were leaving. She could have stayed there to chat with them both all morning. Thomas seemed such a nice, interesting man and Mandy was truly adorable. He was so lucky to have her, even though losing his wife must have been such a tragedy for them both.

'Bye for now,' Thomas said.

'Goodbye,' Mandy said and stuck her little hand into Thomas' big one. 'I will come and see you again soon if you want. I could teach you to walk properly.'

'Oh yes, please,' Ella said, laughing. 'I really need that.' She waved at the little girl as they left. 'Bye, Mandy. See you soon.'

She watched them walking away, Mandy chatting to her father and him replying. She had a feeling they would be lovely neighbours. She looked at Thomas Quinn's tall figure receding in the distance and thought she would like to get to know this man better before she told herself sternly not to rush into yet another relationship. It would only end in tears and misery. But there was no harm in making friends, all the same.

Chapter Four

Lucille's visit to the library resulted in one library card, five books, and two phone calls to join both a reading group and a tai chi group meeting on the main beach every morning at nine. She had also popped into the grocery shop and introduced herself to the owner, Sorcha, and a number of local people who had been queuing at the checkout.

'Nice bunch,' Lucille said. 'They all asked about you and hoped you're recovering. Then I said hello to the postman,' she continued, handing Ella the morning's post. 'Nothing much there. A postcard from the gallery in Paris, your electricity bill and what looks like a bank statement.'

Ella, sitting at the table in the sunroom sketching, took the bundle, laughing. 'I don't even have to open these, do I? You seem to have read it all with your laser eyes.' She flicked through the bundle and was about to put it on the table, but stopped. 'Oh, here's one for you,' she said. 'You must have missed it.'

'Really?' Lucille took the envelope. 'I redirected my post to this address before I left. And before you agreed to have me,' she added with a laugh. 'But I went ahead knowing you would. Didn't want to miss anything important.'

'Is it?' Ella asked as Lucille stared at her letter.

'Uh… No,' Lucille said and stuffed the letter unopened into the handbag she always carried with her. 'Nothing I need worry about.' But her smile as she looked at Ella seemed a little strained and the colour had drained from her face.

'Are you sure?' Ella asked.

'Absolutely.' Lucille regained her composure and her smile looked more genuine. 'So what have you been up to?'

'Nothing much. I had a little rest after my exercises. I fell asleep on the mat in the sunshine.' Ella smiled at the memory of the morning. 'And then I was woken up by a princess.'

'Really?' Lucille stood at the door, looking at Ella.

'Not a real princess, but a gorgeous little girl called Mandy. She's nearly five years old and she and her dad have rented the cottage next-door-but-one for the summer. Very nice man, too.'

'And her mother?'

'She's dead. Mandy actually told me. She said she was in heaven and that she went there two years ago.'

'Oh,' Lucille said. 'That's very sad for them.'

'Oh yes,' Ella said, thinking about the sorrow she had detected deep in Thomas' eyes. 'But he seems such a lovely father. They looked as if they were very close. He's a musician,' she continued. 'And I heard him play the piano early this morning. Beautiful music.'

'Lovely,' Lucille said and snapped the lock of her handbag shut. 'I must see to lunch. I got a quiche at the grocery store. I just need to heat it up. It's getting a bit chilly, so we'll eat in the kitchen, I think.'

'Great,' Ella said and returned her attention to her sketch.

When she was alone, Ella stared out the window, puzzled by Lucille's reaction to that letter she had received. It had been of the kind that looked somehow official. Was it from the tax office? No, couldn't be. Those letters usually had the Irish harp emblem stamped on it. From the bank? Was Lucille in some kind of financial trouble? But that didn't seem possible except if she had turned to internet gambling or something, which would be so unlike Lucille. Was someone trying to blackmail her? Ella immediately dismissed that idea as pure nonsense, laughing at herself at such a silly thought. Too many late-night Netflix movies had put all kinds of fantasies into her head. Ella shrugged and turned her attention to her work, which completely absorbed her during the next half hour, until Lucille called from the kitchen that lunch was ready.

Ella walked slowly into the bright little kitchen that she had painted herself when she moved. She had stripped the brown paint off the original cupboards and painted them a distressed white, adding a wallpaper with a design of tiny yellow flowers, perfect for a country kitchen, giving it a permanently sunny feel. She loved cooking here, especially if she had friends over to dinner, which had happened quite often before the accident.

'I'm going back to the library this afternoon,' Lucille announced as they had lunch. 'I have volunteered to read aloud to the children during story time. Their usual reader is off sick so they thought they might have to cancel. I said I'd be happy to stand in today if they wanted.'

Ella laughed. 'You don't waste any time. You're only here since yesterday and you're already joining groups and doing voluntary work at the library.'

Lucille nodded. 'At my age I have to grab every moment. I love being useful, you see.'

'But you're looking after me,' Ella argued. 'Isn't that useful enough?'

'Ah but this is temporary. No better way to settle into a village than doing little things like this. It's all about goodwill and PR.'

'As in public relations?' Ella asked, intrigued. 'Why do you need that?'

Lucille rose and collected their plates. 'Oh, just to establish a positive image and all that. Important in a new place. So far, I like it a lot, I have to say. But it's early days yet. Will you come with me to the library now that you've had a rest?'

'Yes. I think I can cope with that. I haven't been anywhere since the accident. Plenty of people have offered to take me for outings but I haven't had the courage, to tell you the truth. It's a little scary to walk on crutches anywhere but at home. I'm afraid I'll fall over and hurt myself all over again.'

'You need to get out, though,' Lucille stated. 'How long have you been on those things?'

'Only a little over a week. Before that I had to stay in bed,' Ella replied. 'It's been a very hard time.'

'But now you're recovering. Onwards and upwards, my old dad used to say. No looking back to bad times.'

'I know,' Ella said, suddenly feeling a flash of optimism. Lucille's positive approach was inspirational. 'I'll finish my sketch before we go,' she said getting up from the table. 'I need to decide how I'm going to do the illustrations for this book. It has to catch the imagination of the children reading it and give them an important message at the same time.'

'Make it simple,' Lucille said as she put the dishes into the dishwasher. She pointed at Mandy's drawing on the fridge door. 'Like that one. It's a cat, but it's you as well. It's really expressive.'

Ella looked at the drawing. 'Yes,' she said thoughtfully. 'You might be on to something there. Animals with human faces – yet not human. Mandy, the little girl who called in this morning, made it. It gives me an idea…' She peered at Lucille. 'You could be a fox, you know. A cute vixen who's a little bit sly.'

Lucille smiled. 'I like that idea. Feel free to use my face if there is a vixen in the story.'

'There is. And other animals, too. Hmm… I know a few faces I could use…'

'And this little Mandy girl?' Lucille asked. 'Could she be the heroine of the story?'

'Oh yes, she could,' Ella said, her heart beating faster as ideas formed in her mind. 'I'll have to ask her father if I can use her face – I mean, draw her first, of course, and then use that for the little girl. Brilliant, Lucille. I think you've just got me out of some kind of artistic block.'

'You're very welcome,' Lucille said, looking pleased. 'I'll make coffee and bring it in to you. Then I'm going to read the local paper. I need to know what's going on in this part of the world.'

'Not much, I'm afraid,' Ella said.

'That's what you think,' Lucille retorted. 'Little things are often more important than the big things, you know. They can often grow into something extraordinary.'

'Like the ideas you just gave me. I can't wait to get started.' Excited, Ella grabbed her crutches and made her way to her studio, where she sat down and got out her sketchpad and pencils. She started to quickly sketch animal heads with human faces, starting with Lucille as a vixen, which worked really well. Then the main character, a little girl called Lupita whom she gave Mandy's golden curls and sweet face. She turned Mandy's father into a handsome palomino horse and, like Mandy had done, turned herself into Lupita's cat. Saskia's face was given to a black dog with a pointy nose and glittering dark eyes.

After half an hour of frantic sketching, Ella sat back and looked at what she had drawn. They were only very rough sketches, but she could see how wonderful it would be. More and more ideas popped into her head, turning everyone she knew into some kind of animal or insect. This would be fantastic. The only animal she couldn't find a face for was the bear, the main character of the story. He would have to be moody and broody, even threatening at first, with dark eyes glowing with a mixture of fear and anger which would mellow as the story evolved. Ella racked her brain but couldn't come up with a single face. She pushed the sketchpad away. Better to leave that alone for now. She looked up as Lucille walked into the room with a cup of coffee. She had changed into an ankle-length blue skirt, a white silk blouse, and trainers with a design of flowers and butterflies.

'I called you,' Lucille said. 'But you didn't seem to have heard. So I thought I'd bring you a fresh cup. Then we should go.'

'Great.' Ella quickly drank the coffee in one gulp. 'I like your outfit.'

'It's for the reading. I think the children will like it. We need to get going now, though.'

'I'm ready.'

'Wonderful,' Lucille said. 'And maybe you could try to walk a little if I park a bit away from the library? Just to get you used to being outside among people.'

'That's a good idea. I'm a little nervous still but you're right. I have to get out there.'

'Yes, you do.' Lucille leaned over Ella's shoulder to look at her drawings. 'I like that. Never knew I could look this foxy.'

'Oh, you have fox written all over you,' Ella said with a wink.

Lucille laughed. 'I think you have me taped.'

As Ella looked at Lucille and saw the mischievous glint in her eyes, she thought of the story of going on a cruise that she had told her sons. That had amused Ella, but there was something else, something that Lucille kept to herself. Could that be the real reason for her flight to Sandy Cove?

Lucille parked down the street from the library and helped Ella get out of the car. 'There,' she said. 'It's only a short walk. Take it easy and you'll be fine.'

Ella stood for a while and looked around at the cottages lining the street – their front gardens full of flowers, the curtains in the open windows fluttering in the warm breeze – and the glint of the ocean further away. She hadn't been out of the house for over two months and she suddenly felt as if she had been let out of prison. She looked at the tall Victorian house in the distance where the library was situated and felt as if she was about to run a marathon. It seemed such a long way to walk on crutches and she was afraid she'd fall over if she took a wrong step. Her palms were damp with sweat and she felt herself shaking a little as she started walking on the uneven pavement.

'Every journey starts with one step,' Lucille said beside Ella. 'Come on, girl. You can do it.'

Ella took a tentative step, then another and another, until she was walking at a slow but steady pace, wobbling a little here and there, her palms sweaty, but still continuing until they reached the library. She stopped and panted, smiling at Lucille. 'There. I did it.'

'See? It wasn't that bad, was it?' Lucille said.

'No. Once I got going, it wasn't as scary as I thought.' Ella sank down on the bench beside the entrance door. 'I'll wait for you here, I think, though.'

'Good idea,' Lucille said. 'I'll only be half an hour. And you can sit here and chat to people as they pass. It'll be good for you to catch up with friends and others who haven't seen you for so long.' She patted Ella on the shoulder and went inside, nearly colliding with a tall man on his way out.

'Oh, sorry,' he said and held the door open. 'I didn't see you there.'

'No harm done,' Lucille said, smiling at him as she passed him. 'See you later, Ella.'

'Okay,' Ella said. Then she noticed who the man was. 'Hello, Thomas,' she said. 'Nice to meet you again.'

Thomas looked around and noticed Ella on the bench. 'Oh, hi. Didn't see you there.' He pointed at the door closing behind Lucille. 'Was that the lady who's staying with you?'

'Yes. That's Lucille. She is going to read to the children.'

'Oh, then she'll be reading to Mandy. I just dropped her off for story time.' Thomas paused. 'Mind if I join you? I might as well wait here until it's time to pick her up.'

'Of course.' Ella shifted on the bench. 'Nice to have company.'

Thomas sat down and looked at the crutches. 'How is it going?'

'Slowly,' Ella said with a sigh. 'I'm very impatient by nature, so I find it all very frustrating.'

'I can imagine,' Thomas said. He looked at her for a moment and brushed his blonde hair off his forehead. 'Thank you for being so nice to Mandy earlier.'

'Oh God,' Ella exclaimed. 'No need to thank me at all. She was like a drink in the desert to me. I love kids and she is one of those delightful ones. So chatty and full of wisdom, somehow.'

'She's a little bit precocious, I suppose,' Thomas said with a glint of sadness in his blue eyes. 'Comes from being with adults a lot of the time, I'm afraid. I think I might have been a little overprotective of her since my wife died. I haven't let her mix with other children her age as much as I should.'

'I can understand that. I mean, she's all you have now,' Ella said gently, trying her best to say the right thing. She put her hand on his arm. 'I was so sorry to hear about your wife. Mandy told me she passed away.'

'Thank you. Mandy was only three years old when it happened, so I'm not sure if she remembers much about her mother.'

'No. Maybe not. But I don't think she'll forget completely. She told me she remembered hugs and a song. And a smell like vanilla buns.'

'Did she?' Thomas asked, looking a little brighter. 'I hope she'll never forget those things.'

'The good things will always be there, I'd say. Especially the feeling of being loved.'

Thomas glanced at her. 'You're very astute for someone who's…' He stopped, looking awkward.

'Who's childless?' Ella said with a touch of sadness in her voice.

Thomas squirmed. 'Well, yes. But you might have experience with children all the same. You were great with Mandy this morning. I didn't mean to offend you in any way.'

'I'm not offended at all,' Ella said, touched by his gentle voice and consideration. 'I'll always be sad about not having had children, but that's not your fault. Everyone has some kind of sadness in their lives. Mine is a lot less than yours, though.'

Thomas shrugged. 'Oh, I think it's wrong to compare different kinds of sadness. It's not a competition.'

'You're right. The older you get the more you have to carry,' Ella stated. She sat up straighter. 'It's too nice a day to mope in any case. And Lucille is a great role model. She's eighty-five and always cheerful. Can be a bit tiring but it's also contagious. She arrived yesterday like a whirlwind with tons of luggage and her laptop and a pile of books. She has a huge wardrobe with clothes for every occasion. Today she's wearing her reading-for-children outfit.'

'She looked kind of cosy,' Thomas remarked.

'Cosy?' Ella laughed and shook her head. 'Oh, that's just a façade to create a good image. She calls it PR. I have to say I'm glad she arrived. I needed to be pulled out of my apathy and Lucille is such a tonic.' She paused, remembering what she had planned to ask him. 'Thomas,' she started. 'Would you mind if I used Mandy's face for the little girl in the story I'm illustrating? She'd be the little girl who tames the bear.'

Thomas smiled. 'What a lovely idea. Mandy will be thrilled. I don't mind at all.'

'Oh, good,' Ella said, relieved. 'I had to ask, of course, but I was hoping you'd like it.'

Thomas was about to say something but was interrupted by Mandy coming out through the door holding hands with another little girl with dark hair. 'Story time is over,' she said. 'This is my new friend. Her name is Hannah Primoss.'

'Primrose,' the girl corrected. 'Hannah Primrose.'

'What a pretty name,' Ella exclaimed. 'Hello, Mandy and hello, Hannah Primrose. My name is Ella Caron.'

'And this is my daddy, Thomas,' Mandy said, pointing at her father.

'Hello,' Hannah said shyly, letting go of Mandy's hand and holding it out to Thomas, who shook it.

'Did you enjoy the story?' Ella asked.

'Oh yes,' Mandy said. 'The lady reading it was so funny. She acted the voice of everyone in it.'

'What story was it?' Ella asked.

'It was *Pippi Longstocking*,' Mandy replied. 'She's a very strong girl who lives all alone with her horse and her monkey and she can do *anything*.'

'I loved her when I was little girl,' Ella said. 'In fact, I still do.'

'Mandy,' Thomas said. 'Ella is going to put you into the story she's illustrating. She's going to use your face for the little girl who tames a bear.'

'Oh!' Mandy exclaimed, putting her hands to her cheeks. 'Will it hurt?'

Ella laughed. 'No, of course not. I'm going to draw your face, not chop it off.'

Mandy let out a delicious giggle. 'I knew that. I was only joking. Can Hannah be in the story, too?'

'Of course,' Ella said. 'Lupita, that's the girl in the story, has a cat, which will be me, and a dog, too. So maybe Hannah would like to be the dog?'

'What kind of dog?' Hannah asked, seeming doubtful.

Mandy looked at Hannah. 'I think you could be a poodle with that dark curly hair. Would that be okay?' she asked, turning to Ella.

'It would be perfect,' Ella said. 'But maybe we should ask your parents first?'

'I only have a mum,' Hannah said. 'But I think she'll like it. Here she is now,' she continued as a tall woman with short dark hair carrying a baby on her hip came towards them. 'Hi, Mum, I met a new girl and her mummy and daddy.'

'No,' Ella protested, smiling at the woman. 'I'm not Mandy's mother. Just a friend. A new friend,' she added, trying her best to explain. 'I'm Ella.'

The woman laughed. 'Hi, Ella. I'm Maura Primrose. I think we've met at yoga a while ago.'

'Oh yes, of course,' Ella said after a moment's reflection. 'I remember you.'

'But I heard you had an accident. How are you?' Maura asked.

'Not too bad,' Ella replied. 'I'm trying to be more active. This is my first time out of the house today.' She gestured at Thomas. 'But I forget my manners. This is Mandy's dad, Thomas, who has just arrived in Sandy Cove.'

'Nice to meet you, Thomas,' Maura said and shook his hand. 'Your daughter seems to be settling in very well.'

'Yes,' Thomas said, looking at the little girls. 'I'm happy to see that.'

'Me too,' Maura agreed.

'I'm going to be a poodle in a story,' Hannah interrupted. 'Ella is drawing it and she wants me to be in it.'

'What?' Maura looked at Ella. 'Is this something to do with your work?'

'Yes,' Ella said. 'I'm illustrating a children's story. It has all kinds of animals and I thought I'd give them human faces, if you see what I mean.'

'I'm giving her my face,' Mandy said. 'And Hannah wants to be a poodle but only if you let her.' She drew breath.

Maura laughed. 'Well, that sounds a little strange, but I understand what you want to do, Ella. You have my permission to turn Hannah into a poodle,' she said with a laugh.

'Great. Thanks a lot,' Ella said.

'Yay, we're in a story!' Hannah chanted and clapped her hands.

'Fabulous,' Maura said. 'And so nice to see you out and about, Ella.' Her gaze drifted to Thomas. 'Our girls seem to be best friends already.'

'Yes, they do,' Thomas said, smiling at the two little girls.

'Hey, give me your number and we'll arrange a play date,' Maura suggested.

'Or,' Thomas said and took out his phone, 'give me yours and I'll send you a text.'

Maura rattled out her number and Thomas tapped it into his phone. Then she took Hannah's hand and hitched the baby, who was beginning to whine, higher on her hip. 'This is Sean and he's getting cranky so we'd better go. See you soon, Thomas. Hope you continue to improve, Ella.'

'Thanks,' Ella said. 'I'll get back to yoga as soon as I can.'

'We'd better be off, too,' Thomas said and took Mandy by the hand.

'Yeah, we have to buy things for the beach,' Mandy said. 'A bucket and a spade and a swimming ring and a rubber boat and a…'

'Whoa,' Thomas said, laughing. 'That's enough, young lady. I think a bucket and spade will do for now.'

'Sorcha in the grocery store sells those,' Ella cut in. 'She has an amazing array of things in her little shop.'

'We'll pop in there on the way home,' Thomas said. 'Nice to see you, Ella.'

'Bye for now,' Ella said. 'Enjoy the beach.'

'Bye, bye, Ella,' Mandy chanted, blowing kisses before she ran ahead down the street, with Thomas in her wake. He turned and shot Ella a brilliant smile and then ran after his daughter, who rounded the corner with impressive speed.

Ella laughed as they disappeared, feeling brighter after the pleasant interlude. Lucille was right. It had been good to get out of the house and see people. Especially Mandy again, not to mention her handsome dad. Ella thought of Thomas, who seemed such a wonderful father and a truly caring person. They had only just met but she could see that he still struggled with his grief and tried his best to be positive for his little girl. She hadn't reacted to him with her usual light-hearted banter and flirtatious glances, even though she found him very attractive. He was a single parent who had been through the huge tragedy of losing his wife, and that was off limits to Ella.

As she waited for Lucille, her thoughts drifted to her earlier life and her failed relationships that had all started so romantically but ended in tears and misery. She had a habit of falling passionately in love with men who swept her off her feet, promising to love her forever. Then, with Jean-Paul, the romantic proposal, the ring, the fairy-tale wedding and the honeymoon in an exotic place. With him, she had thought she'd have that happily ever after, and a baby in due course. But the baby turned out to be an impossible dream. She remembered each miscarriage like it was yesterday. They took it in their stride, she had thought, Jean-Paul hiding his disappointment before the shouting started and it all crashed and burned. It was as if he thought it was her fault and he didn't seem to understand her grief, he being the one to suffer the most.

It had happened the same way every time. Ella laughed ironically at herself as she thought of how she had been so easily carried away by a pair of velvet eyes, a handsome face or a deep voice. She had thought it would last forever with Jean-Paul, that they would have that perfect family life. And so it had seemed for a while – until the dream of having a family slowly faded.

But that was over now. She had to grow up and realise that the Prince Charming of her dreams just didn't exist. There was no strong man out there who would love and support her forever. That was just something that happened in silly novels. Now she was in her mid-forties with a single life, which wasn't all bad, really. Especially here, in this village where people were so helpful and friendly. She had said to Lucille that nothing ever happened, but there was still a lot of fun to be had if you knew how to look for it. Ella promised herself that when she recovered fully, she would join some groups and clubs and get more active in village life. Lucille was right about that too.

'There you are,' Lucille said as she came out the door of the library. 'Sorry you had to wait, but I was chatting to the staff. They want me to continue reading to the children once a week, isn't that nice?'

'Lovely,' Ella agreed, getting to her feet with the help of her crutches. 'Let's go home now, though. I'm tired after my first day out.'

'Of course you are,' Lucille said, looking a little guilty. 'I should have realised instead of chatting in there. But those girls were so helpful. They downloaded some pictures of harbours in Italy where cruise ships usually stop off. I'm going to send them to Rory, starting with Genoa. That's where this cruise I'm pretending to be on usually takes off.'

'Oh, God,' Ella said with a sigh. 'Are you sure he'll believe you?'

'I hope so,' Lucille replied. 'I'm very good at pretending.'

'Lying, you mean?'

'Well, if that's what you want to call it,' Lucille said gaily. 'But let's get you home. That's enough gallivanting for today. Tomorrow we could go to the beach, and then the next day I think you should try walking a little further down the road. Maybe to the garden centre? We can have coffee there in their cute little shop Sorcha told me about.'

Ella laughed as she made her way to the car. There was no stopping Lucille. She was going to get Ella back on her feet come hell or high water. She suddenly felt, despite a niggling worry, that Lucille's arrival would mark a new chapter in her own life.

Ella's initial misgivings faded away as it dawned on her what a gift Lucille's arrival was and how it somehow connected her with Rose, her mother she missed so much. *Nobody can replace my mother*, Ella thought, *but Lucille being here somehow brings her closer.* Was Lucille's arrival a gift her mother had sent her in some way? Ella started to look forward to living with this unusual woman, who refused to grow old. It wouldn't be easy to get used to Lucille's many foibles and she knew it would be hard to stop her doing what she wanted. Whatever happened, it certainly wouldn't be boring. But it continued to niggle at Ella that Lucille was weaving this tangled web of lies to her family. How long would it take before they discovered the truth?

Chapter Five

Ella's quiet routine was quickly ramped up to days full of challenges. Lucille cracked the whip of her exercise routine and Ella found herself working so hard that her weak muscles were constantly aching. But it didn't take long before she found her strength returning. Lucille also made Ella get out of the house for short walks or a trip in the car to various beauty spots where they would have coffee or lunch if there was a suitable café or restaurant in the neighbourhood, or a picnic if not. Lucille also brought Ella with her to the reading group at the library and other activities she had enrolled in. And she treated Ella to a day at a beauty salon in Killarney where she had a top-to-toe overhaul that included a much-needed haircut, a facial, a manicure and pedicure, which all made Ella feel nearly reborn. This was a huge boost to her self-confidence and, as Lucille put it, made her 'ready to join the human race again'.

But they weren't just out and about; they often spent long evenings at home over one of the delicious dinners Lucille cooked. She made every evening a party and they lingered over a glass of wine, talking, Lucille being very entertaining while she told Ella stories about her mother and about Lucille's 'life before Johnny', as she called it.

'In the late Fifties,' she said one evening during dinner on the terrace, 'we were beginning to live again after that long horrid war and the poverty that followed. Dublin was buzzing with new talent. There were actors, musicians, artists, writers and fashion designers all over the place and I often met them at the pub or at fun parties. I modelled for Sybil Connolly and later that dishy Dane who came to Ireland with his Scandinavian take on female fashion. What was his name again?'

'Ib Jorgensen?' Ella said.

Lucille nodded. 'Yes. That's him. Well remembered.'

'I studied Irish fashion for a bit in art college,' Ella said. 'And my mum often mentioned him when she was reminiscing. I think she had a dress or two by him in her wardrobe.'

'Did she?' Lucille nodded. 'Yes, I can believe that. She must have been quite elegant in her youth. We lost touch when we left school, so I only know what she told me later about her life and her marriage to your father. They had quite a glamorous life, I believe.'

'Very,' Ella said. 'They lived in Germany for a while, then Ireland, then London and then Ireland again. That's why I went to boarding school.'

'And finishing school in Switzerland,' Lucille filled in.

Ella laughed. 'Oh yeah, that was because Dad thought I'd get all the art nonsense out of my head and learn manners and get a real job. Talk about a total failure. I ran away twice and then they took me out of there. Mum knew there would be no point trying to make me forget about being an artist. She was the one who convinced my father to let me go to the École des Beaux-Arts in Paris.'

'And how right she was,' Lucille said. 'Just look at what you have achieved.'

'Until now,' Ella said with a sigh, glancing into the sunroom and the easel with the canvas waiting to be turned into a stunning seascape. 'The accident really put a stop to my painting. Why did I think I could stand by myself on that rickety ladder just to put a finishing touch on the mural? If I had left it alone, I wouldn't have fallen.' She shook her head in disgust at her stupidity. 'I could have been killed.'

'But you weren't,' Lucille said brightly. 'And you've made a remarkable recovery.'

Ella reached across the table and touched Lucille's hand. 'And you came to my rescue when I was feeling so low.'

'I needed to be needed,' Lucille said. 'Everyone does, really. It's by helping others that you help yourself, you know.'

'That's true,' Ella replied. 'But only a more mature person knows this.'

'You mean old?' Lucille asked. She leaned forward and fixed Ella with a steely gaze. 'I don't like that word, it's derogative. I'm not old, it's just that I have lived a long time. There is a difference, you know. You're never old if you don't want to be.'

Ella laughed. 'That's brilliant! And you're so right. I'm never going to be old either.'

'That's my girl,' Lucille said approvingly and raised her wineglass. 'Let's drink to that.'

The new routine continued at a steady pace, which helped Ella get back to work. When she was not on one of Lucille's outings,

Ella worked on her illustrations, which, with Mandy's help, were coming along nicely. Strange how a child could be so insightful, Ella mused. But she realised that children are more ready to live in a fictional world and believe in magic and fairy tales. The illustrations progressed and Ella had nearly all the faces she needed for the animals in the story. All except the bear. She just couldn't find the right face for him. She left that one aside, hoping it would come to her in a flash of inspiration one day.

A surprise visit late one evening introduced a false note into Ella's road to recovery. She was sitting in the sunroom poring over her sketches when the doorbell rang. Startled, she got up and made her way to the front door. Lucille was in Killarney staying the night in a fancy spa hotel where she had gone for an 'overhaul' as she called it. Who could be calling so late? Saskia looking for a bit of a chat before going to bed? But the shape she could see through the glass pane of the door was that of someone taller and broader. Thomas needing help with Mandy, Ella assumed, and opened the door with a smile that instantly died on her lips as she came face to face with Rory.

She stared at him for a moment, not quite knowing what to say. 'Hi, Rory,' she finally managed. 'What are you doing here?'

'Hi, Ella. Long time no see,' he said.

'Uh, yes. It's been a while,' she said awkwardly.

'Last time was around two years ago. At your mother's funeral,' he said. 'A very sad occasion for you.'

'Yes.' She paused, waiting for him to continue. 'But I don't suppose you've come to say sorry for my loss or anything.'

'No. I was in the area, on my way to Waterville for a legal conference, so I thought I'd call in to ask you something.'

'How did you know where I live?'

'Sandy Cove, County Kerry. Coastguard station. That's what I remembered your mother saying. Didn't know which one of the houses it was, but I picked this one at random and struck gold.'

'Congratulations,' Ella said ironically. 'So what did you want to ask?' she added, steeling herself for what he was about to say.

'It's about my mother,' he said.

'Lucille?' Ella asked with fake surprise in her voice.

'That's the only mother I have.'

'I know. So what about her?' Ella asked, hoping Lucille's bright red jacket hanging in the hall was not visible from the front door. She shifted to the side to make sure he couldn't see further into the house. By doing so, she saw him in the light of the setting sun and was reminded of how attractive he was with his nearly black hair and thick eyelashes over those brown eyes.

'Have you heard from her lately?' Rory asked.

Ella widened her eyes. 'Heard from her? In what way?'

'Has she called or sent a postcard or anything like that?'

'Postcard?' Ella said. 'From Tipperary? Why would she?'

His eyes narrowed. 'You're hiding something.'

Ella folded her arms, trying to look assertive despite her stomach contracting with nerves. 'What would I be hiding? Your mother? Under my bed or something?'

'Don't try to be smart.'

'I don't have to try.' Ella moved away slightly. 'Please don't look at me as if we're in a courtroom. Being a lawyer doesn't give you the right to barge in on people and interrogate them like this.'

'I'm just worried about my mother. She told us she was going on a cruise, you see.'

'So?'

'Well, that's not like her at all. She always said that going on one of those cruises would be her idea of torture. You must have heard her say that, too.'

'Not that I can remember.'

He kept staring at her. 'So you don't know where she is?'

'Right now? No idea.'

'So she isn't here, then?'

Ella held up her right hand. 'No, she is not. That's the truth, the whole truth and nothing but the truth, so help me God.'

'I suppose I have to believe you,' he said with a resigned sigh.

'Yes,' Ella said.

Rory nodded. 'Okay.'

'Great.'

'Fine.'

They looked at each other for a moment, the usual tension between them beginning to rise.

'I'd ask you in for a cup of tea,' Ella said. 'But I'm not really in the mood for company.'

'Especially mine?' he said with a lopsided smile.

'You got it.'

'Right,' he said, backing away. 'I'll be off then. Let me know if you hear from her.'

'You mean if I get a postcard? From that cruise she's on?'

He shrugged. 'Yeah, whatever. Bye for now, Ella.'

'Bye, Rory,' she replied, closing the door as he walked away.

She heard a car driving off and breathed a sigh of relief. She didn't think he had guessed that she knew anything and she didn't feel the slightest bit guilty about misleading him. What had rattled her nerves a little had been more about her own feelings and that buzz between them when they were arguing. That hadn't changed despite not having seen each other for over two years. But he was more trouble than it was worth and now she had the added worry of wanting to protect Lucille. But she had done her best to put him off ever calling again. She decided she wouldn't tell Lucille about Rory's visit. It would only upset her.

Ella went back to her drawings, trying to forget about Rory and turn her mind to more pleasant things, such as her lovely new neighbours who were beginning to become close friends. She had spent quite a lot of time chatting with Thomas, who she often met on nice days when he brought Mandy to the beach. They had struck up a casual friendship and Ella enjoyed talking to him about his music and her art projects. She liked his company and discovered what a well-educated and interesting man he was. She knew their friendship could go further if she could only get to know him better, but something stopped her from delving deeper into his life story. There was an immense sadness deep in his eyes, a sadness that created a wall between them that she couldn't get through. He didn't mention his wife much and Ella suspected he would never get over her death. But she hoped her company might help him feel like living again and look forward instead of back.

She often heard him play the piano late at night when she was on the terrace with a cup of tea before bed. The starry sky and the music wafting through the air were both so soothing she would later drift off to sleep in her bed, lulled by the beautiful soft notes that seemed to float into her window on the summer breeze. It was both healing and comforting, even though she knew he played to distract himself from his sorrows. She hoped that he would find solace here, in this beautiful place, like she had herself when she first came here.

Chapter Six

'Excellent,' the surgeon said, looking at Ella's X-rays on his screen. 'Your fracture is all healed up. You're moving better, too.'

Ella smiled proudly; she knew it was all thanks to Lucille that she had come this far in such a short time. It was three weeks since Lucille's sudden arrival at the coastguard station, and here she was, nearly restored to full health.

'It's all due to a lovely friend who came to stay with me nearly a month ago,' she said. 'She made me work so hard, not only physically but mentally. So instead of doing my exercises just when the physio came to the house, I worked every day. And she got me out of the house and gave me this enormous mental energy that made me want to fight like hell to get back to full health. I'm not there yet, though,' she confessed. 'I don't have much confidence, somehow. I'm always worried I'm going to slip and fall and find myself back in hospital.'

The surgeon, a bald man in his fifties with kind eyes, nodded. 'It's a mild case of post-traumatic stress. You feel anxious and frightened that it will all happen again.'

'Exactly,' Ella said. 'How do I deal with that? Will it go away?'

'I'm sure it will,' the doctor replied. 'But it's up to you to deal with it. Where there's a will there's a way, I always tell my patients. But maybe you need therapy? Talking to someone about it might help. Or meditation,' he added.

'Maybe,' Ella said, reluctant to go the therapist way. 'I've tried meditation and even therapy before, after my divorce, and it helped then.'

'Start with meditation,' the doctor said. 'If that doesn't help, do try to talk to someone.'

'I do have someone to talk to,' Ella said. 'Lucille, that friend I mentioned. I know I can talk to her about this, even if she isn't a professional therapist.'

'Whatever helps,' he said. 'You need to get your mental strength back.'

'Yes, I do,' Ella said.

'You look well, all the same,' he remarked. 'Still a little weak, but with pink cheeks and a big smile and something in your eyes that tells me you're not giving up on life. That's a big change from the last time I saw you, I have to say.'

'That's true,' Ella said, casting her mind back to that occasion, when she was feeling as if she would never get better and would always walk with the aid of crutches. 'That was four weeks ago, when I was just getting out of bed and getting used to crutches. I felt so totally broken, both in body and soul.'

'There's a little way to go yet,' the doctor remarked. 'You still can't take risks and you have to keep working on your lower back. It's the weak point after those two months in bed. Your muscles atrophied during that time. But keep doing what you're doing and maybe add some swimming now that the water is warmer. I hope you'll have your confidence back next time I see you. Work on that back and try to believe in yourself.'

'I will,' Ella promised.

As she walked out of the clinic, she thought of how far she had come, despite the lingering trauma. She would try her best to put all the pain and misery out of her mind and go forward. Lucille had been amazing the way she had pushed Ella to do her exercises but most of all to get herself into that can-do mode that was so important when recovering from a serious injury. It wasn't only that, Ella thought. Lucille had changed the whole atmosphere of her little house, which now smelled of home in a different way. It wasn't really a smell, but Lucille's warmth, wit and intelligence had given it such a welcoming feel, which had greatly added to Ella's well-being and healing.

Lucille was waiting in her car, looking at her phone when Ella crossed the car park. She looked up, staring at Ella with a faraway look in her eyes. 'Not good news,' she said darkly.

'What? Of course there is,' Ella said, confused, as she got into the car. 'The doctor was very pleased. He was amazed by my rapid recovery. And that is all thanks to you.' Ella leaned over and placed a kiss on Lucille's cheek.

'Oh, I didn't mean that,' Lucille explained. 'That's excellent news, of course. No, I meant *my* news. My cover has been blown. Rory is on to me. He just sent me a text saying I'm not fooling him any more and to stop sending fake photos of my cruise.'

'How did he know they were fake?'

'Oh, eh,' Lucille said, looking slightly guilty. 'Could have been the photo of the handsome captain. I used one of Stewart Granger I found on some site.'

'Who?'

'Exactly. I thought Rory would be just as ignorant of old film stars as you. Stewart Granger was a real heartthrob back in the days.'

'Oh, God, Lucille. You mad thing. What did Rory say?'

'He demands to know where I am, but I'm not going to tell him.'

'Maybe you should?' Ella suggested. She was tempted to tell Lucille about Rory's visit a few weeks ago, but changed her mind. No need to worry her further as she was already so agitated. 'I mean, he might be worried about you,' she said instead. 'Or he might be missing you. Isn't it a bit mean to keep hiding from your family like this?'

Lucille frowned. 'Maybe a little bit. But I need to get myself organised before I contact them. It's all going ahead as planned, but I need more time. I don't want any distractions before I'm ready.'

'What is going ahead as planned?' Ella asked, mystified.

'My new life,' Lucille said cryptically as she started the car. 'And something really interesting I'm working on. I'm in the right place to find out what I want to know. But' – Lucille raised a warning finger – 'I'm not going to tell you yet, so don't ask any more ques- tions. You'll find out when the time is right.'

'I see,' Ella said, knowing there was no use continuing. She only hoped it would all work out in the end and life would settle back into what used to be her ordered existence before the accident. She needed to start working on her painting, especially that unfinished canvas still sitting on her easel in the sunroom.

Ella studied Lucille as they drove out of Killarney and headed for home. She looked fairly calm, but Ella knew that message from her son had rattled her. During the three weeks since her arrival, Lucille had been busy on her laptop when she wasn't managing Ella's recovery programme or going out to all the activities and groups she had joined. She was up to something, that was quite obvious, even though Ella had thought she was chatting with people on Facebook or maybe even watching movies. Then there was that letter that had arrived, followed by another one two weeks later, which had also been hastily put away unopened. Something was going on that Lucille wasn't telling Ella about and it had nothing to do with her house hunting or her family. Something was making Lucille all flustered and frightened. But what on earth could it be?

It took Rory another three days to find his mother. Lucille had thought she was safe and that nobody would guess where she had gone. Ella thought she'd convinced him that she wasn't in Sandy Cove. But there he was, one misty morning, ringing Ella's doorbell again.

'I'm back,' he said as Ella opened the door in her pyjamas.

'Rory,' she said, startled. She hadn't expected him to turn up like this again or to look at her with that scowl in his dark brown eyes. 'Hi. What a surprise to see you here.'

'Is it?' he asked.

'Yes, of course. I didn't think I'd see you again.'

'You mean you hoped you wouldn't?' he asked with the beginning of a smile. 'We had a few arguments back when our mothers lived together, didn't we? You were pretty stroppy, then.'

Ella stuck out her chin. 'I still am.'

'As I discovered a few weeks ago. I can tell by the look in your eyes you're not going to change.'

'And I suppose you're still as annoying as hell?'

'Even more so,' Rory retorted. 'I can't help it. It's in my nature.'

'That's no excuse for being obnoxious,' Ella remarked, beginning to enjoy their sparring, while desperately trying to think of a way to hide Lucille's whereabouts. She had to convince him and make him leave before Lucille came back from the beach. 'You could deal with it if you tried very hard.'

'Nah,' Rory said. 'Why should I? I like being obnoxious.'

'I remember my mother saying Lucille had spoiled you rotten.'

'So this character flaw is not my fault, then. What a relief.'

'To you perhaps,' Ella said, folding her arms.

'Can we drop this now? I didn't come here to argue with you.'

'Why did you come, then?' Ella enquired.

'To see my mother. She's here, isn't she?' Rory asked, trying to look past Ella into the house.

'No, she's on a cruise in the Mediterranean,' Ella said, trying to keep a straight face. But she was beginning to feel a little awkward standing there in her pyjamas.

'Yeah, right,' Rory said. 'She didn't fool me with that story and neither do you. You managed to convince me last time, but you're not going to succeed this time, so could you stop pretending, please?'

'Oh okay, she's not on a cruise,' Ella said, feeling flustered. She couldn't help notice yet again that with his strong rugby-playing physique, thick black hair and deep brown eyes he was very attractive. There was also something else about him that occurred to her, but it was gone before she knew what it was. 'She's staying here but she's not in right now.' She was telling the truth. Even though it was only eight o'clock on a Saturday morning, Lucille was doing tai chi with her group on the main beach.

'I have the right to see my mother,' Rory said, glaring at her. 'There's no use trying to stop me.' He took a step forward.

Ella backed away. 'If you force yourself in, I'll call the Guards. You have no right to barge in like this. You should know that, being a lawyer and all.'

'What does that have to do with it?' he asked, his voice laced with irritation. 'Lucille is my mother. I have to get her to be sensible. She's eighty-five, for God's sake. She shouldn't be running around the country like this.'

Ella bristled. 'Why not? Lucille might be eighty-five, but she's perfectly fit and an adult, so she's free to do what she wants and go where she wants. And to spend her money on whatever she desires,' she added.

'Well… maybe. But…' Rory paused, looking at Ella, his eyes calmer. He pushed his thick black fringe out of his eyes. 'Okay, I'm sorry. Shouldn't have accused you of lying. And you're right. My mum has every right to do what she wants with her life. And her money.'

'I'm glad we cleared that up,' Ella said coolly.

'Yeah, well but I still want to talk to her. I suppose she's gone for a walk or something?' He paused. 'You can't deny she's living with you. I know for a fact that she is.'

'I'm not denying anything,' Ella said, feeling there was no use arguing about it any more. He obviously knew. 'I just told you she's staying here. But I…' She backed into the house. 'I've only just got up, you know. I was about to get into the shower and get dressed. Lucille should be home in an hour or so. I'm not sure she'll agree to see you, though, but I'll tell her you called. That's all I can do.'

He nodded, looking calmer. 'Okay.'

'Just one thing before you go,' Ella started. 'How did you find out she was here?'

'The post office in Tipperary,' Rory said. 'I called into the branch in town and they told me she had redirected her post to this address. The rest was easy. Should have thought of that earlier, actually.'

'Oh. I see. Are they really allowed to do that? Isn't it confidential?'

Rory shrugged. 'Probably. But the postmaster and I went to primary school together. You know what it's like in a country town.'

'God, yes,' Ella said, laughing as her annoyance melted under his gaze. 'It's the same here. Everyone knows everyone else. It's like one big family. Can be a bit annoying, but mostly it's kind of comforting.'

'So you have family connections here then?' he asked. 'I never knew where your mother was actually from. Only that she and my mother went to that girls' boarding school together. And that you're half French, of course,' he added.

'Yes. That's right. I'm a blow-in from Paris and all kinds of other places,' Ella said, not wanting to reveal the true story of her family connections. She shivered slightly in the cold breeze through the open door. 'But I'm not going to stand here and share the story of my life with you. It's getting cold and it feels weird to be talking to you in my PJs.'

'Sorry. I'll come back later, then,' he said, looking a little self-conscious. 'I completely forgot you weren't properly dressed.'

'Really?' Ella asked pointedly, which made him look even more awkward.

'See you later, then,' he said.

'If I'm here.' Ella started to close the door. 'Could you call your mum first before you come back?' she said as an afterthought through a crack in the door. 'Just to make sure she wants to see you, I mean.'

'She'll see me,' he retorted, flashing her a confident smile.

'I wouldn't count on it,' Ella said and banged the door shut before he had a chance to reply.

Ella stood in the small hall for a moment trying to gather her thoughts. Rory's arrival had startled her, and his behaviour had annoyed her. But she couldn't deny she found him hugely attractive. She always had. That wasn't what excited her the most, however. Her heart raced as she suddenly knew in a flash of inspiration what had occurred to her earlier. She had found the missing ingredient she needed for the book.

Ella didn't give herself time to get dressed but ran into the sunroom, sat down at the table and grabbed her sketchpad. She just had to get that face and those brown eyes down while it was still fresh in her mind. He was perfect for the bear that the little girl in the story ended up taming. He was fierce and threatening at first but Lupita wasn't afraid of his growls or his angry scowl. She managed to calm his hot temper and talk him out of his anger towards humans, showing him that kindness and empathy were far better qualities than strength and defiance.

Ella barely heard the front door open and she gave a start when Lucille walked into the room.

'You're working?' Lucille asked. 'But it's the weekend. I thought you were taking a break.'

'Yes, but…' Ella started, trying to cover her drawing with her hand.

But it was too late. Lucille had seen it over Ella's shoulder. She laughed as she looked at the face of the bear. 'Those eyes remind me of Rory,' she remarked.

Ella turned and put her hand on Lucille's arm. 'I have something to tell you. He's here, Lucille.'

'Rory?' Lucille, her face suddenly ashen, sank down on the other chair by the worktable. 'Here? In Sandy Cove?'

'Yes. He called in when you were at the beach. I couldn't lie to him and deny you were staying here.'

'Why not? You said you would, remember? Why did you change your mind and break your promise?'

'Because he knew. He had checked with the post office in your town and they told him that you redirected your post to this address. The postmaster and Rory were friends in primary school, he said, so he felt he could share that information.'

'That little sneak Colin Murphy,' Lucille muttered. 'He was always a tell-tale when he was a little boy. I see he hasn't changed.'

'I suppose not. In any case I couldn't keep lying to Rory when he already knew you were here. I didn't tell him everything, though. He only knows you're here but not that you're selling the house or anything else.'

'I see,' Lucille said glumly. 'At least he doesn't know what I'm planning to do.'

'He wants to see you.'

'Oh no, I don't think I want to see him right now,' Lucille protested with panic in her eyes. 'I don't think I could cope with him. He'll only force me to go back home. I'll be putting my house on the market soon and he will try to stop me. But I want to move here.'

'I know you do,' Ella said. 'And why shouldn't you?'

Lucille shrugged, looking sad. 'Because my sons will think it's completely cracked. They'll want me to keep the house so they can use it as their country retreat for weekends now and then, and invite friends to stay. But I'm tired of running a B&B for whenever they feel like it. The rest of the time I'm all alone in that big house. I feel much happier here in the village with people all around me.'

'Why can't you tell Rory that?'

'Because he won't see my point of view. He never does. And then he's my little boy – I can never resist him. He always manages to get around me.'

'But how can you avoid seeing him?' Ella asked. 'Wouldn't it be better to let him come here for a chat and get it over with? I don't see how he can make you do anything against your will.'

Lucille looked at Ella for a moment without replying. Then she nodded. 'You're right. I should see him. But only if you're with me. I don't feel strong enough to cope with him on my own.' Her gaze drifted to Ella's sketch. 'You got him absolutely right. Turning him into a bear in that story is perfect. And you have that cheeky glint in the eyes perfectly. That's a danger sign, you know.'

'This bear is tamed at the end of the story,' Ella remarked. 'By a little girl and then they become best friends and set out to save the planet together.'

'That's a beautiful story,' Lucille said. 'But I doubt it would happen in real life. Rory will never be tamed. Many women have tried but never succeeded.'

'Ah, but they didn't have my chutzpah,' Ella said with a wink. 'Just let him try to make you leave and he'll be a bear with a very sore head.' It was meant as a joke to cheer Lucille up, but as she said it, Ella remembered the look Rory had given her before he left, a look that said he thought he'd get his way and convince Lucille to go back to Tipperary. Ella had to make sure he didn't win. Lucille, despite being hyperactive and quite challenging to live with, had become so dear to Ella during the past weeks and she was determined to defend Lucille's right to do whatever would make her happy.

'They don't understand me,' Lucille said. 'I want to live a little before I go. Even if it's not sensible. Life begins at the end of your comfort zone. Do you know what I mean?'

'Oh yes,' Ella said. 'The road less travelled is always the more interesting. Even if you end up in a ditch.'

Lucille nodded. 'Exactly. Life is for living, isn't it?'

'Yes, it is,' Ella said with feeling.

Lucille got up. 'I'll leave you to your work. I have a few things to do myself,' she added.

Ella looked up from her drawing. 'What's on the agenda for today?'

'Uh, um… First a little work on my laptop. Then lunch in the village with a new friend and then I'll be home. And tomorrow…' Lucille paused, her eyes glittering with excitement. 'I'm looking at a house. Will you come with me?'

'I'd love to,' Ella said. 'Where is it?'

'In the main street. Opposite the post office. A dear little cottage that's a bit rundown. But it has potential, the agent said.'

'They always do,' Ella remarked.

'I know, but I think this one is special. I've seen it from the outside already. But I don't know if I'll tell Rory about it. I don't know what to do about him, actually.'

'You know what, Lucille?' Ella said. 'I think you *should* see him. Better to get it over with. Then you can tell him to go back to Dublin and leave you alone once you've made it clear that you're going to live your life your way and nobody else's.'

Lucille sighed. 'You don't know Rory. But I'll try to talk to him. I'll call him in a minute and ask him to come here before dinner.'

'Why not ask him to stay and eat with us?' Ella asked. 'Beat him at his own game and butter him up with food and wine and compliments.'

Lucille laughed and shook her head. 'You're a bad girl, Ella,' she said approvingly. 'Maybe it will work if you help. Flirt with him a little and pretend you agree with him.'

'Of course. And we'll both dress up and turn it into a party. His head will be spinning.'

'Good idea.' Lucille started to walk out of the room. 'Hmm,' she muttered as she fished her phone out of her enormous handbag. 'Beat him at his own game, eh?' She stopped at the door to the living room and punched in a number. 'Rory,' she gushed when her call was answered. 'How are you? I heard you called in.' She paused and listened. 'Oh, never mind that. I'll be happy to see you. Ella is cooking something French tonight and we'd love for you to join us.' Lucille paused and listened. 'You can make it? Seven o'clock all right? Wonderful. See you then, darling.' She hung up and looked at Ella, letting out a giggle. 'He sounded very confused. But he'll come. So we'll have to work out a strategy before he arrives.'

'And get something to cook,' Ella said, thinking hard. 'Maybe you could pick up a few things at Sorcha's on your way home? And see if they have any crab claws at the fish stand in the harbour. I'll write a list for you.'

'I will,' Lucille promised.

Ella chewed on her pencil when Lucille had left, wondering what she could cook that would put Rory in a good mood. Crab claws to start would be great. Then something simple but delicious. As Ella thought of what to serve this man with the brooding dark eyes, she had a feeling the evening would be full of conflict. How could she help Lucille if her son was so good at manipulating her? Ella's stomach felt full of butterflies as she imagined the worst. Then she looked at the face in her sketch and met those eyes. *I will do my best to tame you, Mr Bear,* she thought. *Even if it ends in tears.*

Chapter Seven

By half past six they were nearly ready. Lucille, dressed in one of her colourful tunics with white trousers and silver trainers, laid the table on the terrace as it was nice evening. The sun bathed the slopes in a golden light and the slight breeze ruffled the water of the bay below the cliffs. 'He'll love these views,' Lucille said as Ella, dressed in her signature black T-shirt and trousers teamed with big sparkly earrings, emerged from the sunroom with a plate of crab claws and a bowl of home-made mayonnaise.

'Who wouldn't?' Ella said, pausing to look out over the glittering sea. 'It's a stunning evening, too.'

'Beautiful,' Lucille agreed as the cork came away with a loud pop. 'He'll love this wine. It's from Johnny's wine cellar. I brought a few bottles just in case.'

'Just in case of what?'

'Of this happening,' Lucille said. 'Having to humour someone. You must always have a plan B, you know.'

'What was plan A?' Ella asked, amused.

'Him not finding me,' Lucille explained. 'But if that didn't work, I needed a safety net. Hope for the best but be prepared for the worst, is my motto.'

Ella nodded and put her burden on the table. 'That's true. I often forget. But tell me, is the food okay? I thought I'd keep it simple but now I feel a little nervous.'

'It's perfect,' Lucille assured her. 'Crab claws followed by steak and chips. He'll love it.'

'I prefer to call it *steak frites avec Béarnaise sauce*,' Ella said. 'It's a little different to what you'd get in a pub. The chips, I mean. I cut them very thin and I'll be using my *friteuse* I brought from Paris. And the sauce is homemade, of course.'

'But of course,' Lucille said dreamily. 'I love the word *friteuse*, even though I know it's just a deep frier. It sounds so poetic in French.'

'Everything does,' Ella agreed. 'I do miss France,' she added, feeling a pang of nostalgia. 'Especially Paris.'

'Me too,' Lucille said. 'I was there in the Sixties. I spent two months dancing with the Bluebell Girls, you know.'

Ella forgot about the menu as she stared at Lucille. 'You did? Oh my God, the Bluebell Girls. They were fabulous.'

'The Bluebell Girls were founded by an Irishwoman in the 1930s. Did you know that? Her name was Margaret Kelly.'

'I had no idea,' Ella replied. 'I only know that those girls had to be very tall and that they were one of the dance troupes at The Lido on the Champs-Élysées. But why did you only stay with them for two months? What happened?'

'Johnny happened,' Lucille replied with a wistful smile. 'He spotted me in the line of dancers and came to the stage door after the show. I didn't usually pay any attention to the men who waited outside. We used to try to ignore them and walk past them very quickly. But that night I saw this tall man with a beautiful smile and lovely brown eyes and stopped to say hello. What harm could it do? I thought. He said hello and told me how much he had enjoyed the show in this soft Tipperary accent. I was homesick for Ireland, so I stayed chatting to him. He asked if I'd like to join him for a bite to eat in a little restaurant around the corner. I was starving, so I said yes, even though it was very late. We fell in love over a plate of *coq au vin* and the rest is history.' Lucille sighed. 'We had a whirlwind romance right there in Paris. He had a horse running in the Prix de l'Arc at Longchamp the next day. You know, the most glamorous horse race event in Paris in the autumn.'

'I know. It's a bit like Ascot,' Ella replied. 'I went once. It was wonderful. The elegant crowd, the women all dressed up in haute couture, the beautiful horses. Amazing.'

'Exactly. So of course I went with him and cheered the horse on and it won. He said I was his lucky charm. He proposed that evening at a champagne supper to celebrate. We were married three months later and truly lived happily ever after. Until death did us part,' Lucille added, her eyes glistening with tears. She put her hand on her chest. 'I'm sorry. I didn't mean to tell you a sad story.'

'It was mostly happy,' Ella said, putting her arm around Lucille. 'I mean, you were so in love and stayed that way all through your life together. That's so romantic.'

'You're right.' Lucille took a paper napkin from the table and dabbed her eyes. 'It's a happy story, really. I was so lucky to meet him and to have been happy for so long. He's up there, you know,' Lucille said, pointing at the sky. 'Looking down and cheering me on. Keeping me going until we meet again. That's why I love this place. You can see the stars so clearly here. I imagine Johnny winking at me.'

'Aww,' Ella said, giving Lucille a squeeze. 'How beautiful.'

Lucille pulled away. 'But back to the dinner,' she said briskly. 'I think it's all in place. I don't see how Rory is not going to be in a good mood.'

'Neither can I,' Ella said. 'But you never know with men.' *Especially the moody types*, she thought, remembering her ex-husband, whose mood could change in an instant and be very dark for no apparent reason at all. In fact, most of the men in her relationships had been the same; that was part of what had attracted her to them. She was drawn to men with lively minds and strong feelings, even if that meant a lot of arguments. It had also meant painful break-ups and after the last one, she had vowed not to get involved with that kind of man ever again. At her age, she needed calmer waters, kindness and compassion, not heated rows about things that didn't matter.

Ella sighed and went back to the kitchen, where she put together the ingredients for the Béarnaise sauce and laid out the steaks on a wooden board. The chips had already been fried in the deep frier once and would only need a quick fry-up once the meat was cooking and the sauce was whisked together. A deceptively simple meal that demanded a lot of careful preparation. The easiest thing to prepare were the haricot beans.

Ella gave a start as the doorbell rang. He was here. She mentally crossed her fingers that the evening would go as planned. She smoothed her hair back and took a deep breath before she went into the hall, glancing at herself in the mirror. She looked very good tonight. Black was the perfect colour for her, and the dangly earrings with the glittering stones brought out the green flecks in her hazel eyes, which she had lined with kohl for a dramatic look. She took another deep breath and opened the door.

Chapter Eight

They looked at each other for a loaded moment until Ella spoke. 'Hello, Rory,' she said with a broad smile. 'Welcome. Nice to see you again.'

Rory kept staring at her. 'Wow,' he blurted out before he pulled himself together. 'Hi. Very nice to see you, eh, Ella.' He was still in the jeans, white shirt and a navy sweater that he had been wearing earlier, but he'd shaved since then and brushed his hair.

'Rory!' Lucille gushed behind Ella, holding out her arms. 'I'm so happy to see you.'

'Really?' he asked ironically and kissed his mother's cheek. 'You look great, I must say. Very elegant.'

'Thank you,' Lucille said, looking flattered. 'It's one of my outfits for the cruise.'

'The one you didn't go on, you mean,' Rory filled in.

'Yes,' Lucille said with a giggle. 'But I would have worn this if I'd been on it.'

Rory rolled his eyes. 'As if you would. Did you really think I'd fall for it?'

'You did for a while, though,' Lucille countered. 'But come in and go through to the terrace. We're eating outside as it's such a nice evening.' Lucille proceeded to lead the way through the living room.

Rory glanced at the paintings on the walls. 'Yours?' he asked Ella.

'Yes. All mine,' she said proudly.

'Nice.' Rory pointed at the abstract. 'But isn't that one hanging upside down?'

'Ha ha,' Ella drawled.

'Stop teasing Ella,' Lucille ordered and waved Rory on through the sunroom to the terrace where she stopped and made a sweeping gesture. 'Isn't this magnificent? The south-west of Ireland at its best.'

Rory looked at the view and nodded, putting on his sunglasses that had been sitting on the top of his head. 'Fantastic, I have to agree. Beats the Bay of Naples that you visited on that virtual cruise of yours. Loved the photo you sent. But that was the one that gave you away. It was from ten years ago, it said when I checked the photo on Google. And the handsome Stewart Granger look-alike captain.'

Lucille looked a little sheepish. 'Maybe that was too obvious. How silly of me. Should have paid more attention.'

'Maybe you should,' Rory said, his gaze drifting to Ella. 'I couldn't help notice all the canvases and the easel in the sunroom. Is that your studio?'

'Yes,' Ella replied. 'I do all my work in there, both my painting and drawing. The light is fantastic, even on a rainy day.'

'I can imagine.'

'Maybe we should sit down,' Lucille suggested and pulled out a chair. 'The crab claws might get too warm if we don't eat them right now.'

'Good idea,' Rory said and pulled out a chair for Ella. 'After you, *madame*.'

'*Merci, monsieur*,' Ella said with a smile and sat down.

Rory settled on the chair beside his mother. 'This looks delicious,' he said and passed the platter of crab claws to Lucille.

They started to eat while chatting about trivial things like the weather, what to do and see in the area, local politics and whatever had been in the latest news. But even though the crab claws were a big hit and the views still stunning, there was a tension in the air like a string on a guitar ready to snap. Lucille kept up her sweetness and light act, but Ella could see Rory wasn't buying it. He kept looking from Ella to Lucille, his eyes narrowing when Lucille kept saying how close they had become. 'Ella is like the daughter I never had,' she said, blowing a kiss across the table.

'Oh yeah?' Rory said. 'How lovely for you, Mum.' But he didn't look as if he thought it was lovely at all.

'It is,' Lucille said. 'And now I'm looking for a little house here in the village.'

'You're going to buy a house?' Rory asked, looking alarmed. 'But what about our house in Tipperary?'

'That's *my* house,' Lucille corrected.

'But it's the house I grew up in,' Rory argued. 'It's our inheritance. Martin's and mine, I mean.'

Lucille looked at him for a moment. 'Inheritance? You can't have an inheritance before someone's died. And I'm not going to. For a very long time. In the meantime, I'm going to spend my money and have a little fun before I pop my clogs.'

'Fun?' Rory asked. 'What kind of fun can you have when…' He stopped.

'When your days are numbered?' Lucille asked, raising one eyebrow. 'Nobody knows when they're going to die, you know.

I could have twenty years left for all you know. Remember that my mother lived to a hundred and three. Could have been longer if she hadn't slipped on the ice and broken her hip. Then she got pneumonia and that was the end of her, God rest her soul.' Lucille drew breath and took a swig of white wine. Then she looked at Rory. 'The house is mine and I'll do whatever I want with it. And I'll spend money the way I see fit.'

'I'm not really worried about the money,' Rory said. 'You can blow it all on cruises and fancy clothes for all I care. I just don't want to see that house deserted. It's our home, our family residence. You should be living there, not in this place. And buying some little house here is utter madness. What would Dad say, do you think?'

'He'd say, "Go for it, Lucille,"' she replied. 'He always did.'

'I know,' Rory said with a sigh. 'The two of you were wild.'

Lucille winked. 'We were cool before it was invented. And I intend to remain that way.'

'God help us all,' Rory said with a deep sigh. He glanced at Ella. 'I suppose you're in on this?'

'You mean it's all my fault now?' Ella enquired stiffly.

'Well, I'm sure there's two of you in it.'

'That's right,' Lucille quipped. 'We're a gang. And nobody can tell us what to do.'

Ella suddenly felt uncomfortable as Rory looked from one to the other. 'Uh, I think I'll go and cook the steaks now,' she said and got up. 'How do you like yours, Rory?'

'Very dark on the outside but rare on the inside. But I don't expect you'd know how to do that.'

'I'll give it my best shot,' Ella said.

With that, she walked into the house before awaiting a reply. In the kitchen, she switched on the deep frier for the chips and then heated the frying pan and proceeded to cook the steaks once it was sizzling hot. It didn't take long to whisk together the sauce while the steaks cooked and the chips were finished, Rory's steak needing less than a minute on each side. Ella tried to concentrate on the food while she thought of the conversation on the terrace. Rory was obviously upset about losing his childhood home. But he seemed to forget that Lucille wanted to change her lifestyle and live near people in a place where she would have plenty of human contact, instead of being all alone in a big house in the country. The dilemma was obvious. On the one hand, Rory and his brother wanted their mother to stay in the big family home and look after them whenever they decided to come for a cosy weekend; on the other, Lucille was on her own most of the time in that huge house with nobody to talk to or call in an emergency, or if she was just feeling sad and lonely.

She was putting the sauce into a sauce boat when Rory arrived in the kitchen carrying the plates and a bowl of crab shells.

'Where do I put these?' he asked.

'Just put the plates in the sink. I'll sort them later,' Ella said. 'The crab shells have to go in the bin in the utility room straight away, because they smell to high heaven after a while.'

Rory put the dishes in the sink and stood there for a while with the bowl of crab shells. 'So you know how to cook, eh?' he said, looking strangely at her.

Ella turned and met his eyes. 'Well, I think I managed to cook your steak the way you like them without much trouble.'

'I was teasing you,' Rory said. 'Just to see how you'd react.'

'Were you disappointed?' Ella turned the steaks and checked the deep fryer.

'Not at all,' he replied. 'I was pleasantly surprised.' He entered the utility room. 'I'll just get rid of these and then help you carry out everything. Those steaks look delicious.'

'Dark enough for you?' Ella asked with a touch of irony as she took three warm plates out of the oven.

'Perfect.'

Ella started to place the steaks and chips and the haricot beans on each of the plates. Then she handed Rory a plate and the sauce boat. 'Could you take these out and I'll bring the other plates?'

'Of course.' He flashed her a smile. 'I can tell you're a good cook.'

'When I'm in the mood.'

'And when you're not?'

'I order pizza.'

Rory laughed and walked out, Ella following with the other plates. Once on the terrace, they sat down while Lucille poured red wine from a bottle she had just opened. 'Château Talbot, 2005,' she said.

'From our wine cellar at home?' Rory asked.

'From *my* wine cellar,' Lucille corrected. She sat down and picked up her knife and fork. 'This looks and smells fantastic, Ella.'

Rory seemed to enjoy his steak. He sipped the wine slowly, savouring the flavours. 'How much of this wine have you got left?' he asked.

'I'm not sure,' Lucille replied as she helped herself to salad. 'I brought two bottles of this one and some Beaujolais and then a few of the Chablis, that's all. But I intend to go and get the rest when I'm settled in my own place. That'll take a while, though.'

'You're really going to move here?' Rory asked incredulously.

'Of course,' Lucille replied. 'Why can't you accept that?'

'I'm doing my best,' Rory said, putting down his knife and fork.

'More sauce?' Ella cut in and pushed the sauce boat across the table.

Rory shook his head. 'No, thanks. I'm not really a huge fan of that kind of sauce with steak. You don't happen to have any ketchup?'

Ella looked at him, knowing he was trying to annoy her. 'Oh, no,' she exclaimed. 'How silly of me. I forgot to buy some. I don't use it myself but I should have known you wouldn't be into fine cuisine. Sorry about that.'

'That's okay,' Rory replied. 'I'll just have to manage without it.' He turned to his mother. 'So the house, Mum, have you thought this through? Maybe we should have a family meeting?'

'No need,' Lucille said. 'I have made up my mind. There's a sweet little house for sale in the village that we're going to look at tomorrow. If I like it, I'll put in an offer. And then I'll move here with my dog and my cat and my chickens that Rita Murphy who lives nearby is looking after for me. It'll be grand, I tell you. I'll have enough money to take little trips abroad from time to time as well and stay in those boutique hotels with pools and spas. I'm so looking forward to it.'

'But what are you going to do when you can't manage on your own any more?' Rory asked. 'You'll be living so far from Martin and me.'

'Then I'll either get a housekeeper, or maybe use my plan B.'

'Plan B?' Rory asked. 'What is that, if you don't mind my asking?'

Lucille drained her wine glass. 'I'm going to become a nun.'

Rory stared at her. 'What?' He glanced at Ella. 'Is this something you've cooked up?'

'Absolutely not,' Ella protested. She looked at Lucille. 'A nun?' she asked. 'What do you mean?'

'I would enter a convent,' Lucille said. 'I've been thinking about this for a while. My aunt was a nun and she was very happy until the day she died.'

'Was that the aunt who fell off her bike and broke her leg in Grafton Street?' Rory asked, looking highly amused. 'I always loved that story.'

Lucille nodded. 'Yes. My Aunt Nora. Later called Sister Assumpta. Nuns look after each other and they always seem jolly and smiley to me,' she continued. 'Living in a convent would be a lot better than one of those dreary nursing homes. And it's free and there are no men. Seems perfect to me.'

'You'd be a terrible nun,' Rory said. 'You don't even go to Mass that often.'

'I'm going to start,' Lucille declared. 'I like the look of the little church here. And the parish priest is very nice. I've met him in the grocery shop several times. He has helped me get things down from the higher shelves, and he always lets me go before him in the queue at the checkout. I'm sure he'll put in a good word for me when the time comes.'

'Yes, but will they really accept you into the convent so late in life?' Ella asked, trying her best to keep a straight face. 'If you're old and weak, I mean.'

'I'm sure they will,' Lucille said. 'Why wouldn't they? It's all about being truly Christian, isn't it?' She shot a triumphant look at Rory. 'See? I can manage all by myself without being a burden on my children. Plan A is already in motion, and plan B is just in case plan A falls apart. All you and Martin will have to do finally is bury me with Johnny. Not too hard, is it?'

Rory sighed and pushed away his plate with a half-eaten steak. 'Mum, this is terrible. Why do you think you're some kind of burden? Martin and I do care about you and we want to see you from time to time. If you feel lonely in the house in Tipperary, you could come and live with Martin and Fiona and we could keep the house as a country place for us to go to at the weekends.'

'That's not a very good idea, Rory,' Lucille said, looking suddenly sad. 'I don't want to live with either of you. Martin and Fiona would hate having me there after a while. Especially Fiona. I can't imagine how she'd feel having her mother-in-law in the same house. And I couldn't possibly live in your flat in the middle of town. I want to be independent, have my own front door and my own life.'

'Yes, but…' Rory started.

'Yes, but – what?' Lucille snapped. 'I'm not going to be an older woman who's wilting away by loneliness and ends up being eaten by my cat.'

'Of course not,' Rory said. 'Who says you would? We want to look after you. Can't you see that?'

'I'm perfectly capable of looking after myself.'

'Right now, maybe,' Rory said. 'But you're not getting any younger.'

'Who is?' Lucille asked. She looked at Ella. 'Explain to him, Ella. Tell him how much fun we've had and how I'm already so involved with everyone in the village.'

Ella nodded, looking at Rory. 'Yes, it's true. Lucille has been amazing since she arrived. She certainly shook me up and got me back on my feet. I'm not quite there yet, but she has cheered me up no end. She won't be staying with me much longer, but we'll be seeing each other often. I think her living here in the village is a wonderful idea. So I'm on her side one hundred per cent.' Ella drew breath and kept looking at Rory, daring him to protest.

Rory was silent for a moment. 'Okay. I get it,' he finally said. 'You've said your piece. I don't agree with this at all. I think it's completely cracked. There isn't much I can do about it, though. In any case, I have some news of my own.'

'News?' Lucille asked. 'What about? Are you getting married at last?'

'No,' Rory said, looking annoyed. 'It's about my summer holidays. I'm going to stay here until I go back to work.'

'What?' Lucille said, looking shocked. 'Stay here? Why?'

Rory looked at his mother for a moment. 'Because I want to spend some time with you. I want to try to understand what you're doing and why. The real reason, I mean. And maybe, in time, you'll come to your senses and move back home.'

'But I told you why,' Lucille argued. 'There is no other reason. I won't change my mind, no matter what you do or say.'

Rory didn't look convinced. 'Well, maybe I just want to get to know the area that you seem to be so fond of, then.'

'Where are you going to stay?' Lucille asked, looking worried.

'Lovely little spot on the road to Ballinskelligs,' Rory replied. 'Self-catering accommodation at a place called Riverside Farm. It's perfect for me. A room and kitchenette and bathroom. It's comfortable enough. Just off some great hiking trails. I can hire a bike and cycle around the area, too.'

'And spy on me,' Lucille said, looking crossly at him.

'Oh Mum, that's not how I see it,' Rory said, looking exasperated. 'I can look in on you and be there if you need me. Won't that be nice?' He looked at his mother with tenderness in his dark eyes and Ella could see Lucille softening under his gaze.

Lucille put her hand on his. 'Yes, I suppose it will be. If you behave.'

'Don't I always?' Rory asked, looking the picture of innocence.

Lucille sighed and started eating again. 'Don't look at me like that, Rory Kennedy. You're the image of your father right now. And you know that always gets me right in my heart. But don't think for even a second that you'll manage to stop me living my life the way I want.'

Rory lifted his mother's hand and kissed it. 'I do love you, you know. I only want what's best for you.'

And for you, Ella thought, admiring his performance. Rory turned his head, and when their eyes met, there was a spark of something between them for a split second, like a single note from a violin. It was short and sharp but it made Ella's insides contract. She didn't even know if she liked him and their sparring had been nearly hostile, but it made her feel both nervous and oddly excited.

'You're not eating, Rory,' Lucille said in a motherly voice. 'Are you not feeling well?'

'I'm fine,' Rory said and pulled back his plate. 'I'll finish this and then I'll be on my way. I'm meeting someone in the pub in a little while.' He wolfed down his steak and what was left of the chips. 'Nice meal, Ella,' he said and wiped his mouth on the napkin. 'I was only joking about the ketchup.'

'I knew that,' Ella said.

'But you meant what you said back?'

Ella shot him a fake smile. 'I always mean what I say.'

'Or say what you mean?' he countered.

'Whatever way you want to twist it,' she replied, trying to avoid looking into those brown eyes. He had been rude to her all through the evening and she had been rude right back. But she had enjoyed their sparring, and she suspected he felt the same.

A little smile played on Rory's lips as he looked at her. Then he got up. 'I'll be off then. Sorry I can't stay longer but I had arranged to meet up with these friends before you issued the invitation to dinner here. But now that I'm going to be around for a few weeks, we'll see each other a lot.' He kissed Lucille's cheek. 'Bye, Mum. I'll be in touch soon. Don't sign on the dotted line until I've seen the house. I want to check it out first.'

'You don't have to,' Lucille protested even though there was a happy look in her eyes as Rory kissed her. 'I'll manage very well on my own.'

'We'll see,' Rory said cryptically. He smiled at Ella. 'Nice to see you again, Ella.'

Ella started to get up. 'I'll see you out.' She followed him to the front door, where he turned and looked at her as he opened the door.

'Bye for now, Ella,' he said. 'I hope you continue to improve.'

'Bye, Rory,' Ella replied, admiring his broad shoulders as he walked away. She didn't usually go for that kind of muscular type, but his obvious physical strength matched his personality perfectly. *A very balanced man with huge confidence*, she thought as he disappeared around the house on his way to the pub on the main street. *Even though he seems to have some kind of agenda. But isn't he too old to cling to his childhood home like this?*

'That went well,' Lucille remarked with a touch of irony when Ella came back to the terrace. 'He didn't believe a word I said and now he's going to get in touch with his brother to try and stop me.'

Ella pulled out her chair and sat down. 'This bit about becoming a nun might have been a little OTT,' she remarked, pouring herself more wine.

'I wasn't really serious about that,' Lucille confessed.

Ella took a sip from her glass. 'He seemed to believe it.'

Lucille giggled. 'I know. I nearly laughed out loud when I saw his face as I said it. But I should be careful and not appear too outrageous. He might try to declare me insane and have me put away.'

'That's never going to happen,' Ella protested. 'But I have a feeling he thinks I'm to blame for you breaking out. He was a little hostile towards me.'

'I thought he found you very alluring,' Lucille remarked. 'Judging by the way he looked at you when you didn't notice.'

Ella shook her head. 'I just think he was suspicious of me. He seems determined to get you back to your house anyway.'

'I know.' Lucille sighed. 'He's a little old to be so attached to his childhood home and his mammy being there always.'

'It's hard to believe he's two years older than me,' Ella remarked.

'You're so much more mature,' Lucille said.

'Older, you mean.'

'No, I meant that you're very self-contained and grounded. Must be because of your career and that you love what you do.'

'And where I am,' Ella mused. 'I mean, I don't hark back to my childhood home. But then we moved around so often, I didn't have one as such. I wasn't very anchored anywhere as a child. That could be the reason I jumped into marriage that time. I was looking for a home and a man to share it with. And a family,' she added wistfully. 'But that wasn't meant to be.'

Lucille reached out and took Ella's hand. 'That must have been so hard. I can't imagine how I'd have felt if I hadn't been able to have children.'

Ella sighed. 'Thank you. Yes, it was a huge sorrow. Still is in a way. My husband and I were so hopeful. Every time I got pregnant we went all starry-eyed, buying baby clothes and teddy bears. And then I miscarried and there we were again – heartbroken with an empty nursery. It made me feel guilty in a strange way and then, when I turned forty, I began to realise it would never happen. I felt like such a failure.'

'Why?' Lucille asked, her voice gentle. 'Surely it wasn't your fault?'

'I know that now,' Ella replied. 'But then it seemed that I had failed in doing what I was meant to do – have children. I noticed Jean-Paul pulling away from me at that point. And that made it worse. I felt so lonely during that time before we separated. I'm less lonely on my own than I was with him then.'

Lucille's eyes were full of sympathy. 'I never knew it was so bad for you.'

'I didn't tell anyone. I thought it would be better if I was strong and independent and could manage on my own. A heartbroken woman isn't fun to be around.'

'Did you get help at all? I mean therapy or even someone you could talk to?'

Ella nodded. 'Yes. I had a wonderful therapist in Paris. She was a huge help. And so was Mum. So I slowly began to heal. I buried myself in work and painted like never before, which I found very soothing. And of course, this place has been the best healer, if you know what I mean.'

'I do indeed,' Lucille said, squeezing Ella's hand. 'It has the same effect on me. That's why I want to live here.'

'I understand completely,' Ella said. 'It's a blessed place.' She pulled her hand from Lucille's grip and pushed her hair back. 'So there you go. The sad story of my love life. I never succeeded in finding a man who'd stick with me through thick and thin.'

'You're just a bad picker,' Lucille said. 'Some women keep picking the wrong man for themselves, over and over again.'

'I'm a serial bad picker,' Ella said, laughing. 'But I've learned my lesson. I won't go there again.'

'You should never say never,' Lucille said. 'Could be that the right man for you is waiting around the corner. Or,' she said, looking down the path behind the row of cottages, 'he might be on his way here right now.'

Chapter Nine

Ella followed Lucille's gaze and saw a blonde head sticking up over the rhododendron bushes and recognised Thomas Quinn coming towards them. He beamed at her and waved as he came closer. Ella smiled back, feeling happy to see a friendly face after all the difficult conversations she'd had with Rory. 'Hi, Thomas,' she said. 'Lovely evening, isn't it?'

'Hello, there,' he said. 'Didn't mean to disturb you. I'm on my way to the path that leads out to the other side of the village along the headland to look at the view of the Skelligs.'

'Where's your little girl?' Lucille asked. 'You didn't leave her on her own, did you?'

'No,' Thomas said with a laugh. 'Wouldn't that make me a bad parent? She's on a sleepover at her new friend's house. You might remember meeting her. Hannah Primrose?'

'Oh, yes,' Ella said. 'Of course. Such a pretty name, too.'

Thomas looked at the table with the remnants of their dinner. 'But I'm interrupting your evening.'

'Not at all,' Lucille said, getting up. 'It wasn't much of an evening anyway. We're very happy to see you.' She looked from Thomas to

Ella. 'Why don't you join Thomas on his walk? It's such a gorgeous evening. The views of the Skelligs will be wonderful.'

'But the washing up,' Ella protested. 'I can't leave you with all of that.'

'Nonsense,' Lucille declared. 'It's just a few plates and things. I'll put them all in the dishwasher and turn it on. In any case, I have a few things I want to look up on the internet. Off you go, Ella. It'll be good for you.'

'Oh, but…' Ella looked at Thomas and then the path that wound its way around the headland. It seemed longer than the Great Wall of China to her, as she contemplated walking all that way with her still-weak legs. 'I'm not sure I can hack it,' she said.

'Why don't you try?' Lucille suggested. 'You turn around if you feel tired. It might help if you use your walking stick. Hang on, I'll go and get it.'

'Just a minute,' Ella said and took off her earrings. 'Could you put these in my bedroom? They're a little too heavy to wear out walking.'

'Of course. Won't be a tick.' Lucille took Ella's earrings and disappeared into the house.

'I do need the walking stick,' Ella said to Thomas. 'I'm still feeling very unsure of myself. The stick is like a security blanket in a way. But maybe I'll be holding you back.'

'Not at all. I'm just out for a bit of fresh air anyway. You can hang onto my arm as well,' Thomas offered. 'And we'll be sitting down at the end of the walk, so you'll have a chance to rest before we head back.'

'Well, if you're sure,' Ella said.

'I'd love the company,' Thomas said, looking as if he meant it. 'I've been working all day and now I wouldn't mind a bit of a chat with someone over the age of five.'

Ella laughed, her resolve weakening as she noticed the wistful look in his eyes. He obviously meant what he said, and it struck her that he must be lonely at times. 'Okay,' she said, getting to her feet. 'If you don't mind me limping along beside you. My recovery is painfully slow, I'm afraid.'

'I'm sure it's hard to get back to normal after such an injury,' Thomas said sympathetically. 'Maybe there's also a huge trauma associated with it that might be something you have to deal with. Like being nervous of moving around in case you fall again.'

Ella nodded, touched by his empathy. 'Yes, that comes into it, too. Very much so.'

'You need to lay the ghost,' he said. 'That's what I've been told. Face your fears and look them in the eye.'

'Here you are,' Lucille said, handing Ella her walking stick. 'Off you go now. You'll be fine. That path is quite smooth.'

'Thanks, Lucille,' Ella replied and grabbed the walking stick. Then she made her way to the edge of the terrace, descended the steps and stood beside Thomas, grabbing his arm. 'Let's get going, then.'

'Right,' Thomas said and started walking slowly and carefully down the path towards the end of the headland. 'You all right?' he asked after a while, glancing at Ella.

'Great,' she replied, hanging on his arm, while she kept her balance with the help of the stick. 'It's more my back that's wonky. I don't seem to have found my strength there yet. But this is fine,' she said, feeling more confident as they continued to walk down the path. She looked up at Thomas, who was gazing ahead at the view of the cliffs and the sun slowly sinking into the turquoise water, the jagged outline of the Skellig islands outlined against the darkening sky. His blonde hair blew across his forehead and there was a happy glint in his blue eyes as he looked at Ella.

'This is nice,' he said.

'Lovely,' she agreed.

Thomas stopped when they came to the end of the headland, where there was a rough bench made out of an old log. 'Let's sit down.'

Ella let go of his arm and sat down on the log, putting the walking stick at her feet. 'Such a beautiful spot,' she said.

'Especially tonight.' Thomas joined her on the bench and gazed out at sea. 'Look,' he exclaimed, pointing ahead. 'Gannets fishing.'

Ella peered out over the water and saw what he was remarking on. Big white birds hovered over the surface and then dived straight down into the water barely making a splash, only to appear seconds later with a fish in their beaks. It was an amazing sight and the precision of the dive impressive. 'Wow,' she said, staring at the birds. 'Aren't they so skilled? I could look at them forever.'

'Me too,' Thomas replied. 'I find it a great way to turn my mind away from sorrows and darkness. Nature is a great healer. Especially in this part of the world.'

'Oh yes, I think it is,' Ella said. 'It helps soothe the pain. Except in my case it's more physical.'

Thomas turned his head to look at her. 'I have a feeling it's in your mind as well. A kind of frustration and maybe a little bit of guilt?'

Ella nodded, amazed at how astute he was. 'I feel so stupid to have fallen off that ladder. I should have been more careful and checked that it was steady. But I was in a hurry. I wanted to finish that mural I had been working on for so long. Just one more brushstroke, I thought and climbed up – even though I had been warned it wasn't strong enough and that they would get me another ladder the next day. But could I wait? Oh, no. I was in a hurry as usual, so I climbed up to the top thinking I'd be fine. And then it gave way and—' Ella stopped, feeling nearly sick as the memory of her fall came rushing back. The sickening thud when her body hit the floor, then the pain, her own voice screaming… Ella felt a cold wave go through her as the images flashed through her mind and she shivered involuntarily.

'I'm sorry,' Thomas said. 'I shouldn't have said anything. It brought you back, didn't it?'

'Just for a second,' Ella confessed. 'A very bad second,' she added.

'That's terrible. But I know how it feels when you're suddenly pulled back to something bad that happened to you. You think you've managed to put it in the past but there it is in a flash. It could be a smell, a piece of music, or someone saying something that reminds you of what happened, or the person you lost.'

'Exactly,' Ella said, the sad look in his eyes making her forget her own trauma. 'But in my case it's just something I'll have to learn to deal with. In yours it has to be so much harder, so much more impossible to forget.'

'Oh, I don't really want to forget,' Thomas said. 'Of course, the events around her death are what I must put behind me, but I do want to remember *her* always. My wife, I mean. Mandy's mother.'

'What was her name?' Ella asked softly.

'Louise,' Thomas replied, his voice gentle as he said it.

'Lovely name.'

'It suited her. She was blonde and very pretty. Much younger than me, only in her early thirties. She played the violin in the RTE symphony orchestra. We met when I was replacing the pianist who was supposed to play at a concert. I had to jump in at the last moment. We played Mozart's Piano Concerto No 21. One of his most beautiful pieces. I'll never forget it.'

'Was it difficult to jump in at the last minute like that?' Ella asked.

Thomas smiled. 'No, not at all. I knew it all by heart, which was lucky as I couldn't take my eyes off her as we played. And then, after the concert, we ended up beside each other having drinks in some pub with all the other musicians. We started to chat and stayed there all evening. We didn't even notice when everyone else left. And that was the start of our love affair.' Thomas looked into the distance, a wistful smile playing on his lips.

'How lovely,' Ella said quietly, not wanting to intrude on his memories. She didn't ask questions, feeling he'd tell her whenever he could.

'Yes,' Thomas said, his voice hoarse. 'It was. Too lovely to last.'

'I'm so sorry,' she said and put her hand on his arm. 'It's such a tragedy to lose someone so young. It seems so unfair, somehow.'

'Yes,' he said bitterly. 'Unfair to me, but mostly to Mandy. She lost her mother when she was only three years old. That'll mark the rest of her life.'

'But she has you,' Ella said. 'And you love her so much. She seems very well adjusted and happy.'

Thomas laughed. 'Oh yes. She's a wise old soul, really. And now she's making friends here, which is wonderful to see. She spent too much time with grown-ups who are very sad. Me and Louise's parents. None of us can get over how like Louise Mandy is.'

'I would have thought that would be a comfort,' Ella remarked. 'Like a little piece of her still here, no?'

Thomas looked at Ella for a moment. 'That's a beautiful thought.'

'Like a little gift?' Ella said, smiling at Thomas. 'A gift from Louise.'

'Thank you,' Thomas said, his eyes bright. 'What a wonderful idea. I feel that's also a gift from *you*. I wish I could give you something back.'

'Oh, but you have. You took me on this walk. I wouldn't have attempted it if you hadn't asked me.' Ella looked out over the cliffs and the mountains, at the blue sky and the gannets hovering above the water before they dived in. 'It's the best time to come here. When the sun is sinking behind the Skelligs, making them look even more mysterious.' She pointed at the jagged outlines against the pink and gold sky. 'I always feel the spirits of the monks are hovering above them. Especially tonight.'

'That's true. There is a presence there all right. I wonder what it would have been like to be there in their day. Very challenging, I'm sure.' He turned to look back down the path at the row of houses. 'If we wind the clock forward a bit, we have the coastguard station that is also very interesting. I wonder who named it Starlight Cottages? Nobody seems to know.'

'I don't know,' Ella replied. 'It had that name when I bought my house. I might look it up and see if I can find something.'

'Great,' Thomas said. 'The internet would be a good start, and then you could go to Killarney and see if you could find some old maps or books in the second-hand bookshop there.'

Ella nodded, suddenly excited about this new venture. 'It'd be very interesting to find out how these coastguard stations came about and what life was like here way back then. It would have been in the early 1800s, I suppose.'

'Something like that.' Thomas shot her a look of concern. 'But you're beginning to look tired. Maybe we should go back?'

'I think so,' Ella replied. 'It's a gorgeous evening, but I don't want to stay here until it gets dark. I'd be afraid to trip if I didn't see the path clearly.'

Thomas stood up and handed Ella her stick. 'Let's get going so.'

They made their way slowly back to Ella's terrace, where Lucille had tidied away everything and placed a thermos and two mugs on the table. 'She's like a fairy godmother,' Ella said and unscrewed the top of the thermos, sniffing. 'Camomile tea. Would you like some?'

'No thanks,' Thomas said. 'The night is still young. Too early for good night tea.' He paused and seemed to listen to something. 'Do you hear that?'

Ella stopped for a moment and heard faint sounds of music in the distance. 'It's Irish music from the pub in the main street,' she said. 'They have live trad music on Friday nights.'

'Sounds great,' Thomas replied. 'Hey, do you want to go there with me? I'd love a pint of Guinness, and a bit of craic actually. How about you?'

'Oh,' Ella said with a sigh. 'That would be heaven. I haven't been to the pub for over three months.'

'Could you make it there, do you think? It's only down the lane and up the street. Or I could get my car and drive you.'

'But then you can't have a drink,' Ella argued. She paused for a moment, assessing how she felt. 'You know what?' she said, a new energy flooding through her at the idea of going to the pub, even for a short while. 'I feel so much stronger all of a sudden. The walk and the chat and the gorgeous views have given me a new buzz. I'm sure I'll be able to walk to the pub if I can hang onto your arm like before.'

Thomas stuck out his arm. 'Here it is. Feel free to hang onto me as much as you like.'

Ella followed his advice, and they wandered carefully around the house, up the little lane and down the main street to the pub, where the doors were open and people were spilling out with pints in their hands, laughing and talking and taking little dance steps in time with the lively music that echoed down the street. Thomas and Ella made their way inside where they found a small table by the open window.

'You sit down and I'll get the drinks,' Thomas offered. 'What would you like?'

'A glass of Guinness,' Ella said. 'I think a whole pint would be too much for me. And in any case,' she added with a laugh, 'pints are not very ladylike, as my mother used to say.'

Thomas smiled and nodded. 'I know. Silly idea. But in any case, you're always a true lady whatever you do.' He pulled out a chair. 'Please. Sit down and I'll be back soon.'

And you're a real gentleman, Ella thought as she watched him weave through the crowd on his way to the bar. She sat back, enjoying the music that had changed to a slow, lilting ballad played on the tin whistle. She glanced out the window at the people in the street having fun, then back at the crowd inside, suddenly seeing someone at another table. *Rory*. She had forgotten he had said he was meeting someone here tonight.

She tried to disappear behind a group standing near her table and peered out, trying to see who Rory was with. She could see he was talking animatedly to a woman with long red hair. Then his gaze drifted and he seemed to sense her eyes on him. Ella whipped her head back, but their eyes met before she had a chance to duck behind the group standing nearby. As they looked at each other, Rory lifted his pint in a salute, a little smile playing on his lips. Then he turned back to his companion, leaving Ella staring at him, her feelings a mix of embarrassment and elation as she again felt that tiny buzz that happened every time they met.

When Thomas came back with their drinks, Ella greeted him with a warm smile, grabbing her glass of Guinness and drinking deeply before she drew breath and laughed. 'Like a drink of water in the desert,' she said. 'I can't remember when I enjoyed anything more. There's nothing like draught Guinness in a real pub.'

Thomas sat and started on his pint, smiling when he put it down. 'No, there is nothing like it.'

'It's not just the Guinness,' Ella said, looking around the pub, tapping her feet to the music. 'It's also being out like this, seeing people, listening to music with a good friend. All that is so great. I haven't had the energy to do it until now. And nobody to go with, really, even though I have plenty of friends in the village. But they're all so busy and I think I might have been a bit of a pain to look after.'

'I'm sure you weren't,' Thomas protested. 'I can't imagine you being demanding in any way, even when you were immobile.'

'I tried my best not to be,' Ella said with a sigh. 'But I didn't quite succeed, I think.' She sat up straighter. 'But hey, why go on about it? This is so much fun.'

'It's great,' Thomas agreed. 'The band is very good.'

The music changed to a livelier tune, and they smiled at each other as they listened, the noise making any kind of conversation impossible. When the song ended, Thomas asked Ella if she wanted another glass of Guinness and she said, 'Yes, please,' with such enthusiasm it made Thomas laugh.

'You look like it's Christmas.'

'That's how it feels. As if I'm across some kind of barrier,' Ella said. 'I might even walk home on my own without the dratted stick.'

'No, you won't,' Thomas said sternly. 'We will walk back the way we came and no arguments. No need to get too gung-ho because you've had a few drinks.'

'You're right,' Ella said, calming down. 'I was feeling nearly giddy from all this excitement.'

'I'll go and get you that glass,' Thomas offered. 'Wait here and no shenanigans while I'm gone.'

'I promise,' Ella said. 'I won't move.'

The music started again and a few people got up to dance to the lively jig, their shoes clicking on the wooden floor. Ella watched them, amazed at their quick footwork, enjoying this impromptu show.

'Great, aren't they?' a voice said in her ear.

Ella looked up and found Rory beside her, a pint in his hand. 'Fabulous,' she shouted back as the music reached a crescendo.

'You checking up on me?' Rory asked in her ear.

'Of course not.' Ella moved away from his hot breath, even though she didn't really mind being so close to him. 'I'm here with a friend,' she shouted over the din of music. 'I had forgotten you'd be here.'

Rory laughed. 'Oh, yeah, that's a likely story.'

'It's true,' Ella insisted. 'I was just dying for some Guinness and Thomas, my friend, was going to the pub so I decided to go with him. Here he is now,' Ella said as Thomas arrived at the table carrying their drinks.

'Here you go.' Thomas handed Ella her glass as he looked at Rory.

'Thanks,' Ella said. 'This is Rory, Lucille's son. Rory, this is Thomas, my neighbour.'

'Hello,' Thomas said and held out his hand. 'Thomas Quinn.'

'Rory Kennedy,' Rory said as they shook hands. 'So you just happened to come here, then?'

'Eh, yes?' Thomas said, looking mystified. 'Why wouldn't we?'

'On a date?' Rory asked.

'Well,' Ella started. 'Not really. But is that any of your business? Or is there a law against being in this pub on a Friday night?'

Thomas looked from Rory to Ella. 'You'll have to explain what's going on here,' he said with a gleam of annoyance in his eyes as he looked at Rory.

Rory grinned. 'Nothing much. Except that Ella fancies me, but hates herself for it.'

Ella rolled her eyes. 'Oh please. Just go away.'

Rory held up his hands. 'Of course. I didn't mean to intrude. I'll leave you folks to continue your date.'

'It's *not* a date,' Ella said, beginning to feel angry.

'It sure looks like it from here,' Rory retorted. 'But whatever. I have to get back to my gang. A walking group who's staying at the farm,' he added, waving at the red-haired woman. 'Have a nice evening. Nice to meet you, Thomas.'

Thomas nodded, then turned to Ella as Rory pushed through the throng. 'What was that all about? You two looked like you could murder each other.'

'Good idea,' Ella said through her teeth. 'He makes my blood boil.'

Thomas sat down. 'Why?'

'Because he's trying to stop Lucille living her life the way she wants. It's all about property and land and stuff. A bit complicated.'

'Sounds like the typical Irish story,' Thomas remarked, starting on his pint. 'Any family row is always about property.'

'Very true,' Ella said and took a swig of her drink. 'Even between couples.'

'I know. It'll never go away.'

Ella drank a bit more and then looked at Thomas. 'I'll just finish this, and then I think I'll go back home. I'll be fine walking with the stick if you want to stay.'

'No, I'll go with you,' Thomas insisted. 'I want to go home anyway. I need to check my emails and do a little more work on my compositions. My agent thinks I could have enough for an album, if I include some classical music. So I'm working hard before I go to Dublin to audition to this record company. I'm also going to try for a permanent position at the RTE symphony orchestra.'

'When are you going?'

'Next week. Tuesday, probably.' He finished his pint and got up, holding out his hand. 'Will we go, then?'

Ella grabbed her stick, took his hand and slowly got up. They made their way through the crowd and found Rory, the red-haired woman and two men outside, chatting. He nodded and Ella shot him a polite smile before she walked away on Thomas' arm. She could nearly feel Rory's eyes on her back, but she didn't turn around. Thomas led her down the street at a slow but steady pace and they arrived at Ella's front door a few moments later.

'Here we are,' Thomas said. 'Home safe and sound.'

'Thanks for a lovely evening,' Ella said.

'I should thank you,' he said. 'I hadn't planned to barge in on you like that.'

'You didn't. I'm glad you arrived just then, when I was feeling a little low. It was a happy accident and then the pub was such fun. It made me feel nearly normal again.'

'That's good,' he said, looking up at the house. 'These houses are so interesting.'

'Yes, they are. But I don't know much about them except that they were built around the 1830s to guard the coast. Must have been exciting in those days,' Ella said.

'Must have been,' Thomas agreed. 'Well, good night. I hope you'll sleep well,' he said and started to walk away.

'Good night and thanks again,' Ella said, watching Thomas make his way down to his house, thinking about what he had told her earlier. So much pain and sorrow and then trying to do his best for his little daughter. He was such a gentle, sweet man, of the kind she had wished to meet after the turmoil of her failed relationships.

Rory and his dark, brooding eyes popped into her mind. He was such a contrast to Thomas, from whom she only got warm, friendly vibes, but without that spark of electricity she had felt with Rory. He was so suspicious of her and always ready for a fight. *I don't want that kind of thing any more*, she thought as she opened the door and went inside. *No more drama and heartache. And no more thrill and passion*, a little voice whispered inside. Ella told the voice to be quiet and to forget all about Rory Kennedy. For now anyway. She could tell he was about to cause a lot of trouble. But she would be strong and do her best to help Lucille to get what she wanted. Whatever it took.

Chapter Ten

The viewing of the cottage Lucille wanted to buy took place just after lunch the next day. Ella and Lucille walked up the street together, Ella now without a walking stick, confident after the night out and the walk with Thomas out to the headland and to and from the pub. She was sure that her weakness was as much in her head as in her body and that confidence was the best medicine. She had to grab Lucille's arm from time to time when she wobbled, but when they arrived at the cottage, Ella felt steadier on her feet and could walk on her own up the garden path to the front door.

Ella looked up at the house, taking in the flaking paint of the façade, the warped window frames and the missing slates in the roof. 'It's very rundown,' she remarked. 'And the garden is a wilderness.'

'It all needs updating a bit,' Lucille said. 'But look at where it is. Right in the middle of the village, the library only a stone's throw away, Sorcha's shop on the corner, and the pharmacy and vet's across the street. Talk about convenient.'

They were interrupted by the creaking of the gate as a woman came into the front garden. 'Hello,' she said, 'I'm Finola from Murray's estate agency. You're here for the viewing?'

'That's right,' Lucille said. 'I'm Lucille Kennedy and this is my friend Ella Caron.'

'Nice to meet you.' The woman took a bunch of keys from her bag. 'I have the keys here. Do you want me to show you around, or would you prefer to have a look around on your own?'

'I think we'd like to be on our own,' Lucille replied. 'What do you think, Ella?'

'Yes. That's a good idea,' Ella replied.

'Grand, so,' the woman said and handed Lucille the keys. 'I have another house to show, so I'd be grateful if you could put the keys into the post box at the gate. The front door key is marked with a green dot. Watch out for the loose floorboard in the hall. See you later,' she added then walked off.

Lucille found the front door key and the door opened with a loud creak after a little bit of pushing and shoving from both her and Ella. Then they went inside and looked around a tiny hall, stepping over the loose floorboard and continuing into a corridor where a staircase rose to the first floor. They passed the staircase and entered a room to the left with a cast-iron fireplace and a window overlooking the street. Lucille glanced around and went to look out the window. 'Lovely snug little room. The perfect living room for me. I can see everyone passing by from here.'

'It's not very big,' Ella remarked. 'And the wallpaper is a bit depressing.'

'I'll get it painted a pale yellow. And I'd have off-white wool curtains. I have two small sofas that can go on either side of the fireplace and there's my Danish coffee table on the oriental rug from the library in Tipperary,' Lucille said, sounding as if she was already moving in.

'Yes, but it will need new windows, and you'll have to dryline the walls,' Ella said. 'These houses weren't very well built, actually.'

'I know,' Lucille said, knocking on the wall beside the fireplace. 'What's on the other side? Let's go and see the rest.'

They walked on, finding a smaller room beside the living room. 'This wall could be knocked down,' Lucille said. 'And then I'd have a bigger living room. Look, that window looks down over that cute garden and I can see the ocean from here. Wonderful. I bet the kitchen has the same view.'

The kitchen was the best room so far with the original beams and solid oak cupboards and a flagstone floor. They could see an overgrown garden through the large back window, and further out wonderful views of the sea. There was a solid fuel stove, but no electric cooker, fridge or freezer. A lean-to addition housed what could be a utility room.

They stepped into the garden and discovered it was quite large and sunny, with a small greenhouse and a shed at the bottom that Lucille thought might become a henhouse. The panoramic views of both the mountains and the sea were the best part of the garden, which would need an enormous amount of work.

'This will be both expensive and take a long time,' Ella declared, looking up at the house. 'And we haven't even seen the upstairs yet.' She had initially been enthusiastic about this new venture for Lucille, feeling it would be wonderful for her to buy a little house and move to the village where she was already making friends. But when Ella saw the state the house was in, she began to see how much work it would entail. 'The bedrooms might be a lot worse,' she remarked. 'Maybe this wasn't such a good idea after all,' she added, wondering how Rory would react when he found out.

'Let's take a look at the bedrooms,' Lucille said, undeterred, and walked back inside, climbing the stairs slowly. 'I'll need a stairlift here, too,' she said.

'You can have mine,' Ella said, climbing carefully behind her. 'I won't need it once I'm back to my full strength. You can see I'm already managing without one quite well.'

'That's a good idea,' Lucille replied as she arrived at the top of the stairs. 'Nice landing up here. Three bedrooms. Perfect. Then there's plenty of room for Martin and Fiona and the kids when they come to stay.'

Ella peered into the bathroom. 'Look. A rolltop bath,' Ella said, buoyed by one of the rooms at least. 'And the wash hand basin is one of those old-fashioned ones. You *could* make this really cute, I suppose.'

Lucille started to say something but was interrupted by a knock on the front door. 'That'll be Jason,' she said. 'I asked him to come around to have a look. He used to be an architect so I thought I could ask him for a bit of advice.'

'To look at the structure of the house?' Ella asked as they went downstairs.

'No, to make up a list and give me a ballpark figure for the work.'

They quickly made their way downstairs and Ella opened the door. Jason, a tall man with greying dark hair, smiled at her. 'Hi,

Ella. Lucille asked me to come around and take a look at this house, just to give her some estimates.'

Ella smiled and opened the door wider. 'Come in. I didn't even know you and Lucille knew each other, and then she tells me you're a qualified architect.'

'I was in an earlier life,' he said as he stepped inside. 'But now I design furniture, as you know.'

'Of course.' Ella led the way into the living room, where Lucille was waiting, having taken a notepad out of her handbag.

'Hello, Jason,' Lucille said. 'Thank you for taking the time to come around to look at the house.'

'No problem,' Jason said. 'I already had a look at the outside. You'll need a surveyor, but my first impression is that the construction is solid and the roof okay, except for a few slates here and there. That's a good start. But the windows will need to be replaced as most of the window frames look in bad shape.'

'Excellent,' Lucille said. 'I mean about the exterior. I know the windows are bad and all need to be replaced,' she added and scribbled something on her notepad. 'So we'll concentrate on the interior, then.'

'Yes,' Jason agreed, looking around the room. 'I think you'll need to insulate the walls for a start, and maybe the floors as well. You could keep the floorboards. The timber is very nice, but lift them and put insulation underneath and you'll still have the period feel with added warmth.'

Lucille nodded and kept writing. 'I want to knock that down,' she said, pointing at the wall. 'Just to make this room bigger.' She made a sweeping gesture with her pen. 'And then do a job on the kitchen without ruining that lovely old-fashioned look. Follow me and you can have a look for yourself.'

Jason nodded and followed Lucille into the kitchen, Ella in tow. They then went upstairs and Jason knocked on walls, opened windows, bounced on floorboards and generally gave the rooms a thorough examination. They returned downstairs and explored the garden – Jason much impressed by the size and aspect of the outdoor space.

'This will be a fabulous garden one day. But it will need a lot of work.'

'I'll have it landscaped,' Lucille said. 'And the shed and greenhouse will also be rebuilt.' She looked at Jason. 'So, what do you think? Is this property worth all the work?'

'It will be very expensive,' he replied. 'But yes, if you don't mind spending quite a lot, I think it'll be a real little gem in the end. A place where someone could be very happy.'

'Someone like me,' Lucille said with a happy smile, putting away her notebook. 'I know it'll probably cost an arm and a leg and a bit more, but it'll be my forever home, my very own place. I never had that, you see. I moved into Johnny's home when we were married and then he very generously left it to me. But I never really felt it was mine. I know the boys will be a little cross when I sell it, but their father left them a tidy sum and some land, so they're fine financially.'

'But not emotionally,' Ella said. 'I have a feeling the house is very important to them.'

'So is my money,' Lucille said darkly, closing her handbag with a loud snap. She looked apologetically at Jason. 'Sorry, Jason. I didn't mean to drag you into all that family stuff.'

'I don't mind,' Jason said. 'I know what families can be like. Anyway, as I look around this house, I think it's important to keep the period charm. You could even try to find all kinds of things in architectural salvage yards. There's one near Kenmare, I've heard. But whatever about that, you will have to find yourself a builder if you go ahead with this project. We had a good one when we did up Lydia's house, but it was a bit of a struggle to keep them at it, if you know what I mean.'

'How long would this work take?' Ella asked.

Jason shrugged. 'No idea. In theory, it shouldn't take more than a few months, but this is Kerry and builders have their own rules around here. You'd need to be at them all the time to get them to finish.'

'Don't worry,' Lucille said, a determined look in her eyes. 'I'll be on their backs the whole time. I might even set up camp in the garden. They won't get away from me.'

Jason laughed. 'I'm glad I'm not a builder working for you. I'm looking forward to seeing this house restored. I liked it ever since I moved here four years ago and was hoping it would be brought back to life. You're really doing the village a huge service, Lucille.'

'Ah, thank you,' Lucille said, her cheeks pink with pleasure. 'That's a wonderful thought.'

'I mean it.' Jason started to walk towards the house. 'But I have to go. Let me know if you want me to draw up a plan for any builders, and don't forget to have the house surveyed before you sign the contract.'

'I promise,' Lucille declared. 'Thank you again for taking the time and trouble to come, Jason. I really appreciate it.'

'You're very welcome, Lucille,' Jason said. 'Bye for now.'

'Bye and thanks, Jason,' Ella said.

'Such a nice man,' Lucille said when Jason had left. She looked up at the house and sighed happily. 'It's going to be so exciting to wake this house up from its long sleep. I feel like the prince kissing Sleeping Beauty.'

Ella followed Lucille's gaze, but even though she knew Lucille imagined the house and garden all newly restored and gorgeous, all she saw was a near ruin with broken windows, missing roof slates and flaking paint on the façade. It would be a mammoth task to make it habitable, never mind turning it into the gem Jason had talked about. 'It'll be incredibly tough to do what you plan,' she said. 'Are you sure you want all that stress and pain?'

'Oh yes, I am,' Lucille replied. 'It will be a huge challenge but I think it'll be very exciting.'

'But you might regret it once the problems crop up.'

Lucille's eyes glittered strangely as she looked at Ella. 'Regret it? Never. Ella, this project will save my life.'

They walked through the house again, looking into every nook and cranny, Lucille writing down a few more details on her notepad as she muttered to herself. She looked so absorbed in her task that Ella decided to leave her in the living room while she went into the kitchen to have a last look around before they left. When it was updated, it would be a very nice, bright kitchen, she realised as she glanced through the window and imagined how Lucille would cook for friends on summer evenings while looking out at the newly planted garden. It was the middle of summer now, so the house would probably not be finished until early spring next year, if everything worked out according to Lucille's plan. She would have to put an offer on the house and then it might take a month or so before the conveyancing and all the legal details had been ironed out. Ella knew the house had been on the market for more than a year, so the owners would want a quick sale.

A noise at the back door gave Ella a start. Then a dark head appeared and she saw who it was. 'Rory,' she said. 'What are you doing here?'

'What do you think?' he said, as he stepped inside.

'That you're checking up on Lucille,' Ella said.

'I'm just having a look at this house. It's for sale, isn't it?'

'Obviously.'

He looked around. 'It's a wreck.'

'With potential, though,' Ella said, meeting his gaze.

'Maybe. But potential could be quite expensive and take a long time and effort. It's too much for an old woman to take on, you know.'

'Depends on the woman,' Ella remarked. 'I think Lucille is well able to tackle this. It'd be good for her.'

'Or the stress would kill her.'

'I doubt that very much,' Ella countered. 'She's as tough as an old boot and as sassy as a whole army of much younger women. I wish I had her strength and commitment to a project she's passionate about.'

'You look like you're ready for a fight,' he remarked, looking amused.

'I'm determined to do what I can to help Lucille,' Ella replied. She folded her arms and glared at Rory. 'Why are you so suspicious of me?'

'Suspicious?' he asked. 'Are you kidding? I'm terrified of you.'

'Oh yeah, I bet.'

They stared at each other for a while until Rory's eyes softened. 'Look,' he said. 'I love my mother and I want the best for her. Of course, it might look a bit selfish to try to make her stay in that big house all alone. I can see that it's very lonely when we're not there. But moving here and taking on this wreck is not the answer to that.'

'Why not?' Ella asked, not quite believing the earnest look in his brown eyes.

'Because it's too much for her. I'm sure we could solve the problem some other way. Like getting a carer for her or something.'

'A carer?' Lucille's voice from the door made them both jump. 'Like a nurse or something?' she asked angrily. 'Why on earth would I need that?'

'Well, maybe not right now,' Rory said, looking a little sheepish. 'But the time will come...'

'No, it won't,' Lucille snapped walking into the room. 'That time will never come. But if you keep going on like this, Rory Kennedy, the time will come when I cut you off completely. So you can either stop trying to prevent me from living my life the way I want, or never see me again.'

'What?' Rory exclaimed, looking more than a little shaken.

'I mean it,' Lucille said. 'Ella, I have a lot of phone calls to make and things to do. Let's go back to the house. I'll be waiting outside.' She walked out of the room, her heels smattering on the floorboards and then the front door slammed.

Rory stared at Ella. 'She has never spoken to me like that before.'

'Well, then maybe it was time she did.'

'Did she mean it?' he asked, his face suddenly pale.

'It sounded like it. I've never seen Lucille really angry; she's always so positive and sweet. But I think she's hurt that you don't trust her.'

'Does she appear... normal to you?' Rory asked. 'I mean, generally.'

'Perfectly,' Ella said. 'Except for the fact that she seems at least twenty years younger than her age. She's as sharp as a tack, you know.'

'Okay,' Rory said without much conviction. He made a sweeping gesture. 'But this... I mean... It's such a huge undertaking. It could all end in disaster.'

'Who knows? Could be the best thing she ever did. Or the worst,' Ella said, heading to the door. 'But it's her decision. And in the meantime Lucille will have had a lot of fun. See you around, Rory. Bye for now.'

'Bye, Ella,' Rory replied with a flicker of a smile. 'I'll stay out of Mum's way from now on. But I'll be keeping an eye on things from a distance.'

'A great one, I hope,' Ella said and disappeared out of the room before he had a chance to reply.

She walked down the corridor deep in thought. What had at the beginning seemed like just a family tiff now looked a lot more complicated. She had seen the hurt and anger in Lucille's eyes as she had listened to her son, but Rory had also been very upset. The tension between them was obvious and there had to be something more serious going on than just the fact that Rory wanted to hang onto his childhood home. A man like that, a highly qualified lawyer, couldn't possibly be that immature. There was something about the house in Tipperary that made Rory want to keep it in the family at all costs. He didn't know that Lucille was planning to sell it, but when he found out, he'd be even more upset than he was right now.

Then there was another niggle in Ella's mind. The fact that Lucille seemed so frantic somehow. And then… those letters and the phone call she'd just hung up on… Lucille had also seemed quite stressed at times, staying up late, working on her laptop, closing it quickly whenever Ella came into the room as if she didn't want to reveal what she was doing. Ella was sure it wasn't about blogging or online chatting. What was Lucille hiding?

Chapter Eleven

'I'm sad,' Mandy said as she sat on Ella's beach blanket the next morning.

'Why are you sad, sweetheart?' Ella asked, drying her hair after a long swim. They were on the main beach and Mandy had wandered over to Ella as she came out of the water, asking if she could sit on her beach blanket for a bit. That swim had been the first time Ella had truly enjoyed her newfound strength. The water was crystal clear today and she had found herself swimming further than ever before, lost in the sensation of the cool water on her skin and the silence as she floated on her back looking up at the blue sky. This was utter bliss. Her thoughts drifted to Lucille, who had been so kind when Ella had spoken about her sadness. It had been the first time in years that Ella had talked about it. But it had felt good to finally share it with Lucille. It had been cathartic somehow, making it possible to finally close that door.

'I have to go to Dublin with Daddy and I don't want to,' Mandy said, interrupting Ella's thoughts.

'Why not? I thought you were going to see your granny and grandad.' Ella scanned the beach, trying to find Thomas.

'Yes, that's the problem,' Mandy said, burying her toes in the sand. 'I don't like staying with them. They're always so sad.'

'Oh, I see,' Ella said, turning to look at Mandy. 'Maybe it's because they miss your mummy so much.'

Mandy nodded. 'Yes, that's it. And they look at me and sigh all the time because I look so like Mummy. But Daddy misses her too and he is not sad all the time. And if I go to Dublin, I can't go to Hannah's party. She will be five on Friday and she's having a party with a bouncy castle and I won't be there.' Mandy drew a ragged breath, looking as if she was about to burst into tears.

'I can see why you're sad about that,' Ella said. She looked at Mandy for a moment while an idea popped into her head. 'How long does your daddy have to be away?'

'All week,' Mandy said, sounding as if it was more like a year.

'That's not so long,' Ella said. 'But...' She looked around the beach again. 'Where is he?'

'Over there,' Mandy said, pointing at someone coming out of the water. A tall man with blonde hair in red swimming trunks who Ella saw was indeed Thomas as he drew nearer.

'Hi, Thomas,' Ella called and waved. 'Mandy's over here with me.'

Thomas smiled and started towards them. 'Hi,' he panted as he arrived. 'Thanks for looking after Mandy. I told her to come and sit with you if she got lonely. I hope you don't mind.'

'Not at all,' Ella said, leaning back on her elbows, squinting at him against the bright sunlight. 'I was happy to have her company. But there's something I want to ask you.'

'Okay,' Thomas said. 'Hang on a minute till I go and change. Won't be a tick. You stay there, Mandy.'

'Okay,' Mandy said. Then she turned to Ella. 'What are you going to ask him?'

'Just wait and you'll find out,' Ella said, looking mysterious.

'Can I stay here when you ask him?' Mandy wanted to know. 'Or are you going to tell me to go away while the grown-ups talk about things children don't understand?'

'You can stay here,' Ella said and scooped Mandy into her lap. 'It's about you, after all.'

'Is it? Why?' Mandy looked up at Ella, her blue eyes wide.

'Hold on, here he comes,' Ella interrupted as Thomas approached, dressed in denim shorts and a white polo shirt. 'Fingers crossed he'll agree.'

Mandy carefully crossed the fingers on both hands and squeezed her eyes shut. 'I won't open them until he says yes.'

Ella laughed. 'But you don't know what I'm going to ask.'

'No, but it has to be something fun,' Mandy declared.

'Right,' Thomas said, crouching on the sand. 'What was it you were going to ask me?'

'It's about me,' Mandy piped up, opening her eyes and wriggling away from Ella's lap.

'Really?' Thomas said, his eyes full of laughter. 'So can we hear it then?'

'Yes,' Ella cut in. 'I was going to ask if Mandy could stay with me when you go to Dublin.'

'Oh.' Thomas sat down on the sand. 'Well, eh…'

'Of course I can!' Mandy squealed. 'That will be much better than going to Dublin. And I can go to Hannah's party and play on the bouncy castle. Please, please, Daddy. Say yes,' she pleaded, kneeling in front of Thomas, her hands together. 'I'll be sooo good and I'll eat my dinner all up and sleep all night, I promise.'

Thomas laughed looking at Ella. 'Oh my God, what a performance. But yes, that's fine if you don't think it would be too much trouble.'

'What trouble could a five-year-old girl be?' Ella asked. 'Lucille and I will be delighted to have her. She can sleep in the spare bed in my room. It'll be like a long sleepover. Won't that be fun, Mandy?'

'Yes it will,' Mandy declared.

'Thank you so much, Ella,' Thomas said.

'You're welcome,' Ella replied. 'It's all organised, then. You're leaving on Tuesday, is that right?'

'Yes,' Thomas replied. 'I could drop Mandy off at the playgroup before I go and then you can pick her up from there at lunchtime. I'll pop in to you with her things before I leave.'

'Brilliant,' Ella said. 'And maybe you could text me her different play dates for the week so I can make up a schedule?'

'I will,' Thomas said.

'Hannah's party is on *Friday*,' Mandy piped up. 'We have to buy her a present before that.'

'We will,' Ella promised. 'We could go to Killarney or Dingle to get it and then have lunch in McDonald's. Would you like that?'

Mandy nodded. 'Yes, I would.' She suddenly noticed a group further down the beach. 'Look,' she said, pointing. 'There's Hannah and her mum and the baby. Can I go and tell her I'm staying with you and that I'll come to her party?'

'Off you go,' Thomas said. 'But come back here then. It's nearly time to go home for lunch.'

'Okay.' Mandy got up, brushed the sand from her shorts and then ran across the beach as fast as her little legs would go. 'Hannah!' she shouted. 'I don't have to go to Dublin with Daddy, I'm staying here with Ella.'

Thomas and Ella watched the two little girls jumping up and down and hugging each other. 'Well, that made her day,' Thomas said, resting his arms on his knee. 'I have to say I'm really grateful, Ella. I didn't know what to do, to be honest. I knew she didn't really want to come with me now that she has settled in so well here and made so many friends. She can keep going to the little art group at the library and the summer playgroup at the primary school like before, just to give you a break. And she has several play dates lined up that I would have had to cancel if she had gone with me. So you won't have to mind her all the time. I couldn't ask Maura as she has her hands full with Hannah and the baby. Being a single mother of two small children and working full time is no joke, I'm sure.'

'I would say that's hard work,' Ella agreed. 'But I'm truly happy to have her and Lucille will be delighted. So no problem at all.'

'I'll miss her, but it's better for her to stay here where she can have a bit of fun. And I'll try to be back by the weekend, so I'm sure she won't even notice I'm gone.'

'She is really loving it here,' Ella remarked.

Thomas nodded. 'Yes. It's so good for her to be here.' He looked at Ella. 'And for me, too.'

Ella looked away from his gaze so full of warmth and friendship. He was the kind of man she had always hoped to meet. Kind, loyal, dependable. Someone to lean on who would never let her down. His good looks and his beautiful daughter made him even more attractive. But as she smiled back at him, trying not to drown in those deep blue eyes, she suddenly wondered if it wasn't all a little too perfect. She had always been drawn to danger and mischief and there was none of that with Thomas. But those things had always brought her misery in the end, she told herself. It was time to grow up and forget dangerous men. Wasn't it?

Lucille was all smiles when Ella came back from the beach. 'It's all going smoothly,' she said as she sipped coffee on the terrace. 'The house in Tipperary is going on the market soon and I have a surveyor lined up to look at the cottage in the village.'

Ella sat down on the chair opposite Lucille. 'Brilliant,' she said. 'You didn't waste any time.'

'No time like the present,' Lucille said with a cheery smile. 'I need to get my skates on if I'm to do this and I want to book the builders before they go on their summer break.'

'You're right,' Ella said. 'But don't you feel sad about leaving your lovely big house?'

'Not at all,' Lucille said briskly. 'It was sadder rattling around in all the rooms with the ghosts and the memories. The cottage holds no such things. It'll be all new and exciting.'

'You're amazing,' Ella said. She sat back on the chair and relaxed in the sunshine. 'It's a lovely day.'

'But clouds are gathering on the horizon,' Lucille remarked, pointing out to sea. 'We have to enjoy it while we can.'

'That's true.' Ella sat up again. 'Look, Lucille. I'm getting a bit uncomfortable about keeping the sale of your house from Rory. It was all very well to pretend you were on a cruise. But this is different. Don't you think you should tell him about it?'

Lucille frowned. 'No. I need a little more time.'

'To do what?' Ella asked, feeling slightly irritated at all the secrecy. 'Is it fair to keep this very important decision from your sons? I mean, it's the house they grew up in. They must have so many memories of their childhood and their father.'

'Please,' Lucille said, her face pale. 'Don't make me feel like a bad mother. I've given so much of my life to them. Isn't it my turn to think of me for a change?'

'Yes, but—' Ella started.

'But nothing,' Lucille snapped. 'The subject is closed and you will say nothing to Rory. You promised.'

'Okay.' Ella realised that she wouldn't get any further with Lucille. Better to change the subject and keep things on an even keel for now. 'I have some news,' she said brightly. 'We're going to have a houseguest this week.'

Lucille brightened. 'Oh? Who's coming to stay?'

'Mandy. Thomas is going to Dublin and will be away until the weekend. Mandy didn't want to go, so I offered to take her. She'll be staying with us and she'll sleep in the spare bed in my room.'

'Oh,' Lucille said. 'Are you sure that's a good idea? It's a huge responsibility.'

'I know, but it'll be all right. Mandy is very well-behaved and I think she likes me. I feel much stronger now than when you arrived three weeks ago, so I'm sure I can cope with her.'

'She adores you,' Lucille said. 'And her father is also very fond of you.'

'Oh, I don't think so,' Ella said, squirming slightly on her chair. 'He's just a very kind man. He's nice to everyone. I don't think he gives me special treatment.'

'He does give you special looks, though,' Lucille said with a wink. 'How do you feel about him?'

Ella thought for a moment. 'I like him a lot. He's very good-looking in that clean-cut way. He's a wonderful father too.'

'Do you feel attracted to him?' Lucille wanted to know. 'I mean, in that special way that gives you a buzz every time you're with him.'

'I don't know him well enough for that,' Ella protested. 'But I think, in time I could grow to like him.'

'He's a very nice package,' Lucille stated. 'Talented, stable, good-looking, kind and caring.'

'Oh yes, all of that,' Ella said with feeling. 'I like his company too and he's a very talented musician. What's not to like?'

'And then, of course, there's that gorgeous little girl.'

'She's adorable.'

'Oh yes,' Lucille agreed. 'But…'

'But what?'

'Make sure it's the father and not the child you're falling for.'

Ella laughed. 'Of course not. That would be silly.'

Lucille got up. 'Women have fallen for sillier things. But enough about that. I'm meeting one of my tai chi girlfriends for lunch at The Two Marys'. And I should tell you that I have to go to Tipperary in a day or two to meet the estate agent who will be selling the house. I need to get everything ready to be photographed and make sure all valuables have been put away. They're putting the house on the market at the weekend. And…' She paused, looking unsure. 'Some of the art and antiques will be sold at an auction later this month.'

'Oh,' Ella said, taken aback. 'How are Martin and Rory going to react to that?'

'I'll have to tell them eventually. I will ask them to pick out anything they might want before that. They'll probably want some mementoes from their childhood home.'

'That could lead to more arguments and trouble,' Ella warned.

'I know. But I have decided to share the proceeds with them from both the sale of the house and whatever the auction makes. That might calm them down a bit.'

'I hope it does,' Ella said. 'When are you going to Tipperary?'

'Wednesday. Mandy could sleep in my bed while I'm away if you like.'

'Oh thanks,' Ella said. 'I'll see what she wants to do.'

'You'll manage on your own with her?' Lucille asked.

'Oh yes, of course,' Ella replied. 'No problem at all. In any case, she will be at playgroups and that little art course and a lot of other things too nearly every day, so I'll have plenty of time to work on the illustrations.'

'How is that going?' Lucille asked.

'I have nearly finished the sketches and will be sending them to the publishers for approval next week.'

'I had a look at them this morning,' Lucille said. 'They're terrific. Did you ask permission from the people whose faces you've used, or is it going to be a surprise?'

'I've told nearly everyone and nobody has complained so far. They were all quite excited about it.' Ella paused. 'Except Rory. I haven't said anything to him yet. Do you think I should?'

Lucille stopped on her way into the house. 'I'm not sure. He's sulking right now because of what I said to him. He hasn't been in touch at all since I told him off at the cottage. It makes me nervous, really. It's not like him to be that silent. But I'm going to let him stew, even though all I want to do is tell him I didn't mean what I said.'

'Good idea,' Ella agreed. 'But you must talk to him eventually. Make him see things from your point of view.'

Lucille nodded. 'I will when he's had a while to calm down. I'll be off now. Bye for now.'

Ella looked at the door closing behind Lucille, going over their conversation in her mind, remembering especially what Lucille had said about Thomas. *Do I like him only because of Mandy?* she asked herself. *Is the idea of a family with him and Mandy luring me into finding him more attractive? Am I still looking for that child I wanted but couldn't have?* There were no answers to her questions, so she pushed them out of her mind and went into the sunroom to work on her illustrations, knowing it would distract her from her doubts and worries.

Chapter Twelve

Ella came back to reality more than an hour later as she heard footsteps on the terrace. She blinked and looked up from her work as a shadow fell over her drawings. She turned and focused on the figure, thinking it was Lucille. But the person standing there was a lot taller and broader. Ella realised it was Rory, who now knocked on the sunroom door.

Ella got up and opened it. 'Hi,' she said, her voice stiff. 'What are you doing here? Lucille isn't home.'

'I came to talk to you,' he replied, his eyes a little wary. 'If you have the time.'

'I'm working,' she replied, glancing at her watch. 'But I see it's past lunchtime and I haven't had anything to eat, so I'll take a break.'

'I'd appreciate it,' he said. 'May I come in? It's starting to rain, actually,' he continued as large drops began to smatter against the windows.

Ella opened the door wider. 'Okay. Go and sit down in the living room. I'll go and make myself a sandwich. I'll be back in a minute. Do you want anything?'

'No thanks, I've had lunch.'

'I'll bring you coffee, then.'

'That'd be great,' he said as he entered.

Ella went into the kitchen and quickly made herself a cheese sandwich, catching sight of her reflection in the window. She realised how messy she looked, with stains on her white T-shirt from the dark graphite pencils she used for drawing, one of them stuck into her hair. There were smudges on her nose, and her black linen trousers were both baggy and creased from sitting so long. She had dressed for comfort, not style but now she felt slightly awkward about looking so unkempt in front of Rory. Not that she cared what he thought about her, but it felt like a disadvantage all the same. She quickly cleaned her face with a dampened towel, pulled the pencil out of her hair and tried her best to smooth it. There was nothing to be done about the T-shirt or the crumpled trousers, but she was at least cleaner and tidier. Then she suddenly remembered something and her heart nearly stopped. She had forgotten to put away the sketches she was working on. The ones with the bear. He wouldn't recognise himself in the sketches, but Lucille had given her a photo of Rory, which she had propped up on her worktable. She forgot all about her appearance as she hurried out of the kitchen. She had to hide those drawings and the photo before Rory saw them.

But it was too late. When Ella rushed into the living room, she could see Rory through the glass door to the sunroom, where he was standing at her worktable, looking from the sketchpad to the photo with a strange expression. He looked up as Ella approached and when she came through the door, he held up the page. 'What is this?' he asked. 'Some kind of caricature of me?'

'No,' Ella exclaimed, snatching the sketchpad out of his hand. 'It's the illustrations I'm working on for a children's book. I'm using interesting faces for all the animals and the people around here are wonderful subjects.' She stopped and drew breath. 'Your face, and your eyes… they're so… so…'

'Bear-like?' he asked.

'Well, yes. But I didn't mean it as an insult at all. It's actually quite a compliment. Well, at least everyone else thinks so,' she babbled nervously.

'Were you going to mention this to me?' he enquired, his voice silky with a slight edge. 'Or would I have discovered it in this book if I happened to go into a bookshop?'

'Of course I was going to ask you,' Ella protested. 'Eventually. When we were on more friendly terms.'

'And when would that be, do you think? When you've finished supporting my mother in her hare-brained scheme of maybe selling my childhood home and then moving to this little village in the wild west of Kerry?'

'I'll always support her,' Ella declared, squirming as he mentioned the possibility of the house being sold. 'And so should you if you truly love her.' She avoided his gaze and hoped he wouldn't press her further about Lucille's intentions.

'Of course I do,' he argued. 'That's why I don't want her to do something she might regret. I want her to have a few happy years before… well, you know. Can't you understand that?'

'Before what?' Ella asked. 'Before she dies? Or before she is totally incapacitated and has to go into a home? How do you know what's going to happen to her in the future? We could both be dead before her.'

'I suppose.' Rory pushed his black hair out of his eyes and sighed. 'Could we stop this? I wanted to have a civilised conversation with you so I can try to explain where I'm coming from. I don't want you to think I'm constantly worrying about my inheritance.'

'Even if that's what you constantly do?'

Rory suddenly laughed. 'You really are a tough cookie. You're not going to let me off the hook, are you?'

'I don't know what you mean,' Ella said, trying not to join in Rory's laughter. It was a little bit ridiculous to behave like school-children and going around in circles like this. But she couldn't stop herself. She always had that odd urge to argue with him every time they met. She had never been able to resist needling him.

'Of course you know what I mean,' Rory snapped. 'But let's leave that alone for now. Did you say coffee earlier? And shouldn't you eat something? Low blood sugar can make you bad-tempered.'

'I'm not the slightest bit bad-tempered,' Ella said. 'But I will go and get that sandwich and the coffee. Then we can talk. In a civilised way.'

'That would be a first,' Rory remarked.

Ella shot him a thin smile and went back to the kitchen to get the sandwich she had made and the coffee from the coffee machine. When she came back into the living room with a tray, she found Rory still in the sunroom, flicking through the sketchpad.

He looked up as she arrived. 'These are damn good,' he said as he looked at the drawings. 'I think I recognise a lot of these faces. Is this my mum as a vixen?'

'That's right,' Ella said. 'Clever of you to see that.'

'Brilliant.' He looked at Ella again. 'It looks like a good story. And hey, I don't mind you using my face for the bear. I kind of like the idea now that I've seen these.'

'Are you feeling all right?' Ella asked, putting the tray on the coffee table. 'You're not your usual feisty self today. It's not like you to be so pleasant to me.'

'It's the prospect of fame that excites me,' he said with a lopsided smile. 'I mean, if this book is a huge hit, I can tell my friends I modelled for this famous artist.'

'Ha ha.' Ella gestured at the tray. 'Sit down and have your coffee, will you? I even opened a packet of chocolate chip cookies for you.'

'I'm honoured.' Rory sat down on the easy chair while Ella settled on the sofa, grabbing the sandwich.

She ate quickly while Rory drank his coffee and nibbled at a cookie. 'So,' she said, when she had finished her sandwich and drunk some water. 'What was it you wanted to say to me?'

He put his mug on the table. 'I just thought that maybe I could explain the situation with the house from my point of view.'

'I would have thought your point of view was fairly obvious.'

'If you jump to conclusions, yes. It's easy to judge looking at it from the outside – or even just from one angle.'

Ella wiped her mouth on a paper napkin. Her heart softened as she saw the frustration in his eyes and knew somehow that there was more to his side of the story than she had thought. 'Okay,' she said. 'Go on. Tell me. I'll try not to argue with you this time, even if it's hard to break the habit of the past years.'

'I think we fell into some kind of silly game of one-upmanship from the very beginning,' he remarked. 'My fault as much as yours. We both enjoyed the sparring, though, didn't we?'

'I love a challenge,' Ella said with a cheeky smile. 'And I loved needling you.'

'Me too. Which is not helping here,' he said.

'I'm listening,' Ella said. 'And I won't start a fight.'

'Good.' He looked at his hands for a moment, then back at Ella. 'It's quite a complicated issue with feelings and emotions and grief all mixed up together. It's about my relationship with my father and how he loved that house and the land. It wasn't in the family since the Middle Ages or anything, but my great-grandfather bought it all when he was quite young and my father wanted to pass it on to his children and grandchildren. Then he met my mother and brought her to the house, where they were very happy all through their marriage. Martin was born quite soon after they married and then I came along eight years later.'

'Oh. I didn't know he was that much older than you,' Ella said. 'But then I have only met him once or twice when my mother lived in the house.'

Rory nodded. 'I know. He was probably there at other times than you, I think.'

'I suppose. But go on.'

'Right, well…' Rory paused, looking thoughtful. 'I was the baby in the family when I grew up. My mother doted on me and my father – well, he and I were true kindred spirits. Even though he loved both his sons equally, he and I shared the same interests. Horses and dogs and sport. Riding, swimming, hiking, skiing – we did them all together while Martin was more studious and didn't like sports that were risky. He ended up playing golf and tennis at school while I was more into rugby.' Rory touched his nose. 'Hence the slightly battered face.'

'It suits you,' Ella said without thinking.

He laughed. 'I thought you said you were going to behave.'

'I meant it,' she replied, her cheeks hot. 'It adds to your... eh, rough charm.'

There was a glint in his eyes for a moment. 'Well, thank you, says the bear.'

Ella laughed.

Rory cleared his throat and sat up straighter. 'So as you might have gathered, my father and I were very close. And when he died suddenly' – Rory paused, his face suddenly pale – 'it was as if my whole world stopped. I was there, you see. I saw him fall after jumping that fence. And just before that, before we rode off... My father and I were talking about the house and the farm and how he was leaving it to my mother in his will but that she had promised it would stay in the family and she would pass it on to Martin and me to run together. He left it to her in his will because he wanted her to have the security of owning it outright so nobody could take it from her. But...' Rory paused. 'Now I'm worried she will sell it.'

'Oh,' Ella said, taken aback by the pain in his eyes.

'That house means so much to me. Much more than to Martin in a way. We both inherited some land and a sum of money, but the house and gardens went to my mother on the understanding that she would leave it to us the way my father wanted. But now... I'm not sure what her plans are. Is she selling it?'

Ella hesitated. Should she tell him? But, no, she had promised Lucille. 'I don't know,' she said, the lie nearly choking her. She cleared her throat. 'But I see why you're so worried.'

'Yes.' Rory's eyes were full of emotion as he looked at Ella. 'I don't understand why she would be doing this, why she'd sell the house when she promised my father she wouldn't ever do that.'

Ella thought for a moment. 'She might be planning to let it, though. But her reason for wanting to come here is because I think she's trying to be relevant. To be accepted as part of a community where she can be useful and not seen as someone old and vulnerable. She can't do that out in the countryside in Tipperary.'

Rory nodded. 'Okay. Fine. But then she could move into the local town there and let us have the house.'

'But she wants a change of scene,' Ella said. 'In a part of the country where she has family connections.'

Rory looked puzzled. 'What family connections could she have here?'

'She said she was trying to find out more and would tell me when she had the whole picture. She's doing some kind of project, she says,'

'Oh.'

Ella nodded, wondering fleetingly if it was wise to keep the truth from Rory. Lucille was his mother and he seemed to truly care about her. She knew he often used charm to get his way, but the expression in his eyes told her he was upset and worried about his mother. Maybe he was right? Lucille might be a strong, capable woman, but she was, after all, eighty-five years old and might at any moment come down with some ailment or other that would make her very frail and helpless. Was that why she wanted to live in this small village, near people who might give her a helping hand?

'I think you should talk to her. Tell her what you told me just now and how you feel about it. Then she might change her mind and maybe you can find a solution together that will make all of you happy.'

'Would that make her give up this mad scheme of buying that wreck and go back home?' Rory asked.

'No. She's determined to move here.'

'Why?' Rory asked, looking exasperated. 'Is it because she wants to live close to you?' His eyes were suddenly suspicious. 'Or are you trying to convince her? I know you've become close during this time.'

'It has nothing at all to do with me,' Ella protested. 'I would never try to talk her into doing something like that. But I think she's really scared.'

'Of what?'

'Of being ill and alone and not have anyone nearby if she should need help.'

'But we…'

'You go down to Tipperary for weekends and have a great, relaxing time,' Ella said. 'Then you go back to Dublin to work and she's on her own during the week. She says most of the people she used to socialise with are dead and that it takes half an hour to get into town. She was happy there when my mother lived with her. The two of them loved their life there. But now…' Ella stopped, the memory of her own mother overwhelming her.

'But now your mother's gone,' Rory said, his voice suddenly full of sympathy. 'And you had to cope with that accident as well. I'm really sorry, Ella. I never said anything to you about that. It must still be hard for you.'

'Yes,' Ella mumbled, blinking away the tears. 'It is. But I'm getting better. Except for feeling stupid about using that ladder.'

'Who supplied the ladder?' he asked.

'The hotel. Why do you ask?'

'Because if you can prove it was their fault, you could sue them.'

Ella shook her head. 'No, I don't want to do that. I knew that ladder was unsteady and insisted I'd use it, despite them saying they'd get me a better one in a couple of days. I could have waited but I was in a hurry to finish the mural. All my fault for being impatient.'

'But you'd still have a case,' he argued.

'You're thinking like a lawyer. I know suing them would be bad for my reputation and if it came out, nobody would commission me for that kind of work again. Please, let's not talk about it. I'm trying to forget it and move on.'

'Yeah, but I've been such an insensitive idiot. I never even mentioned it.'

'You were worried about Lucille.'

'You're very understanding,' Rory said.

'Why wouldn't I be?' Ella sat back against the cushions and looked levelly at Rory. 'I'm glad we had this conversation. I know where you're coming from now. And I get why you're upset about the house. I also understand Lucille. I think she's doing the right thing to come and live here, you know. It would be the best thing for her and it would make her happy.'

'I suppose in a way it would.'

'In every way. Not for you and your brother, but for her. But maybe there is a solution? Could you and your brother buy the house from her and whatever land comes with it?'

'We couldn't afford it. If she's selling, it'll go on the market with an asking price of around a million.'

Ella blinked. 'Wow. Are you sure?'

'A Georgian house that big? Definitely. It's got six bedrooms, four reception rooms, three bathrooms and a top-notch kitchen. Of course it will. Mum kept up the repairs and had the house redecorated about a year ago. There isn't a thing out of place. And the garden is beautifully landscaped, as you know. But I thought she was doing that for us, not for herself. It breaks my heart to think that she would be so selfish.'

Rory drew breath and finished his coffee. 'So there you are, the ugly truth about me and my feelings.'

'Not ugly at all,' Ella argued. 'I'm only sorry that I didn't realise all of this. And maybe Lucille doesn't either? I don't think she's being selfish exactly, just trying to survive. Maybe she thinks you need to learn to manage on your own? Isn't it time you did?'

Rory looked at Ella while his eyes changed from anger to frustration and then something else that she couldn't quite decipher. It was like watching clouds drifting across the sun, the sky constantly changing from dark to light. 'You've made me think,' he finally said. 'And it's not all nice.'

'I only meant to…'

'I know,' he said. 'I'm beginning to see that you're the piggy in the middle here and that's very hard.'

'Yes,' Ella agreed. 'But I didn't know how you felt.'

'How could you until I told you the whole story?'

'I should have known your motives weren't in any way nasty.'

'And I should have realised what a tough time you've been through. I hope you can forgive me.'

'Of course I do.' Ella suddenly smiled. 'Is this some kind of watershed moment? When we make peace and become friends?'

'I wouldn't go that far,' Rory said with a wry smile. 'Let's just say we've buried the hatchet.'

'That's a good start.' Ella got up and stretched her back. 'Sorry, but I still get a little stiff when I sit for a long time. And I was sitting on that stool drawing for quite a while before you arrived.'

Rory rose from the chair. 'You probably want to lie down for a bit.'

'Yes, I think I should.'

'I'll leave you alone now. Thank you for listening.'

'You're welcome. I'm glad we talked.'

'Not that it would solve anything.'

'You never know,' Ella said. 'In any case, I see the problem from both sides.'

'And you believe me?' he asked, looking unsure.

'Yes, I do. But you have to talk to Lucille. Tell her how you feel.'

'I will.'

'If there is anything else, I'd be glad to help,' she added, although she had no idea what that could be.

'I'll give you my number, so you can call me if you come up with anything.'

Ella picked up her phone from the coffee table. 'Good idea.'

Rory read out his number and Ella typed it into her list of contacts. Then she quickly sent him a text so he had hers. 'Great,' he said, putting his phone back in the pocket of his jeans. 'I'll be off then.'

Ella walked to the sunroom and held the back door open, peering out. 'It stopped raining. Did you come by car?'

'No, I cycled here. I parked the bike at the side gate.' He stopped by the door and looked at Ella. 'Do you think you could have a word with my mother, too? Find out what her plans are?'

'I'll do my best,' Ella promised. 'There has to be a solution to all of this, something that'll make everyone happy.'

Rory let out a snort. 'That'd be the day.'

'I'm glad we're on better terms, though,' Ella said, meeting his eyes that were no longer hostile.

'I'll miss the fighting,' Rory said with a grin. 'But I'm sure it won't be long before we're at it again.'

Ella laughed. 'Yeah, it's too much fun for it to stop. See you soon, Rory. I'll let you know if there are any developments.'

'Great. Bye for now,' Rory said and swiftly left the house.

*

When Rory had gone, Ella forgot about her aching back, sat down at her worktable again and looked at her drawings. She picked up a pencil and turned to a clean page, starting to sketch without thinking. Rory's face grew on the page, not as a bear, but as himself, with the black hair, the square jaw, the slightly crooked nose, broken in some rugby match long ago. Then the eyes, dark with long lashes and that slightly forlorn look she had noticed just now when they had talked about his childhood and the promise Lucille had broken.

Ella paused, her pencil in the air as she thought about what he had said. She felt very much like a piggy in the middle now, as Rory had said, torn between wanting to support Lucille and feeling sorry for Rory and his grief over his dad. How could she help resolve the conflict between mother and son without getting hurt herself? She put her work down and got up from the table, her back now screaming for a rest. She slowly walked upstairs and went to lie down on her bed, still thinking about Rory and his plight. How horrible it must have been to witness the death of his father who he loved so much. No wonder he was so moody and so quick to anger.

She heard the front door open and knew Lucille must be back from her lunch. Ella didn't know how to tackle the dilemma or even how to begin to speak to Lucille. It was a good thing that she was leaving for the stay in Tipperary the day after next. It would give Ella a chance to think about the whole issue and how she could help resolve it in some way. Then she remembered that Mandy was coming to stay tomorrow. What a happy accident that she had offered to take her for the few days of Thomas' absence. It would be such fun to look after this enchanting little girl.

All thoughts of Rory and Lucille and the house floated out on the breeze from the open window as Ella made plans for Mandy's stay and all the things they would do together. She had never minded a child for any length of time – only an hour or two to give a friend a break from time to time. This would be different, putting her meagre child-care skills to the test. But she had always dreamed of having children and she looked forward to the week ahead with great joy and a tiny bit of trepidation. The dream might be very different to the reality of minding a child who had been through so much sadness.

Chapter Thirteen

Mandy's arrival the following day pushed all concerns about Lucille and her family problems from Ella's mind. She was astonished at the amount of stuff that was essential for a small girl of five. The little hall was suddenly packed with a big bag of clothes, a car seat and a large cardboard box with Mandy's favourite toys.

'Good Lord,' Lucille grunted, trying to squeeze past the pile. 'You'd think she was moving house. How long is she staying? A year?'

Ella laughed. 'I think Thomas is being overprepared. He arrived this morning with all this, saying some of it was "just in case" and that I probably wouldn't need half of it. I think he's a little nervous because this is the first time they've been apart since Mandy was born.'

'Very brave of him to let her stay here,' Lucille remarked.

'He was a little pale, I have to say. I offered to look after her so he could have a little time to himself. Now he can concentrate on his work without having to worry about Mandy. He knows how much she loves it here. She has settled in here so well and has so many little friends already. But this is the first time they've been apart, so maybe it's hard for him to be on his own.'

'He's a good father.'

'Wonderful,' Ella said. 'And I'm honoured that he trusts me with his little girl. She's so precious to him. It's huge for him, so I just need to make sure everything goes smoothly.'

'He'll be phoning and texting all the time,' Lucille stated.

'I know.' Ella checked the pocket of her jeans. 'But I don't mind that. It's natural for him to be nervous. I'll have my phone with me at all times and I already promised I'd text him updates, like when I've picked her up from the playgroup. And he'll call to say good night to her every evening.'

'Sounds like you have it all sewn up,' Lucille said, taking her linen jacket from the row of pegs on the wall. 'I'm off to meet the surveyor. I want to hear what he has to say about the house. I'll be back for lunch.'

'Okay,' Ella said absentmindedly while she grabbed the bag with the clothes. 'I'll have this sorted before then.'

'See you later,' Lucille said as she left.

Ella's phone rang in her pocket just as the door had closed behind Lucille. It was Thomas.

'Hi,' Ella said. 'Did you forget something?'

'No, but I just wanted to tell you that there is a small box in the bag with cough medicine and paracetamol if she should come down with a cold or a fever or something. And some plasters and antiseptic cream if she falls and scrapes her knee or cuts herself or—'

'Thomas,' Ella interrupted. 'I've got this. It'll be fine. Mandy is going to survive and so will you.' She paused, remembering the worried look in his eyes this morning as he said goodbye. 'But if you're that worried, maybe you should take her with you to Dublin after all?'

'No. I can't do that to her. She'd be devastated if she misses Hannah's party. And she is very excited to stay with you. It's me. I'm feeling a little wobbly, to be honest.' He paused and Ella could hear him sigh heavily.

'Of course you are,' Ella soothed. 'But you should do this. You should go to Dublin and try not to worry. Mandy is in good hands, you know. I think it'll be good for you to have a break. You'll feel a lot better when you come back, I'm sure.'

'You're right,' Thomas said after a long silence. 'I know you'll look after her very well. It's just that it felt so strange to be driving along the road without Mandy chattering beside me, telling me to stop for ice cream and asking "Are we there yet?" every five minutes. But I'll get through this. I won't call you until tonight when it's her bedtime.'

'Good,' Ella said. 'It'll be hard for you to be on your own for the first time. But try to concentrate on the music and the audition. It's important for both of you that it goes well. Put on some music on the car radio for your drive, stop in Adare and have a lovely, peaceful lunch all by yourself and enjoy being on your own.'

'I will.' Thomas laughed. 'You're a tough taskmaster. Thanks for the pep talk.'

'You're so welcome. Good luck with everything. And thank you for letting me have Mandy and for trusting me.'

'You're a star, Ella,' Thomas said and hung up.

Poor man, Ella thought as she went to put Mandy's car seat into her car that was parked on the driveway outside the house. *He's so lost and lonely, missing his little girl who is all he has after the loss of his wife. Even if it's good for him to manage on his own, he won't truly heal unless he finds someone to share his life and help carry the burden of bringing up his child.* Was that someone Ella? She wasn't sure, even if the thought of having Mandy in her life for good was like a dream come true. Then she chided herself for thinking like that. The only woman who could possibly step into the shoes of Thomas' late wife had to be truly in love with *him*, not just the idea of being a mother. *Could I make myself fall in love with Thomas?* Ella asked herself as she hung Mandy's clothes in the wardrobe and made up the spare bed. Real, true love wasn't like painting by numbers, she knew from experience. It just happens without rhyme or reason. Which was why it was so very dangerous.

Mandy rushed out of the primary school building with the other children and ran up to Ella, who was waiting at the gate. She waved a drawing in the air. 'I drewed the beach and all the people that were there,' she said. 'And I did a dolphin and seagulls too. Is there a dolphin in your story?'

Ella took the drawing and glanced at it. 'That's a really good picture, Mandy. But no, there are no dolphins in the story. It takes place in the forest, you see.'

'Oh.' Mandy stuck her hand into Ella's. 'That's okay. You can put a dolphin into the next one. Like Fungie, the dolphin that lives in Dingle Bay. He's very tame, you know, and you can go and see him on a boat.'

'I know,' Ella said as they started to walk down the street. 'I thought we might do just that tomorrow if it's a nice day. But if it rains, we could go to Ocean World and look at all the fish and marine life in the aquariums there. Would you like that?'

'Oh yes, please,' Mandy said. 'But I hope it doesn't rain because I really, really want to see Fungie. That would be my favourite.'

'Let's hope the rain holds off, then,' Ella said, squeezing the warm little hand in hers.

'Has Daddy gone to Dublin already?' Mandy asked as they walked.

'Yes. He left a few hours ago. He'll be there soon.'

'Far away from here,' Mandy said.

'Are you sad about that?' Ella asked.

'Not yet. But maybe I'll miss him a little bit when I go to bed and he won't be there to tell me a story.' Mandy looked up at Ella. 'But I might watch a movie with you on TV instead. Then I'll forget about being sad.'

'You think that'll help?' Ella asked, amused by Mandy's ability to reassure herself.

'If you give me popcorn, it might.'

'I will,' Ella promised.

'And you'll let me stay up *very* late?'

'We'll see. Let's have lunch and I'll think about it. I'll make chicken sandwiches and then you can have an apple and strawberry yogurt. How's that?'

'Fine,' Mandy said. 'And then I have a play date with Rebecca. She lives on the other side of the beach in a white house with a blue door and she has a brother called Patrick and a poodle dog called Rufus.'

'You'll have a busy day,' Ella replied as they arrived at Starlight Cottages. They hurried inside at the same time as rain started to smatter against the windows.

Only minutes later, Lucille ran inside, slamming the door behind her. 'Phew,' she said. 'I just made it before the downpour.' Her gaze focused on Mandy. 'Hello, Mandy. Welcome to our house.'

'Hello, Lucille, the story lady,' Mandy said. 'Do you live here?'

'I'm a houseguest,' Lucille said. 'Just like you.'

'How did the survey go?' Ella asked as she helped Mandy take off her rain jacket.

Lucille hung her raincoat on a peg and tided her hair. 'Very well. No real problems except a little damp here and there and a settlement crack in the back wall. So I will go ahead and make an offer.'

'Oh.' Ella didn't quite know what to say. If she hadn't heard Rory's story, she would have been delighted and very excited for Lucille. But now her feelings were mixed. She understood Lucille's motives for wanting to move to Sandy Cove and she fully supported that part of the story. She had become increasingly fond of Lucille and felt she somehow filled the void her mother had left when she died. Lucille was important to her and she was happy they would be living so close to each other. But then there was Rory and his emotional bond with the place where he had grown up. She wanted to ask Lucille again if she couldn't speak to Rory properly before making any definite decisions – maybe if she involved Rory in the process and took the time to listen to him, he'd be on board. But then Mandy pulled at the leg of Ella's trousers.

'I'm hungry,' she told Ella.

'Oh, sorry, sweetheart,' Ella exclaimed. 'I nearly forgot about your lunch.'

'But I didn't,' Mandy said. 'And my tummy is rumbling.'

Ella laughed. 'I know. Mine too. Let's go to the kitchen and make the sandwiches. Come on, Lucille, I'm sure you're hungry too. We can talk while we eat.'

'That's rude,' Mandy said as they entered the kitchen. 'You should *never* talk with your mouth full.'

'That's not what I meant,' Ella said, taking a loaf of bread from the breadbin. 'We will talk while we're having lunch but not with our mouths full.'

'Can I have peanut butter instead of chicken?' Mandy asked, moving on to the more important issue of what would go into her sandwich.

'Yes, you can,' Ella replied. 'I even remembered to buy it.'

'Well done,' Lucille said behind them. 'I'll lay the table while you make the sandwiches.'

'Thank you, Lucille.'

They soon sat together at the kitchen table enjoying sandwiches and tea, with Mandy glugging down a glass of milk, quickly eating her yogurt and then sliding off her chair saying she wanted to go upstairs on the chairlift, which she did with Lucille's help, gliding up with a blissful smile, declaring it was great gas and that she'd ask her father for one in their house in Dublin.

The rest of the day went off well. In the evening, after a discussion about bedtime, Mandy had a long session in a bubble bath. Then she settled into the bed in Ella's bedroom just as Thomas called from Dublin to say good night. Mandy chatted with her father for a long time, telling him all about her play date and then, having said 'night, night', she held out the phone.

'He wants to talk to you.'

Ella took the phone. 'I'll talk to him downstairs.'

'Good,' Mandy said and yawned, looking angelic in her pink pyjamas. 'I think I might go to sleep now, but leave the light on.'

'I will,' Ella promised.

'You can hug me good night if you want,' Mandy offered.

Ella smiled and hugged Mandy, briefly burying her nose in her neck. 'You smell delicious.'

'It was those bubbles,' Mandy said and yawned again as she fought to keep her eyes open. 'Night, Ella,' she mumbled.

'Night, night,' Ella whispered as she slipped out of the room and gently closed the door. 'She's asleep already,' she said to Thomas on the phone.

'That's great. She sounded happy.'

'I think she is. She had quite a busy day, though.'

'It's good for her.'

'I hope so,' Ella said as she walked down the stairs, the phone to her ear. 'How about you? Are you okay?'

'Fine, but missing Mandy. This house seems so empty without her.'

'Of course it does. It must be hard for you to be back there on your own.'

'Not as hard as I thought. I'm sitting here with a beer watching an old movie and it's kind of nice not to have to worry about Mandy. Tomorrow I have to practise all day for the audition and go to a few meetings and if I'd brought Mandy I would have had to park her with her grandparents, who are not hugely fun to be with for a five-year-old.'

'She says they're very sad.'

'Yes, they are when they're with her. Mandy reminds them too much of Louise at the same age, so it must be difficult. I'm hoping they'll come and visit me in Sandy Cove. That might help lift their spirits.'

'That's a good idea. It might help them to see Mandy in a different environment.'

'I hope so. Anyway,' Thomas continued. 'I'm really grateful that you're looking after her this week.'

'It's a pleasure,' Ella said.

'But I'm sure you have stuff to do, so I'll let you go,' Thomas said.

'Yeah, I need to catch up on my work. I have a deadline for next week so the illustrations need a little polishing. Good night for now, Thomas.'

'Good night. I'll talk to you tomorrow,' Thomas said and hung up.

Ella put away her phone and went out to the terrace to take in the cushions that had got wet in the rain. Thomas had sounded relaxed but a little lost, as if a piece of him was missing. His good humour hadn't seemed quite genuine. Ella suspected that he was trying to cheer himself up and be brave even though he must be missing Mandy. But he had a busy few days ahead of him, which would be a good thing.

Ella had just put the things from the terrace in a corner of the sunroom when her phone rang. She checked the caller ID before she answered, surprised by the name.

'Rory? What's up?'

'Are you alone?'

'Uh, no. I'm minding a little girl called Mandy, who's asleep upstairs, and your mum is in the kitchen making herself a cup of tea.'

'I didn't mean that kind of alone, I meant as in can anyone hear you?'

Ella sat down at her worktable. 'No, not right now.'

'Great. I just wanted to ask you something.'

'Okay, what?'

'Does my mother seem ill in any way? I mean, is she on any kind of medication?'

'Uh, no. Not as far as I know,' Ella replied, surprised. 'She's quite proud of the fact that she has normal blood pressure and so on without pills. She told me that quite recently. Why do you ask?'

'Oh, just something I was wondering about. She seems so frantic, don't you think? As if she has found out she only has a year to live or something and she's making sure that year, or whatever time is in her head, is going to be spectacular.'

'Oh.' Ella thought for a moment. 'I'm not sure I agree with that. Yes, maybe at her age, she might think her time is limited.' Ella stopped for a moment to think. She was tempted to tell Rory the truth about Lucille's plans for the house in Tipperary, but then changed her mind. That was Lucille's secret to reveal when she felt she could, even if Ella thought it wrong to keep it from her sons. And she did seem fine – apart from seeming concerned about whatever was in those letters. 'She seems very content most of the time,' Ella continued. 'In fact, I think she's blooming. She loves company and is doing all kinds of things. Above all, she wants to be useful and part of the community. The only thing she seems to worry about a little is mental health, and maybe that's why she wants to move here, where she will never be lonely.' Ella drew breath.

'Maybe,' Rory said, not sounding convinced. 'I might be overthinking this.'

'I'd say you are,' Ella agreed. 'You should try to make up with her. Apologise, and then try to see her way of thinking. Talk to her, explain how you feel instead of arguing.'

'Easy for you to say as an outsider.'

Ella bristled. 'Outsider? Here I am *living* with your mother, and you call me an outsider? I know more about what's going on with Lucille than you do. But you haven't bothered to see this from her side at all, have you? Try to at least walk a couple of metres in her shoes and not just think of yourself all the time!'

'Don't hang up,' Rory exclaimed just as Ella was about to end the call. 'Please, Ella. Let's not start fighting again. Don't be mad.'

'How can I help it when you're being so self-centred all the time?'

'Am I? What about her? Isn't she only thinking of herself?'

'She's trying to survive.'

'Aren't we all? You think my life has been easy?'

'Nobody's life is easy, Rory. But you have to make your own luck, not expect others to do it for you.'

Rory sighed. 'Oh please. Don't you think I know that? All I want right now is to try to save the house for the family. Not for me, but for Martin's children. That's what my dad would have wanted. He trusted Mum to fulfil her promise, but she seems to have forgotten all about it. I want to know why, and I also want to know what she's hiding from us.'

'I know,' Ella said, beginning to see the whole picture. 'I do understand, Rory. But I also understand Lucille. In any case, I don't think she's keeping a secret from you to do with her health. She's definitely hiding something but I don't think it's that big – it's something connected to Sandy Cove. She said just this morning she was working on something on the internet. But then she got all coy and said she wasn't ready even to tell me.'

'The internet?' Rory asked, mystified.

'Yeah. She's on her laptop most evenings and she's spending a lot of time in the library as well. Not to mention her trips to Killarney from time to time for what she says is shopping. But she doesn't come back with anything.'

'That's very strange. She used to be the queen of retail therapy.'

'I know. My mother used to laugh about that.' Ella glanced at the drawings scattered all over the large table and caught sight of the bear. In that sketch, he was beginning to soften, to leave his anger behind and start looking around at all the other animals, noticing that their habitat was also threatened. 'We have to work together,' she said, thinking out loud.

'Yes,' Rory said, his voice gentle. 'We do. Fighting is not the answer. Is it?'

'No,' Ella whispered into the phone as she saw through the glass door that Lucille was crossing the living room with a tray. 'She's here. I have to go.'

'Bye for now,' Rory said, his voice still soft. 'Talk soon.'

'We will,' Ella said, then hung up and smiled at Lucille through the glass door. She got up and walked into the living room.

'I made you some camomile tea,' Lucille said, sitting down in the sofa.

'Thank you.' Ella took the mug and sat down beside Lucille. 'I'll be going to bed soon. I think Mandy is already asleep.'

'Unusual for a child that age,' Lucille remarked. 'Normally they'd feel out of sorts in a new place. But she seems very secure. Must be her father's doing.'

'I'm sure it is.' Ella stifled a yawn. 'God, I'm tired. I think I'll go to bed when I've finished my tea. How about you?'

'I'll stay up for a bit longer,' Lucille said. 'I'll be off to Tipperary early tomorrow. Will you be all right minding Mandy on your own?'

'Of course. No problem,' Ella assured her. 'She's going to the playgroup in the morning and then I'll take her to Dingle to see if we can go on that boat trip and buy a present for Hannah. That way we don't have to go to Killarney.'

'Sounds good.'

Lucille's phone rang just as Ella put her mug on the tray and got up. Lucille picked it up, glanced at the phone and then replied. 'Hello,' she said. 'I'm… uh…' She glanced at Ella. 'Just a minute,' she said into the phone.

Ella headed swiftly for the door. 'It's okay. I'm going upstairs. Night, night,' she mouthed.

Lucille blew her a kiss and turned her attention to her phone. 'It's okay,' she heard Lucille say. 'I can talk now. Thank you for calling me back.'

Ella only barely heard what Lucille said next as she walked upstairs, but then, when she was finally in bed, she remembered what it was: Lucille had asked the caller what time it was – in Australia.

Chapter Fourteen

'Ella,' a voice said in her ear. 'Ella, wake up!'

Ella blinked and slowly opened her eyes. 'Uh… Mandy? What time is it?'

'This time,' Mandy said and held the alarm clock in front of Ella's face.

She peered at it. 'Five o'clock? Far too early. Please go back to bed.'

'Why?' Mandy asked. 'The sun is up and I finished sleeping.'

'But the sun rises very early in the summertime,' Ella tried to explain. 'That does not mean we have to wake up.'

'Why?' Mandy put her finger in her mouth and stared at Ella through her fringe, which had flopped into her eyes. She pushed it up with both her hands. 'My daddy is often up at this time playing the piano.'

'That's because he finds it hard to sleep. I don't,' Ella replied, half-asleep. She tried to pull the duvet over her head.

'But you're awake now.'

'Because you woke me up,' Ella replied. 'Come into my bed for a minute.'

'Okay.' Mandy climbed into Ella's bed. 'But we won't sleep, okay?'

'No,' Ella said. 'I'll tell you a story.'

'No, sing me a song.'

Ella sighed. 'What song do you want me to sing?'

'The happy birthday song. That's my favourite.'

'Okay. *Happy Birthday to you, happy birthday to you…*' Ella sang softly in Mandy's ear, which made her giggle.

'Again,' Mandy ordered when Ella had finished.

'Oh God,' Ella groaned and sang the song again. Then again and then Mandy wriggled out of bed and announced she wanted breakfast, so Ella had no choice but to get up, put on her dressing gown, then they went down to the kitchen, where she poured Rice Krispies into a bowl. But Mandy turned her nose up at that and announced she wanted Coco Pops and if she couldn't have that she didn't want anything at all. Except orange juice and a banana. And maybe a bar of chocolate she spotted on a shelf in the larder.

Slightly frazzled, Ella gave Mandy what she wanted, even the bar of chocolate, feeling too tired to argue. Then she turned on the early morning cartoons on TV and parked Mandy on the sofa with a blanket around her. She collapsed beside the little girl and fell into a fitful sleep until Lucille walked in and stopped in the middle of the room, laughing.

Ella lifted her head and looked at Lucille. 'What's so funny?'

'You,' Lucille said. 'The perfect childminder.'

Ella laid her head down again. 'What's the problem?' she mumbled. 'Everyone's happy and I managed to catch a little sleep after being woken up at dawn.'

'No problem at all,' Lucille said, still laughing.

'Shh!' Mandy hissed, glaring at Lucille. 'I'm watching *Dora the Explorer* and I can't hear what she's saying.'

'Sorry, darling,' Lucille whispered and waved at Ella to follow her into the kitchen.

'What's up?' Ella asked as Lucille made coffee for them both.

'Nothing. I just thought I'd see if you needed anything before I go.'

'Thank you,' Ella said with a sigh and sat down at the table. 'That's very kind. I hope we didn't wake you up.'

Lucille smiled. 'Not at all. Small children never wake me up, except if I have to mind them.' She put a mug of coffee in front of Ella. 'Here. Drink up. You have a long day in front of you.'

'Thanks.' Ella took a deep gulp of coffee. 'I don't think it'll be that bad. Mandy has the playgroup this morning and then we'll be going to Dingle for our outing.'

'I know, but small children can be very tiring. Just don't let her get the upper hand.'

Ella laughed. 'I don't know what you mean. Mandy is a little angel.'

'Oh, but she has her daddy wrapped around her little finger. Make sure she doesn't do that to you. Stay strong and you'll survive,' Lucille said and sailed out of the kitchen.

Ella shrugged and sipped her coffee. Lucille was inclined to dramatise things. What possible trouble could Mandy cause?

At nine o'clock that evening, Ella was half-lying on the sofa trying to stay awake to watch the evening news. It had been, as Lucille predicted, an exhausting day. First, Mandy had kicked up a fuss about practically everything, starting with what to wear to the playgroup and eventually, after some tough negotiations, settled on a pair of pink shorts, a blue sweater that was too warm for this sunny day and her red wellies. Not what Ella would have wanted, but she decided it was easier to let Mandy have her way. Then there was the argument about what snack she should bring and how buying sweets on the way to the playgroup was not a good idea. Then there was lunch and the fish fingers Mandy declared were 'boring' and she wanted a hamburger and chips with ice cream to follow. But Ella didn't give in and told her that was all there was. Mandy pouted for a bit and then ate the fish fingers as if she was making a huge sacrifice.

At one point Ella decided to have a little talk with Mandy. She sat down at the kitchen table while Mandy ate the last bits of her food. 'Look, sweetheart,' she said gently. 'I'm sorry if things aren't the way you'd like. But I'm doing my very best. I know you must miss your daddy very much, but he'll be back soon and then everything will be fine.'

Mandy looked at Ella from under her fringe. 'Are you going to tell him I was bad?'

'No, I won't.'

'But you were cross with me.'

'Maybe a little bit,' Ella said, taking Mandy's hand. 'But not really.'

'I won't tell on you either.'

Ella couldn't help laughing. 'Okay. That's a deal. We won't tell on each other. Can we be friends now?'

Mandy nodded. 'Yes, we can. Is there any ice cream in your freezer?'

'I think there might be,' Ella said getting up. 'Vanilla only, though.'

'That's okay,' Mandy said graciously. 'When are we going to see Fungie?'

'We'll go when you've finished your ice cream and I've had coffee.' Ella glanced out the window. 'But it's raining, so we'll have to skip the boat trip and go to Ocean World instead and look at the sharks.'

Their visit to Dingle town went off without a hitch and they both enjoyed Ocean World, wandering around the huge fish tanks, looking at all the amazing marine life gathered there. They laughed at the penguins, gazed at the huge sharks swimming around looking 'very scary', as Mandy declared and then shopped for Hannah's present in the Ocean World gift shop. Mandy picked out a huge plush dolphin named after the famous tame counterpart in Dingle Bay. Then they drove back in high spirits and the day ended well with just a tiny argument about bedtime, which Ella won.

Lying on the sofa, she smiled as she went over the day in her mind. Mandy had a strong will, so she decided that the power battles they'd had were quite normal and nothing to worry about. She hoped tomorrow would be a little better.

Ella gave a start as her phone rang and she picked it up from the table. 'She's fine, Thomas,' she said. 'You only just said good night and now she's asleep. No need to worry.'

'What?' a deep voice asked.

Ella laughed and turned on her back. 'Hi, Rory. Sorry. I thought it was Mandy's father. She's the little girl I'm minding.'

'Fussy parent?' Rory asked.

'No, I think he's just lonely.'

'I see. And how are you?'

'Exhausted.' Ella sighed. 'She woke me up at five this morning and then, apart from a short nap, it's been a hectic day. I only managed to work for two hours while she was at playgroup and then it was all go, with an argument about practically everything. This girl has a real attitude despite her sweet appearance.'

'You're not related, are you?' Rory enquired.

'Ha ha,' Ella drawled. 'So to what do I owe the honour of a call from you?'

'Nothing much. I just thought I'd see if you had discovered anything new about Mum.'

'Not really. Except…' Ella stopped as something popped into her tired brain. 'I did overhear her on a call from Australia yesterday. And it was a long conversation. Any idea what that could be about?'

'No.' Rory was silent for a moment. 'Australia? Hmm. It kind of rings a bell now that I think about it. But it's a very faint bell. I have a feeling my parents were discussing Australia a long time ago, when I was about twelve or so. I think it sparked off a row about someone in Mum's family, but I can't for the life of me remember why.'

'Let it rest and you might remember it.' Ella stifled a yawn.

'Am I boring you?'

'Not yet. But keep talking and you might.'

'You're just tired.'

'Mm,' Ella mumbled, beginning to like the sound of Rory's deep voice in her ear, and the teasing between them. 'What did you do today?' she asked. 'Anything fun?'

'I went for a hike up the mountains but then it started to rain so I had to head back down again. I would have kept going if I'd brought my rain gear but the sun was splitting the rocks when I set off.'

'That's Kerry for you. Always ready to slap you in the face with a wet rag.'

Rory laughed. 'That's a perfect description.'

'I know. What about that walking group?' *And the woman with the red hair I saw you with in the pub*, she thought.

'They moved on to the Dingle peninsula to climb Mount Brandon. But I'll stay here for the duration.'

'Of what?' Ella asked, even though she knew.

'Of my mother's mad scheme and my campaign to get her to change her mind. I'm hoping to solve the problem in a way that makes everyone happy.'

'That'll take a lot longer than your holiday,' Ella remarked, sitting up on the sofa, now wide awake.

'That's why I've taken a long leave of absence from the department,' Rory said. 'I need to think about my own situation, as a matter of fact. Job, life and so on. I feel I've come to a kind of crossroads, somehow.'

'I know what you mean,' Ella said. 'Me too in a way. This accident has made me think about what I want to do professionally.'

'In what way?'

'Well, it's a bit complicated, but I'm beginning to really enjoy doing illustrations. Especially this book. I might get into that more and maybe brush up on my graphic design skills.'

'You're very good at those drawings. Really impressive work, I have to say.'

'What?' Ella asked, startled by his warm tone. 'Is that a compliment?'

'Not a compliment,' he corrected. 'I stated a fact.'

'Oh. Well, in that case I'm doubly flattered. I think,' she added, feeling suddenly confused. 'So what about you? What do you want do with your life?'

'Something that makes me happy and fulfilled,' Rory replied wistfully. 'And the civil service is not it. I don't quite know where I am at the moment. I just broke up with someone, which was very painful. So I need to recover from that.'

'Oh. I'm sorry,' Ella said, sensing he didn't want to talk about it. 'That's always a bit hard.'

'More than a bit in my case. But we couldn't get all the components to work, so we decided to end it.'

'That sounds more like running some kind of machinery than having a relationship,' Ella couldn't help remarking.

'You know what?' Rory said after a moment's silence. 'In a way it was. But the pieces wouldn't come together. I'm trying to get over that. Like doing a system reset, if you know what I mean?'

'You want to get back to who you were before?'

'Exactly. In the meantime, I'll enjoy this wonderful place and I'll also try to reconnect with my mother. I'm beginning to see why she loves it here so much, though. The countryside is stunning, but it's more than that.'

'I know. It's mostly the people around here,' Ella agreed. 'I always think of that quote by Yeats when I try to analyse it. "There are no strangers here, only friends you haven't met."'

'Well, I wouldn't go that far,' Rory said. 'I'm sure there are people you'd prefer not to meet and some that wouldn't ever be your friends even in this village. But yeah, folks around here have been great so far, if a little rough around the edges. Hey, could we meet up sometime?' he asked in the same breath. 'I mean, when you're not exhausted and minding a five-year-old with attitude. I hear your voice fading away here.'

'Mm, yeah, I'm getting a little sleepy,' Ella said, her eyes heavy. 'I think I'll go to bed, actually. Better to keep the same hours as Mandy.'

'So how about it?' Rory asked.

'How about what?'

'Meeting up when you're not half-dead.'

'Maybe,' Ella said.

'Great. Half past seven on Monday night in the Harbour pub?'

'Well…'

'See you then,' Rory said and hung up.

Ella laughed and shook her head. Typical. Not that she'd mind having a drink with him, but the way he had just assumed she'd come was annoying. She had a good mind to stand him up. That would teach him not to take women for granted.

Too tired to decide whether she liked or loathed him, Ella went upstairs and opened the door to Lucille's bedroom to check on Mandy, who, looking like a little angel, was fast asleep, her eyelashes fanned over her cheeks.

Ella smiled and gently closed the door and then, after brushing her teeth, went into her own room. She had made up Lucille's bed earlier so she wouldn't wake Mandy, and she lay down and pulled the duvet over her, still thinking of Rory and the vibes between them.

He had said he was recovering from a difficult break-up, so she was sure he wasn't even thinking of her in any kind of romantic way. And neither was she. But it was nice that they got on better, that their arguments could be more for fun than actual animosity. But who was he really, this moody man with the dark eyes? Friend or foe? Ella wasn't sure. The only thing she knew was that she wanted to make peace between him and his mother. But first she had to find out what was behind Lucille's decision to move here. And most of all, what else she was hiding.

Chapter Fifteen

A strange face loomed in front of Ella's eyes the next morning. A face with a huge red mouth, black eyes and red cheeks. 'Whaa!' Ella screamed. Then she woke up fully and saw who it was. 'Mandy? What have you done to yourself?'

'It's just a little make-up,' Mandy said, smoothing her hair. 'I found it in the bathroom. Do you like it?'

'Eh, well… Not really,' Ella said, trying not to laugh at the huge red mouth, the black rings around the eyes and the two pink circles on Mandy's cheeks. 'There's too much of it for a start and you're too young for make-up. That's Lucille's best Chanel lipstick, I see.'

'I like the colour.' Mandy ran to the full-length mirror and admired herself for a moment. 'Lovely, darling,' she said to herself, pouting her lips.

'Lovelier without it,' Ella said. 'What time is it?' She grabbed her phone and peered at it. 'Eight o'clock. Thanks for letting me sleep.'

'You slept a long time,' Mandy said, turning to Ella. 'I've been awake for hours.'

'What have you been doing while I was asleep?' Ella asked.

'Weeell,' Mandy started. 'I played with my teddy and looked at the pictures in the story book we read last night. And then… I went downstairs and played a little bit with your computer. I like the big screen.'

'What?' Ella stared at Mandy. 'You mean the PC in the sunroom?'

Mandy nodded. 'I pressed the button and the screen came on.'

'I must have forgotten to turn it off last night,' Ella said, jumping out of bed. 'What did you do on it?'

'I just pressed a few buttons and looked at the pictures and then… pouf, it all bisappeared,' Mandy said, looking slightly worried. 'But it's not broken, cos it's making a sound.'

'Oh my God!' Ella raced down the stairs and ran to the sunroom where she sat down at her PC, looking at the screen where images flickered, then died as she tried to get her various programs to start. Then the screen went blue with the text 'Attempting repair' before it turned black and died with a whining sound. Oh God, this was a real disaster. She had scanned her drawings into the computer yesterday and then started on the graphics, which she had worked on for a long time prior to doing the sketches. Then she was going to combine it all in her final designs. 'Weeks of work is in here,' she sobbed. 'What am I going to do?'

'I'm sorry,' Mandy said, standing in the door, her shoulders slumped. 'I didn't mean to break your work.'

Ella looked at Mandy, torn between anger and pity. Mandy looked so crushed, and she could see a tear making a groove through the plastered-on make-up. 'Come here,' she said.

Mandy's chin wobbled. 'Are you going to tell me off?'

'No. It was stupid of me to forget to turn off the computer.'

'It was all your fault?' Mandy asked, looking brighter.

'In a way.' Ella buried her face in her hands. 'Oh God, this is such a disaster.' She took a deep breath and started the computer again. The screen lit up, looking normal, but then it turned blue again with that text and a tiny circle going round and round. 'I'm not very good at computers. I should have done a course when I started doing graphics but I thought I could manage without it,' she muttered.

Mandy touched her arm. 'I'm sad for you.'

'I'm sad for me too,' Ella said with a sigh. She scooped Mandy onto her lap and squeezed her tight. 'It's okay. I'll get it fixed somehow. It's not really the end of the world.'

Mandy sighed deeply. 'But it's making me sad.'

'Let's go and have a scrummy brekkie,' Ella suggested. 'I bought Coco Pops yesterday. And we'll have toast with jam.'

'And chocolate buttons?' Mandy said hopefully.

'That's for your snack at the playgroup. Can you wait until then?'

'I'll try,' Mandy said bravely. She jumped off Ella's lap and ran off to the kitchen.

Ella sighed and followed, wondering how she was going to get her computer fixed in a hurry. She began to realise that a five-year-old, even one as cute as Mandy, was a lot of work and that minding her was not the cosy, cuddly Disney movie she had thought it would be. How on earth did parents cope with not one but several small children and manage to hold down a job at the same time? It seemed an impossible task. But maybe she wasn't cut out to be a mother?

Later that morning, when a cleaned-up Mandy had been deposited at the playgroup, Ella sat down at the computer and tried to start it up without success. Her agent had sent a text message saying the deadline for the finished drawings had been pulled forward and she now had to send them on the following Monday at the latest. He said he had also sent her an important email she couldn't look up because of her broken-down computer. A lot of the designs were, of course, in that dratted machine that now stared at her with a black screen. If she couldn't get this one started, she'd have to consider buying a new computer and start from scratch, which meant there was no way she could meet the deadline and then she'd be in breach of contract to the publisher. Ella bit her lip as she looked up computer repairers on her phone and gave a start as it rang. It was Rory, she saw on the screen.

'Yeah?' she snapped. 'What do you want?'

'Sorry, did I call at a bad time? Or is it always a bad time with you?'

'Right now is a very bad time,' Ella said and then, to her horror, burst into tears.

'What's the matter?' Rory asked, sounding suddenly concerned.

'It's my computer.' Ella sniffed and tried to sound at least like an adult, but failed. 'It's broken,' she sobbed, 'and I don't know what to do. All my work files have disappeared. It's a disaster.'

'How did that happen?'

'A five-year-old girl waking up at dawn happened. She had nothing to play with so she saw the computer blinking at her. You can guess the rest.'

'Oh. I see. Do you use a cloud by any chance? Dropbox or Google Docs or…'

'No. Stupid, I know, but there you are. I am officially completely brainless.'

'You're not alone,' he said. 'Not in being stupid but in not backing up your work. You'd be surprised at how many people fail to do that. But fear not, I'll come around to take a look. I know a few things about computers, so…'

'Oh, great,' Ella said, feeling a little brighter. She doubted Rory could fix it, but it would be nice not to be alone. He might even know someone who could help. Mandy would be at the playgroup for the next few hours, so she could try to retrieve some of her files at least. She quickly tidied away the breakfast dishes and went upstairs to freshen up and rinse her red eyes with cold water. No need to resemble the wreck she felt like. While she was drying her face, she heard a car come to a screeching halt outside the house. She peeked through the window and saw Rory get out of a silver Golf and she ran down the stairs and opened the door, shooting him a wan smile.

'Hi. Jaysus, that was quick! But thanks for coming. Sorry about the nervous breakdown earlier.'

'No need to apologise,' Rory said as he came inside. 'Anyone who's lost several weeks of their hard work would feel like crying.'

'That's for sure,' Ella said with feeling. 'I still have the sketches I did, of course, but if I have to start doing the graphics from scratch, I won't be able to meet the deadline. Come on in. The computer is in the sunroom that I use as a workroom.'

'I know the way,' Rory said as he marched across the living room and into the sunroom, where he sat down at the desk by the wall. He pressed the switch on the PC. 'Let's see what happens.'

'Nothing, that's what,' Ella said. 'It just says attempted repair or something and then gets stuck there.'

'Let's try this.' As the computer started up, Rory held the power button for around ten seconds and the computer shut down. 'I'll repeat this three times and then we should get to some kind of page. It's the "command prompts" I'm after.' As Rory repeated the action a few times, a blue screen appeared with several boxes. 'Aha!' he said, sounding satisfied. 'Here we go.'

'Here we go – what?' Ella asked. 'What are you doing?'

'Never mind,' Rory said without taking his eyes off the screen.

'Will you be able to fix it?' Ella asked, wringing her hands.

'I hope so.'

'You hope? Is that all you can say?'

'Right now, yes.' Rory shot her an irritated look. 'Could you make me a cup of coffee?'

'Okay. If you're sure you don't need me.'

'I've never been more certain of anything in my life,' Rory grunted.

Realising she was disturbing him, Ella went into the kitchen and made coffee for them both with her Nespresso machine, while she prayed to God in heaven that he'd manage to fix her computer. That was the most she thought he could do. Retrieving her lost files was another matter, and she was sure they had all disappeared into cyberspace never to be found. She nearly started crying again as she thought of the lovely designs of the forest and the flora and fauna. She thought she had created such a gorgeous, magical world in those images, perfect for the story, but now she might have to start from scratch.

But when she went back to the sunroom she saw a sight that nearly made her drop the two cups of coffee. The lovely images she had created filled the screen and Rory was staring at them, looking very pleased with himself.

'You did it!' Ella exclaimed, putting the coffee on the worktable beside the desk.

Rory beamed at her as he stood up. 'But of course. Did you doubt me?'

'No... Yes, I mean...' Ella sat down on the chair, staring at the screen, her eyes filling with tears of relief and happiness. 'It's amazing,' she whispered, turning to look at Rory. 'I could hug you for this.'

He held out his arms. 'Be my guest.'

For a split second, Ella was ready to fall into his arms and feel that strong body against hers. But then alarm bells rang in her mind and she laughed. 'Nah, that'd be too soppy. But I am truly grateful. You have no idea what a disaster it would have been if all this had been lost. It's been so hard to keep working as I recovered from the accident, but I forced myself to sit down for at least an hour every day, even if my back was killing me. And then when I thought it had all been for nothing...'

Rory picked up his cup from the table and sipped his coffee. 'That little monkey nearly ruined all you had worked so hard for. I'm sure you wanted to kill her.'

'Well, yes, at first,' Ella admitted. 'But then I realised she's just five years old and didn't mean any harm. She was up early and got bored, despite the toys she brought. It was my fault for not getting up in time to make sure she had something to occupy her.'

Rory handed Ella her coffee. 'Here. I'm sure you need it.'

Ella took the cup. 'Thanks.' She drank the coffee as she met Rory's eyes. 'Don't you like children?' she asked.

'Of course I do. I love kids normally. That doesn't mean I think they should misbehave.'

'Did you ever want to have children of your own?'

Rory shrugged. 'I never really thought about it. I'm quite close to Martin's children. Sarah and Alex are teenagers now but I enjoyed being the fun uncle when they were small. I used to take them to the cinema and babysit at weekends when Martin and Fiona wanted a break. Fun evenings with popcorn and movies on TV. That made up for not having kids of my own. The woman I was with had two teenage children. But it didn't work in the end.'

'So those were the components you were talking about that didn't work?'

'Some of them, yes,' he replied curtly.

'I see.' Ella could tell by his tone he didn't want to talk about it.

'Right,' he said, putting his cup on the table. 'I'll be off, so.'

'Okay.' Ella got to her feet and was about to give him a kiss on the cheek as a thank you, like she would normally have done with anyone else. But something stopped her and she stood there, feeling awkward. 'Thank you so much for your help,' she said instead. 'You saved my life.'

'Not really, but I know what you mean,' he replied. He flicked his hand in a goodbye gesture. 'Bye for now. Give me a shout if you have any more trouble. And please look up Dropbox or any of the cloud services and get a subscription.'

'I will.' Then something suddenly occurred to Ella. 'Hang on.'

He stopped on his way out of the room. 'Yes?'

'What was it you called me about earlier? Before I told you about the computer disaster.'

He looked blankly at her. 'Oh that. It was about Australia and my mother's family. But I think I'll do a little research before I talk about it. I don't have much to tell you right now.'

'I'll wait until you do, then,' Ella said, turning back to the computer.

'Grand. See you at the pub on Monday night. Unless you want to cancel that?'

'No, I'll be there,' Ella said. 'Looking forward to it.'

'Me too,' he said, turning on his heel and walking out of the room.

Ella laughed to herself as she switched to check her emails. He had looked a little grumpy but she could tell he was softening towards her. He now seemed to see her as an ally instead of an adversary. But was she really? She had been very supportive of Lucille from the start, but ever since Rory had told her his side of the story, she'd started to feel terrible about keeping the truth of Lucille's plans for him. She found herself sitting on the proverbial fence, not quite knowing which side was right. She realised how alike Lucille and Rory were, both using charm to get what they wanted.

But as Ella considered both sides, she began to find Rory's arguments the more compelling. Was this because she was beginning to feel attracted to him? She hoped not. That would cause more trouble than it was worth. Thomas was the kind of man that would be right for her: kind, considerate… Oh God, this was getting so confusing. She had hoped looking after Mandy would take her mind off Rory and how she felt about him. She had also thought it would bring her closer to Thomas and show him how good she was with children. But Rory kept popping up and ruining her plans, constantly confusing her.

Ella shook off those thoughts as the computer started up again without a problem, and turned her attention to her emails, two of which were from her agent, the latest making her heart beat faster.

She read it twice as she held her breath. How incredible! Here was the break she had been hoping for, her chance to get into illustrations in a big way. All thoughts of Rory, Thomas or any other romantic notion disappeared as she considered what this would lead to. It could change her life completely.

Chapter Sixteen

Ella tried to digest what she had just learned and turned to her work while it all sank in. Her agent's news was amazing, but it also made her a little nervous. Could she do this? It would involve graphic techniques she wasn't sure she'd mastered quite yet. But she had started to love working like this and knew that if she applied herself, she'd manage it in the end. She was dying to share this news with someone, but there was no one around right now. Lucille was in Tipperary and Thomas in Dublin and Lydia, with whom she had become close friends, was in Boston with Jason for the summer visiting his family. Then, almost on cue, her phone rang and she saw it was Rory.

'Hi,' he said. 'I'm sitting on top of a mountain looking out over the bay. I can see the coastguard station from here. It just occurred to me that you need to restart your computer after re-installing some of the apps. Have you done that?'

'No, but I will,' Ella said. 'Thanks again for helping me. I thought I was going to have a nervous breakdown.'

'You're welcome,' he said. 'Happy to help a lady in distress.'

'How very gallant you are.'

'You sound surprised. I'm not always the grump you have come to like so much.'

'That's nice to know. And...' She couldn't hold it in any more; she just had to tell someone, even if it was just Rory. 'I just got an email from my agent with some exciting news.'

'Such as?'

'He told me that there is a possibility that the story will be developed into a cartoon strip, and maybe even an animated movie. He's negotiating with publishers and film makers right now.' Ella drew breath, her heart beating as she thought of this amazing break.

'Wow, that's incredible,' Rory said, sounding impressed. 'Congratulations.'

'Thank you. I shouldn't really tell anyone, but I couldn't hold it in any more. It means that I will be able to keep doing illustrations, which is what I've started to really enjoy.'

'What about your painting?'

'I can do that too, but it won't be as important as before.'

'I see. Great.' He stopped for a moment. 'As I look down on your house, I'm thinking about the history of the place, and about the people who have lived there through the years. I have been looking up the coastguard station on the internet and connected it with that discussion of my mother's family years ago that developed into a row. I can't remember the details, but some of it came back to me when I was reading about the place.'

'Go on,' Ella said, momentarily distracted from her drawings.

'It was about Mum's mother's relations. They were called Brosnan, which is quite a common name in Kerry, isn't it?'

'Yes, I think so,' Ella said, intrigued. 'And...?'

'There was some sort of scandal in that family that my dad was teasing my mother about. She took huge offence and there was a lot of door-slamming and harsh words until they made up. Then it wasn't mentioned again.'

'Oh.'

'And then when I was looking it all up yesterday, I discovered that there was a Brosnan living in Sandy Cove in the 1840s, who got into trouble with the law.'

'Really? That's interesting. Lucille never mentioned this to me.'

'She doesn't like to talk about that side of the family. I have a feeling that my father's family were a bit snooty about her, as they had a more upper-class background. Landowners and academics and so on.'

'Maybe that's why she wants to relocate?' Ella suggested. 'To forget all about the snooty relations?'

'Why should she?' Rory asked. 'Most of the worst ones are dead anyway.'

'Ah, but it could still give her a sense of satisfaction.'

'Hmm,' Rory said. 'No, that sounds a little far-fetched. Anyway,' he continued, 'I'm going to keep walking here. Gorgeous views and fantastic exercise. Then when I come down to the cottages where I'm staying, I can have a dip in the river to cool off.'

'Sounds great,' Ella said. She checked her watch. 'I have to go and collect Mandy from the playgroup in a minute. Thanks for calling. I'll do as you said with the computer.'

'Grand. See you soon, then,' Rory said and hung up.

Ella went back to her work, the conversation fresh in her mind. She had deduced before that Lucille's husband's family had looked down their noses at her. Marrying a dancer might not have been accepted in those circles in the 1950s and then when they found out about the misdemeanour of one of her ancestors, they had probably sneered even more at her. But Lucille had actually mentioned that her family had connections with Sandy Cove. That must be part of the reason why she had come here to Sandy Cove and wanted to live here.

Ella shook her head and turned off her computer. Enough about Lucille. Now she had to concentrate on Mandy and try to entertain her until it was time for bed. And tomorrow she would wake up early to make sure there were no more disasters. It seemed suddenly years until Thomas would be back to take over. Thank God for that party at Hannah's house. That would occupy Mandy for hours and hopefully make her tired enough to sleep for a little longer.

Hannah's mother, Maura, lived in a big white house on the outskirts of the village. Ella had heard on the grapevine that Maura had inherited it from her parents when they died. She lived there with her two children, working from home as an accountant and book-keeper. The garden surrounding the house was a little overgrown but lovely with wild flowers competing for space with roses and shrubs. A gravelled path snaked its way through the long grass around the house to the back lawn where a bouncy castle had been erected. Mandy squealed with joy as she saw it and threw Hannah her present before she ran towards it, took off her shoes, and started to bounce, the skirt of her party dress flying.

Maura, walking across the lawn, laughed as she watched Mandy. 'Here's someone who's having a good time already.'

'That's for sure,' Ella said. 'She has talked of nothing else all week.' Ella looked around the garden teeming with children and turned to Maura. 'How on earth do you cope?'

'Cope with what?' Maura asked over the din of children running around shouting at the tops of their voices.

'With looking after two small children on your own, and a job as well,' Ella replied. 'And then giving a party like this. I only have to mind Mandy for a couple of days and I'm already exhausted.'

Maura laughed. 'Of course you are. They're very tiring. But you get into a kind of routine after a while. And you learn to watch them out of the corner of your eye while you do other things. And I have a brilliant childminder who comes to the house during the week.'

'I see,' Ella said, admiring Maura's casual look that didn't show the slightest sign of stress. Her short dark hair was brushed back from her face, her discreet make-up was perfectly applied and her blue T-shirt looked newly ironed. This was a sharp contrast to Ella's messy hair, baggy trousers and wrinkly shirt. She hadn't had time to freshen up between catching up on her work, collecting Mandy from playgroup and getting her ready for the party. 'It probably takes years to get into it.'

'It's more about having an organised mind, I think. And being relaxed about a lot of stuff. Thomas is very good at that.'

'Is he?' Ella asked, intrigued. She knew Thomas was good with Mandy but the way Maura talked about him was almost wistful.

'Oh yes. All children seem to take to him big time.'

'Maybe it's something you're born with,' Ella suggested, wondering how much time Thomas spent at Maura's house.

'I think it has more to do with an instinct that kicks in the minute you become a parent,' Maura said.

Ella shrugged. 'I suppose. I wouldn't know as I haven't experienced it.'

'But you're great with Mandy, Thomas says.'

'Does he?' Ella asked, feeling a sudden warm glow at hearing that Thomas had talked about her in such a positive way.

'Oh yes. All the time,' Maura said.

'Well, that's nice to know. I was flattered that he trusted me to look after Mandy.' Ella paused. 'I hope all goes well for him in Dublin.'

'Oh.' Maura looked surprised. 'Hasn't he told you? It didn't go well at all. He didn't get that job with the RTE symphony. He was quite down about it. He'll be back a bit earlier than planned. Tomorrow, I think he said. But he wants to surprise Mandy, so not a word to her,' Maura added with a wink.

'Of course,' Ella said. 'I'm sure he did call me, but I've been so busy I must have missed it.'

'Yeah. Probably,' Maura said. 'But now you'll have to excuse me. I have to take control of this rowdy lot and feed them cake and play games and make sure nobody gets killed.'

'Do you need a hand? I could stay and help,' Ella offered.

'That's very kind of you,' Maura said. 'But I have plenty of help. My childminder is in the kitchen preparing the cake and my aunt will be around soon to help out. You go and enjoy the break and come back at around five to pick Mandy up.'

'Great,' Ella said. 'I hope you survive.'

'Of course I will,' Maura said with a grin. 'I'm an old pro, after all.'

'See you later then,' Ella said, feeling intimidated by Maura's excellence. Here was a woman who truly had control of her life. She didn't have a man in her life, but she didn't seem to need one at all. A truly complete, self-contained woman who was happy on her own and managed her life perfectly. That was the official image, but, Ella mused, as she moved away, those children had a father somewhere and there must have been a painful separation at some point. Not even perfect Maura would have sailed through that unscathed. Maybe she screamed into the darkness sometimes, or cried when she was all alone? Not that Ella wished this cheerful woman to be unhappy but it made her strength all the more admirable.

With the sounds of children's voices only a distant echo, Ella walked on, enjoying the warm sun on her back, the cries of the seagulls and the glorious views of the coast ahead of her. A lovely day that should not be wasted, or spoiled by dark thoughts. But Ella couldn't help thinking about what Maura had said, and that Thomas had called her to tell her the bad news instead of sharing it with Ella. Apart from the good night call to Mandy last night, he hadn't called to talk to Ella in private. Why didn't he feel he could confide in her?

She sat down on a low wall and stared out to sea, oblivious of the stunning views. She had hoped to get closer to Thomas by looking after Mandy but maybe he didn't see her that way? Or maybe he had a closer friendship with Maura because they were both parents…

Her thoughts were interrupted by her phone pinging in her pocket. Ella pulled it out and looked at the text from Rory that said: *Mother disappeared. U know where she could be?*

Ella stared at the message for a moment. Then, not knowing quite what to do, she called Lucille's mobile. It rang a few times and then switched to her voicemail. 'Lucille, please call me,' Ella said after the tone. 'Rory is very worried about you.'

Just as she hung up, the phone pinged again. A text message from Lucille. *Don't worry. I'm fine, but I won't be back for a while. I'll be in touch when I can, but until then I will observe radio silence.*

Ella looked at the message, not knowing whether to laugh or cry. Radio silence? That sounded like something from a spy movie. What was Lucille up to? Something strange was going on. Was it something to do with that phone call to Australia? Or the sale of the house? Or was she in some kind of danger? Ella found Rory's number and called it.

'Hi,' she said when he answered. 'I just got a strange text from Lucille. She says she's fine but won't be back for a while and that she will observe radio silence until she'll be in touch again.'

'Radio silence?' Rory asked. 'Is she being held against her will by some terrorists?'

'Yeah, that's what it sounds like.' Ella snorted a laugh. 'I don't think you need worry. She's up to something, that's for sure, but I'd say she's enjoying whatever it is. And also having fun playing the mystery woman.'

'Hmm.' Rory was silent for a moment. 'You're probably right. I got a bit of a fright when I heard from my brother that she wasn't in Tipperary. Nobody has seen here there. The house doesn't seem to have been put on the market yet anyway. Martin and the family are staying there for the weekend, so if she appears, he'll be able to talk to her.'

'Maybe she knew he'd be there and is avoiding them?' Ella suggested.

'Could be. But we'll just have to wait until she decides to appear again.'

'Exactly.' Ella got up from the wall. 'But she might be a while.'

'That's frustrating,' Rory said sourly. 'But we can drown our sorrows on Monday anyway. See you then,' he said and hung up.

'And you have a lovely day, too,' Ella muttered, putting the phone in her pocket. She resumed walking, feeling less and less cheerful. What a sourpuss he was when things didn't go well. While it was good thing that they got on better, she was still constantly reminded of how moody he was. And how wrong he would be for her, even though she felt such a strong physical attraction every time they met. But that was all it was, of course. They weren't compatible in any other way. Her thoughts turned to Thomas and how calm and accepting he was of everything, even though his sorrow came through occasionally. But surely time would heal the grief and he would be able to consider a relationship again. A man like that wouldn't want to be on his own for the rest of his life. *Time,* Ella thought, *maybe that's what he needs. And maybe that's what I need too, instead of rushing ahead as usual.*

Chapter Seventeen

It was Saturday, and Thomas would be back sometime today, so Ella had taken the day off work to get the house and herself spick and span. She had managed to catch up after the computer disaster and now she wasn't worried about meeting the deadline any more. She just needed to check it all through before she sent it off.

Deciding to try her best to be more like Maura, Ella spent the morning tidying up the house, and baked a lemon sponge, Mandy cracking the eggs and 'helping' by stirring the batter and licking the spoon. Then, while Mandy watched cartoons on TV, Ella washed and blow-dried her hair, put on a newly ironed linen shirt and her cleanest pair of jeans. She looked nearly as polished as Maura, she thought as she examined herself in her bedroom mirror. And the house was tidy and smelled of newly baked cake. Thomas was sure to be impressed. Thank God her health was so much better. She felt nearly back to her old self, and that was very much thanks to Lucille in so many ways. Now she could manage on her own as the morning's work had proved.

Ella smiled and patted her hair, feeling a huge sense of achievement. It wasn't as hard as it had seemed to get her act together with the housework and achieve this well-groomed look at the same time.

All it took was a little organisation and a bit of effort. Minding a five-year-old wasn't hard once one got into the swing of it. She didn't think she could have found time to do any work on her illustrations as well, but then, unlike Maura, she didn't have any help at all.

Happy with the way she looked, Ella went downstairs to check on Mandy, who, judging by the sound from the TV, was still watching the cartoons. The cake would be ready in a few minutes, so she had plenty of time to tidy away the toys in the living room. When he arrived, Thomas would find a perfect house, a happy child and a newly baked cake on the table to go with his coffee. Not to mention a beautifully groomed babysitter.

Pleased with her morning's work, Ella came into the living room. 'Mandy,' she said cheerily, 'maybe it's time to turn off the TV. The cake is nearly ready, and—' The words died on her lips and she stopped dead, looking around the empty room strewn with toys.

Where was Mandy?

The sofa where she had been sitting was empty, the door to the sunroom open and the back door as well. Ella rushed outside but found the back garden deserted, the gate swinging open, and she felt panic rise in her chest. Where had Mandy gone? Not down the steep steps to Wild Rose Bay, she hoped, running along the path to the fence that had been erected there, but that gate was locked. Ella felt a brief sense of relief. At least Mandy hadn't been able to go down there. She looked around and scanned the path on the other side that led to the headland and started to run along it. There was nobody about as it was windy with a light drizzle, not pleasant walking weather at all.

A cold hand of fear squeezing her heart, Ella ran on, her sandals squishing on the muddy path, trying her best to dodge the puddles.

Why oh why did Mandy have to run off just now, when Thomas was about to arrive? But where was she? There was no sign of the little girl on the winding path, and it was difficult to see far ahead in the mist. But as she rounded the last bend, feeling her heart might burst, she spotted Mandy, sitting on the rough bench with something in her lap.

'Mandy!' Ella shouted. 'Come here. What are you doing out in the rain?'

Mandy turned her head and looked at Ella. 'I was saving *him*,' she said, holding up her burden, which Ella now saw was a very wet white kitten that meowed pitifully, trying to struggle out of Mandy's grip. 'He was lost,' Mandy said. 'I tried to catch him but he ran off so I followed him.'

'Where did you find him?' Ella asked coming closer.

'He came into the garden and kept meowing and meowing, so I thought I'd catch him and bring him inside. But then he ran away into the rain. I just caught him.'

'But where did he come from?' Ella asked.

'From his mummy's tummy,' Mandy said.

Ella sighed. 'I know, but where does he live?'

'I don't know,' Mandy replied. 'He just came into your garden.'

'Okay. We'll have to try to find out where he belongs.' Ella held out her hand. 'Come on, we have to go back now. You can't sit here in the rain.'

'It's not really raining that much,' Mandy argued. 'Just a little bit.' She held up the struggling, meowing kitten. 'Here. Can you carry him? He's a bit prickly.'

Ella carefully lifted the kitten out of Mandy's grip and held him to her chest, where he relaxed and started to purr loudly. 'He seems to have calmed down. Let's go back now.'

Mandy jumped down from the bench. 'Okay. Let's go and eat that cake.'

'Oh, no,' Ella groaned. 'The cake. I forgot to take it out of the oven. It'll be burned to a cinder.'

'What's a cinder?' Mandy asked as they started back down the path.

'Something black and burned.' Ella took Mandy's cold little hand while she held the kitten to her chest with the other. 'But we can buy a new cake from the bakery instead.'

'After lunch?'

'That's right. After lunch,' Ella promised, hoping Thomas wouldn't appear until the afternoon so she could recover from what had happened and tidy up.

No such luck, however. The doorbell rang just as they stepped into the house. 'Go and see who it is,' Ella said, looking around for a safe place to put the kitten.

Mandy ran to the hall and wrenched open the front door, squealing 'Daddeeee!' as she discovered who was standing on the doorstep.

Ella heard Thomas laugh in the hall as she put the kitten into a cardboard box where he immediately settled and started to lick his wet fur. She looked down at her mud-splattered shirt and jeans and put a hand to her hair that was hanging in wet strands around her face, where the mascara was sure to have slid down her cheeks. Not the pretty picture she had prepared. The smell of burning suddenly hit her nostrils and she rushed into the kitchen to turn off the oven and take out the black mess that had been a lemon sponge cake she had hoped would impress Thomas.

'Ugh.' Ella waved the oven glove to disperse the smoke and opened the window.

'What happened?' Thomas asked as he entered the kitchen with Mandy hanging off his neck.

'Well,' Ella started, 'this was supposed to be your homecoming treat. But things happened and…' She stopped. 'It's a long story.'

Thomas eyed her bedraggled appearance. 'Did you go jogging in the rain or something?'

'No, she was looking for me,' Mandy said with a giggle. 'I ran after the kitten and then Ella got worried and ran after me and we got all muddy and wet. Even the kitten is wet. And Ella forgot to take the cake out of the oven.'

'You're pretty muddy and wet yourself, young lady,' Thomas said and put Mandy down on the floor. 'And so am I,' he said, glancing at his white polo shirt that bore the marks of Mandy's enthusiastic welcome home. He glanced at Ella. 'I hope it hasn't been too stressful for you to mind Mandy.'

Ella managed to laugh. 'Stressful? Not all. We've had a lot of fun, haven't we, Mandy?'

Mandy nodded. 'Yes, we have. And Ella only got mad at me once, but I said sorry and then we were friends again.'

'What happened?' Thomas asked.

Ella waved her hand. 'Nothing worth talking about. Hey, let's go out to the living room before we're asphyxiated.'

'We should really go home,' Thomas said. 'We've troubled you enough. I'm sure you have other things to do.'

Ella pinched her wet shirt. 'Yeah, like getting cleaned up.'

'The kitten is asleep,' Mandy announced, looking into the cardboard box. 'Maybe we could take him home?'

Thomas looked at the kitten curled up in the box. 'He's very cute. I'm sure he belongs to someone, Mandy. Someone who might be missing him.'

'We could keep him for a little while,' Mandy suggested. 'Until we find out where he lives.'

'That's a good idea,' Thomas said, lifting the box. 'I'm sure Ella doesn't want a kitten tearing around the place.'

'Not really,' Ella confessed. 'He's lovely, but I don't think I want a pet just now.'

'Of course you don't,' Thomas said. 'You've had enough to do these past few days. But now I'll take over.'

'Thanks,' Ella said, relieved she was no longer responsible. 'I packed Mandy's clothes earlier. The bag is in the hall. Only the toys to pick up but I can do that later. I'd ask you to stay for lunch, but…'

'Why don't I take you both out for lunch?' Thomas suggested. 'The two Marys do great hamburgers. It's very popular with families on Saturdays.'

'Sounds great,' Ella said, her mood lifting. 'I could do with one of their delicious hamburgers.'

'And chips,' Mandy cut in. 'And ice cream.'

'Of course,' Thomas said, patting Mandy's head. 'It's Saturday after all. We'll go home and clean up and meet you there in half an hour.'

'Great,' Ella said. She took the box from Thomas. 'Maybe better to leave him here for now. I'll tuck him up and then maybe we can ask around after lunch if someone has lost him.'

'And if nobody has, we'll keep him,' Mandy stated. 'That's a good deal, don't you think, Daddy?'

'I'll think about it,' Thomas said, looking doubtful.

Ella helped Thomas carry Mandy's bags to his house and then ran back home to change. Her heart sang as she changed into clean clothes, not caring what she put on. Thomas hadn't seemed to worry about what she wore or that the homecoming she had planned had ended in such a mess. And now they would be having lunch together, in what felt nearly like a real family... Ella pushed the thought away, knowing that it came more from her affection for Mandy than anything to do with Thomas.

The Two Marys' café, housed in a thatched cottage above the main beach, was packed with families. Children ran around the tables chasing each other, shouting and laughing and there was a delicious smell of grilled meat. Thomas had grabbed a big round table by the window, from where he waved at Ella standing by the door. 'Over here, Ella!' he shouted.

'You managed to get a table,' Ella said. 'I'm impressed.'

'No, it was Maura,' Thomas said. 'She was already here and asked me to join them. She's gone to order with the girls. I said to get hamburgers and chips for everyone. That okay with you?'

'Fine,' Ella said, trying to look cheerful even though she felt disappointment settle on her like a damp flannel. This day was going from bad to worse. But she smiled at Thomas as she sat down and put her hand on his. 'I was so sorry to hear things didn't go so well in Dublin.'

'Who told you?' he asked.

'Maura.'

'Oh. Well yeah,' he said with a shrug. 'Could have been great, but maybe it was better it didn't work out. It would have meant a lot of trips to Dublin during the summer. I want to stay here as long as I can. It's so good for Mandy.'

'She's really thriving,' Ella agreed.

'She is. Oh, and I meant to tell you, I saw Lucille at the RTE studios in Donnybrook when I was there for the audition.'

'What?' Ella asked. 'Lucille? At RTE? What would she be doing there?'

'We didn't talk to each other. I saw her as I walked in and she was on her way out. In fact, she looked a little upset that I had spotted her. Tried to hide behind a pillar in the lobby.'

'Are you sure it was her?'

Thomas nodded. 'Absolutely. She was wearing a bright red tunic, white trousers and those silver trainers I've seen her in before. Nobody could copy that look.'

'No, that would be hard.' Ella stared at Thomas. 'I wonder what's going on. She's been a little weird lately and then she disappeared and told me not to contact her. She said she'd be in touch when she was ready.'

'Sounds a little peculiar,' Thomas remarked. 'But I'm sure she's fine and has her reasons. Try not to worry.'

'I will,' Ella said. 'And I hope you're not too upset about the audition.'

'Not really. That's show business, as they say. And it's nice to be back,' Thomas replied. 'Such luck to run into Maura and Hannah, don't you think?'

'Fabulous,' Ella said with a thin smile, pulled back to reality and her dashed hopes of a family kind of occasion with Thomas and Mandy. It had all been in her imagination anyway.

'Mandy was so happy to see Hannah,' Thomas continued with a laugh, not appearing to have noticed Ella's glum expression. 'You'd think they hadn't seen each other for weeks the way they carried on.'

'They're great friends,' Ella said. 'Hannah is such a sweet girl.'

'The perfect friend for Mandy,' Thomas said. 'Hannah's very like her mother.'

'I suppose she is,' Ella said, thinking about how brightly Thomas spoke of Maura. 'Where's the baby?' she asked.

'He's with Maura's aunt. He's teething, apparently, so a bit grumpy. Maura didn't get much sleep last night, but she still wanted to take Hannah to lunch, because she promised. Such a fantastic mother. I wouldn't be able for all of that,' Thomas said, his voice warm.

'Hi, Ella,' Maura said behind them.

Ella turned and discovered Maura carrying a tray with drinks. Her eyes looked tired but apart from that, she was the picture of perfection with her pristine white shirt, a blue sweater across her shoulders and her hair brushed back from her face. 'Hi, Maura,' Ella said. 'Do you need help with that?'

But Thomas had already shot up to take the tray, which he placed on the table. 'There. Thanks for getting the drinks.'

'The orders are on the way.' Maura sat down on the chair Thomas pulled out for her. 'So nice to see you, Ella. I didn't have time to chat yesterday with all the kids running around.'

'It was a lovely party, Mandy told me,' Thomas cut in. 'A bouncy castle and a magician, no less.'

'She had a ball,' Ella said. 'She was so excited afterwards it took her hours to go to sleep. Which earned me an extra few hours this morning,' she added with a laugh.

'I hope her early mornings haven't been too hard,' Thomas said apologetically.

'A bit,' Ella had to admit. 'But as it was only for a few days, I didn't mind. I just went to bed early and it was okay. There was no way I could change Mandy's sleeping pattern in such a short time.'

'Funny how it's so difficult,' Maura cut in. 'I've tried to delay Hannah's bedtime but she conks out in the sofa anyway and then I have to carry her to bed.'

'It's their circadian rhythm,' Thomas said. 'I read about that recently.'

Maura nodded. 'I know. I read that article too. Interesting, wasn't it?"

Thomas and Maura fell into a conversation about small children and their sleeping habits while Ella's thoughts drifted. What Thomas had said about Lucille had startled her and she wondered what on earth Lucille was doing in Dublin. And in the television studios of all places. Was Rory right to worry about his mother's mental health? Or was Lucille on some kind of mission? It was all so strange and there didn't seem to be any rhyme or reason to her behaviour.

Mandy and Hannah joined them at the table at the same time as their orders arrived. They all fell on the food and ate in silence while Thomas and Maura kept an eye on their daughters, mopping up spilt ketchup and wiping their mouths from time to time, while laughing and chatting mainly about children and the trials and tribulations of being single parents. Ella looked at them, not being able to join in. It suddenly struck her that she wasn't the one Thomas was having a family time with. It was Maura.

Chapter Eighteen

Back home after the disappointing lunch, Ella threw away the burned cake and tidied up the living room, piling Mandy's toys into the hold-all. She laughed at herself when she thought of the effort she had made to be the perfect 1950s housewife. *What was I doing?* she wondered. *Was I trying to push Rory out of my mind by trying to impress Thomas and casting myself in the role of Mandy's new mummy, imagining us as some kind of family?*

She shook her head at her delusions as she fluffed up the cushions and wiped little fingerprints off the coffee table. The reality bore no resemblance to her dream. She had been rushing ahead without thinking. That kind of relationship took a long time to nurture. Better to let things drift for a while and give everyone some space. And she needed a little peace to finish her project in any case. Matters of the heart would have to wait.

The kitten had woken up and was wandering around the living room, meowing and glaring at Ella with his green eyes. She carried him into the kitchen and put a saucer of water on the floor, which he lapped up in no time. She found a tin of tuna and put the contents in a plastic bowl and offered that to him, which he also gobbled up very quickly. Then he sat on the floor and started to clean his face,

Susanne O'Leary

making Ella smile. 'Who do you belong to?' she asked. She gave a start as she heard footsteps in the living room. Ella went to see who it was and discovered that Saskia had just walked in.

'Hi, Ella,' she said. 'Sorry to barge in, but the door was open. I'm just back from Donegal and thought I'd call in to see how you are.'

'Hi, Saskia,' Ella said. 'I'm really happy to see you back. How did your trip go?'

'I had a lovely time,' Saskia replied. 'And I found some gorgeous pieces of seaglass for my jewellery collection on the beaches there.' She paused and looked at Ella. 'You look fantastic, Ella. Nearly back to your old self, I see.'

'Oh yes,' Ella said, stretching up her arms above her head. 'All thanks to doing my exercises religiously every morning. And Lucille making me get out and about, too.'

'Wonderful.' Saskia's gaze fell on the kitten. 'You got a cat?'

Ella laughed. 'No, this is not my cat, it's a stray or a runaway kitten from somewhere that just wandered in here and caused a lot of trouble.'

'Gosh,' Saskia said, looking startled. 'Has he done a lot of damage?'

'Not as such,' Ella tried to explain. 'He only ruined the image of perfection that I was trying to impress Thomas with. Long story.'

'Have you had a bad day?' Saskia asked.

'You can say that again,' Ella replied.

'Do you want to tell me about it?'

'Yes,' Ella said, looking at Saskia's kind face. 'I really need a friend right now. And wine.'

'I'm right here,' Saskia said, 'Where's the wine?' She laughed.

'There's a bottle of white in the larder,' Ella replied. 'Won't be chilled but who cares?'

They settled on the sofa in front of a fire Ella lit as it was still quite chilly with rain beating against the windows. Saskia cuddled the kitten while Ella poured them each a glass of wine.

'So,' Saskia said, 'tell me what's been going on since I've been away.'

'I don't know where to start,' Ella said with a sigh. 'First Lucille disappeared and refuses to tell us where she went.'

'Us?' Saskia asked.

'Rory and me. I've been… Well, we've kind of joined forces to try to figure out what's going on with Lucille.'

'Aha,' Saskia said.

'There's no "aha" at all,' Ella said. 'We're just friends and I really hate him anyway.'

'Of course you do,' Saskia soothed, her eyes dancing. 'What else has been going on?'

'Nothing that I could control,' Ella replied, taking a gulp of wine. Then she told Saskia about the past week and how it had all ended earlier today. 'Wonderful, don't you think?' she said.

Saskia shrugged. 'I wouldn't worry about it. Thomas didn't seem shocked or disgusted, did he?'

'Not really. But then Thomas is hard to read. He never flies off the handle or shows when he's annoyed.'

'Nice man, but he seems hard to get to know,' Saskia remarked. 'Rory is more interesting. Not that I've seen much of him, of course.'

'I've seen *more* than enough of him,' Ella said with a sigh. 'I prefer talking to Thomas. He's so calm and so thoughtful.'

'But Rory helped you fix your computer,' Saskia said as she helped herself to more wine. 'That makes him some kind of hero in my book.'

'Yeah. He saved my life,' Ella said. 'And he was here in like three seconds after I had told him what happened, even though he was about to go hiking up the mountains.'

'And you still hate him?'

'Uh, well, maybe not so much after that,' Ella confessed, trying not to think about Rory and what effect he had on her. 'But we're still arguing all the time.'

'Sounds like fun.' Saskia laughed.

'Not always,' Ella said, making a face. 'We get on a bit better now. But I'm sure he'll be really shocked to find out that I've been hiding the truth from him.'

'What truth?' Saskia asked.

'That Lucille is selling his childhood home. Lucille made me swear not to tell him, but I'm finding it increasingly hard to lie to him all the time. He keeps mentioning that it's what he *thinks* is happening and I just keep staying silent.'

'Gosh,' Saskia said. 'That must be very difficult.'

'It's becoming nearly impossible. And I'm sure if Rory finds out I knew, he'll think I'm such a horrible liar.'

'And does that bother you?' Saskia asked with a smirk. 'If you're interested in him, maybe you should tell him the truth?' she suggested, looking thoughtfully at Ella.

'No, I'm not interested in him in that way,' Ella protested despite her heart skipping a beat as she thought of Rory. 'I'm devoted to Lucille and I want her to be happy. Rory is too much trouble anyway.

I think calmer waters are better for me. I've had enough of difficult men. I just feel bad for him.'

'So you think Thomas is a better bet?' Saskia asked, sinking deeper into the sofa.

'Yes, maybe. I did think that.' Ella sighed, forgetting her dilemma with Rory and Lucille's big secret. 'I thought I was doing so well when he asked me to lunch. But then…'

'Then what happened?'

'Perfect Maura happened. You know, that tall, cool, dark-haired woman with the two kids. She seems to be able to cope with anything and always looks like a million dollars. I bet she even irons her underwear and her socks.'

Saskia laughed. 'I know who you mean. Maura O'Sullivan. And yes, she always looks her best. But I always thought that perfect façade was her armour that she hides behind after all that's happened to her.'

'All? What do you mean?' Ella asked, taking a sip of wine. 'I've only lived here five years, so I don't know everyone's life story.'

Saskia shifted carefully on the sofa so she wouldn't disturb the sleeping kitten and put her glass on the coffee table. 'Well, for a start, her mother died when she was seventeen. She was the eldest of five children, so she became the mother and brought up her four siblings.'

'How terrible.' Ella was shocked. That sounded like an awful lot for a young girl to take on.

Saskia continued. 'Then, when she was at college studying to be an accountant, she fell in love with a fellow student and they moved in together. Then when she graduated, they both got jobs with high-profile accountancy firms and they moved in together. Hannah was born, just as Maura's father was diagnosed with cancer. She came here with Hannah to look after him, but her partner didn't want to come with her. He only appeared from time to time. Very flash guy as far as I remember. When Maura's father died about two years ago, her partner came here for a bit but then he left when Maura got pregnant with their second child. I think he left the country. Went to America for a job at one of the big banks, I think.' Saskia drew breath. 'Not husband material, I suppose.'

'Or father material,' Ella said, feeling a sense of shame at her thoughts about Maura. 'I had no idea Maura has gone through all that. She always looks so cheerful.'

'I'd say she's often very sad on the inside.' Saskia looked down at the kitten and stroked his soft fur, making him purr loudly. 'He's adorable. I wouldn't mind having him while we try to find his owner.'

'That'd be great,' Ella said. 'You could let Mandy feed him and play with him at your house. I don't think Thomas is that keen on a pet.'

'Probably not.'

'Thank you for telling me about Maura,' Ella said. 'I had no idea what she's been through. She must be so brave and so strong.'

Saskia nodded. 'Yes, I think she is. But then living in this village makes things a little easier. Everyone's so helpful, even if they poke into your business all the time. They seem to know what's going on in your life before you've even said a word.'

Ella smiled. 'That makes me laugh. But maybe it's not funny if you want to keep things private. I wish they'd second guess what Lucille is doing. It's getting on my nerves not knowing. And I'm beginning to think she's being unfair to her children, to be honest. Especially Rory.'

'Could you talk to her about it?' Saskia asked. 'Maybe make her see that she's wrong not to tell her sons about the house?'

'I tried, but you know what? I'm going to try again. In fact, when she comes back, I'm going to give her a piece of my mind. She's really overdoing the eccentric old woman act, doing what she wants without a thought to anyone else's feelings. Even mine.'

Saskia leaned forward and looked at Ella. 'Are you getting angry with her?'

'Yes. I'm sick of all the mystery and the cryptic messages. I know she's having fun fooling everyone. But it's time to lay the cards on the table. That's what I'm going to tell her.'

Saskia laughed and shook her head. 'You're going to get Lucille to behave? I barely know her, but I have a feeling she's quite a tough cookie. Good luck with that, my dear.'

'I mean it,' Ella said with feeling. 'And I'm going to tell Rory that when we meet up on Monday night.'

Saskia looked suddenly excited. 'You have a date?'

'No, just a drink.' Ella rolled her eyes. 'Why does it have to be a date every time I meet a man that I just happen to know?'

'Because you are a beautiful woman,' Saskia stated. 'We're all hoping you'll find someone who'll love you the way you deserve.'

'That's lovely,' Ella said, touched by Saskia's kind words. 'I hope so too. But that's a long way off and Rory is certainly not that man.'

'Are you sure?' Saskia asked.

Ella leaned forward and fixed Saskia with a steely gaze. 'One hundred per cent.'

'Okay,' Saskia said, laughing. 'You've convinced me.'

'That's a relief.' Ella looked sternly at Saskia. 'But I still don't want him to find out about my lying to him.'

'He won't hear it from me,' Saskia promised. 'And what about Thomas?'

Ella sat back. 'I think I'm more in love with Mandy than him. But I'm not sure I'm cut out to be anyone's stepmother. I've found out how exhausting small children can be.'

'If you're over forty, yes,' Saskia declared. 'But most mothers of small children are young and have the energy.'

'That's true,' Ella replied. 'I never thought of it that way. And of course, Maura is a lot younger than me. She doesn't look a day over thirty,'

'I think she's around thirty-five,' Saskia said. She looked at Ella with concern. 'I hope you're not still upset about what happened today.'

'I'm getting over it.' Ella pulled her legs under her and curled up in the corner of the sofa, cradling her glass of wine. 'I'm feeling a lot better. Thank you for taking the time to talk.'

Saskia smiled fondly. 'I enjoyed it. It's nice to have neighbours who are also friends.' She looked down at the kitten. 'And I have a feeling I got myself a new baby.'

'Mandy might be jealous,' Ella remarked. 'But she can always come to you and play with him. If you decide to take him, I mean.'

'I'll give her the job of chief cat minder, if I do,' Saskia suggested. 'And she can help me pick a name.

'Great idea.' Ella yawned and stretched, but stiffened as she heard a car pull up outside and a door slamming. 'Who's that, I wonder?'

'I'll check.' Saskia lifted the cat off her lap, got up and went into the hall. 'It's Lucille,' she called just as the front door opened, bringing with it a cold breeze and a hint of Chanel No. 5.

Ella sighed and laughed at the same time. Lucille was back and would be stirring up trouble again. But how boring life would be without her.

Chapter Nineteen

Ella watched as Lucille returned and settled back into her old routine in no time at all, going to her tai chi group on Sunday morning and joining Ella for a late breakfast on the terrace afterwards, having brought fresh soda bread and scones from The Two Marys', and the Sunday papers. She refused to answer any questions as to her whereabouts during her absence, except to say there would be 'a surprise very soon'. The bottles of champagne she had brought were put in the fridge for 'a celebration' and then she clammed up. Ella tried to speak to her but soon realised there was no use trying to find out what was going on and gave up.

They read the papers in companiable silence in the sunshine and then Lucille put down her copy of *Style* magazine and looked at Ella. 'You're very quiet. Are you cross with me for not telling you where I've been?'

Ella sighed and poured herself more coffee. 'Maybe a little. But more because you made everyone worry. Especially Rory. Was it fair to just disappear like that?'

'He didn't have to check up on me. If he hadn't, he wouldn't know I wasn't in Tipperary.'

'He's worried about you. And it's not just because of you selling the house. It's because he loves you, you know. He might not show it, but he does.'

'I know he does.' Lucille's eyes suddenly filled with tears. 'But he's not being fair. Johnny used to say, "Not all girls are made of sugar and spice and all things nice. Some are made of adventures and whiskey and all things risky." And I was one of those. That's what made him fall for me. I haven't changed and I never will. I wish my sons could accept that.'

'Do you have to sell the house they love to prove it? Or is it for another reason?'

Lucille raised an eyebrow. 'What other reason?'

'Revenge?' Ella suggested. 'Not on them but on Johnny's family. Those that were looking down their upper-class noses at you all those years ago.'

Lucille stared at Ella for moment. Then she took a deep breath. 'I don't know how you guessed it, but yes, maybe that's one of the reasons. Other than that, I don't want to end my days there all alone.'

'That could have been avoided in other ways,' Ella said. 'I have a feeling something, or someone triggered this sudden decision to put the house on the market.' She put up a hand as Lucille started to speak. 'Okay, I know you were feeling desperately lonely after Mum died, so I'm sure you were thinking about moving anyway. But it all seemed to happen so suddenly. And your move to Sandy Cove seemed to come out of the blue. I had no idea you wanted to come and live here until the day you called me.'

'A lot of things happened at once,' Lucille said, looking down at the magazine on the table. 'It was a coincidence that they all happened at the same time, but they made everything fall into place.' She fiddled with the pages of the magazine, looking into the distance as she spoke. 'I didn't want to have to explain myself until I was sure about the details. I didn't want the boys to try to stop me.' She turned her gaze back to Ella. 'And I can't tell you any more right now.'

'Lucille,' Ella said sternly, 'the sale of the house is going to break their hearts. Isn't there any way you could resolve this without that? Can't you at least speak to them about it?'

Lucille looked a little contrite. 'Maybe.'

'Talk to them,' Ella urged. 'Make them see your side of the story. I'm sure you could work out a solution and still buy the cottage here. If they knew *why* you want to move here, of all places, they might see things your way. And if they could buy the house from you, or something, everyone would get what they want in the end.'

'But then I won't be able to get back at that woman,' Lucille said cryptically.

'I don't know who you mean, but I'm guessing it's someone in Johnny's family who hurt you,' Ella said.

Lucille nodded, her eyes hard. 'Yes. But I don't even want to talk about it, if you don't mind.'

Ella stared at Lucille for a moment. Rory's sad eyes as he talked about his father's death suddenly popped into her mind. She grabbed the old woman's hand. 'Lucille, whatever it is about the woman who hurt you, whoever she is, think about Rory. He's desperately worried about you selling the house. He wants it to stay in the family so he can keep going there when he wants, but he also wants it for your grandchildren. I know Johnny left you the house, but don't you think he would have wanted his sons to have it after you passed away? Not that it's going to happen for a long, long time, but...' Ella paused, not knowing how to continue.

Lucille let out a long sigh, pulling her hand away. 'I see that this is important to you. Is it because you have feelings for Rory?'

Ella shook her head. 'No. I'm not sure how I feel. But let's forget about that. I want to ask you a question. Don't you love your children? I mean, if I had been lucky enough to have them, I would be prepared to die for them. Isn't that how mothers are supposed to feel? Even when the children are grown-ups?'

'Yes and no,' Lucille said, looking thoughtful. 'You want the best for them, but you also want them to be independent, to be able to manage on their own. But...' She suddenly looked confused. 'Oh, God, this is making me feel very strange.' Her eyes welled up with tears and she put her hand to her mouth. 'I've been selfish, haven't I? Only thinking of myself.'

'I have a feeling you're frightened of something. Not just of being alone,' Ella said.

'Not frightened, exactly. It's more about bad memories and being haunted by the past. My feelings were hurt a long time ago...' Lucille paused. Then she turned to Ella. 'When I arrived in Tipperary as a new bride, I was always made to feel that Johnny had married down, somehow. I wasn't from their social class, you see. I didn't know how to ride and I didn't go out shooting pheasants at dawn on ice-cold winter mornings, or wade through mud wearing those stupid waxed jackets. I didn't know which fork to use at dinners or what to wear or what to say. It was all so la-di-da with some kind of code I never managed to crack. Johnny didn't care; he actually loved me for being different from them. But *they* cared and sneered at me behind my back. I overheard them talking about me sometimes but I never let on that I knew what they thought of me.'

'Oh God,' Ella said, feeling a dart of pity for Lucille. 'That must have been hard.'

'It was awful at times,' Lucille sighed. 'But then something happened to me when I came here to Sandy Cove. I met people who are so like my own family, even though I grew up in Dublin. Like them, people here don't care about forks and dress codes and all that nonsense. You can be yourself here without pressure to fit in. It's so refreshing and relaxing. That's part of the reason I want to move here. I feel so at home even though I have only just arrived.'

'I know what you mean,' Ella said. 'It's the least stressful place I've ever been in.'

Lucille nodded. 'Exactly.' She took a deep breath as if to steady herself. 'Oh God, I know I've been very stupid and very mean. I wanted to sell that house to get back at Johnny's snooty relatives. I met one of them at a funeral just before I came here. His cousin Janet. I overheard her saying they were all appalled that I owned the house and the land that should have gone either to my sons or to one of their relations. She said... she said I wasn't worthy, not good enough for Johnny and that everyone had said so when we married. Johnny married beneath him, she said. I was vulgar and cheap and uneducated. And he was ashamed of me but stayed with me out of duty for the boys.'

'When did you hear this?'

'At the lunch after the funeral. It was held in a posh hotel. I was in one of the stalls in the ladies' and I heard them talking about me outside.'

'Oh God, how awful.'

Lucille nodded. 'Yes. Horrible auld biddies. They're the ones who are vulgar and cheap, not me.'

'You're a true lady,' Ella said with feeling. 'I've always thought so.'

'Have you?' Lucille asked. 'Really?'

Ella nodded. 'Oh yes. You were always so elegant. You still are.'

Lucille put her hand on her chest, her eyes glistening with tears. 'Oh. How kind of you to say so.'

'I mean it,' Ella insisted. 'You have real class, Lucille. But this doesn't mean that your sons don't deserve that house too. You shouldn't feel you have to act so dramatically to show them who's boss. That house is yours and *they're* wrong.'

'Thank you,' Lucille said with a wan smile. 'Oh, I'm so sorry, Ella. I just feel so overwhelmed. I think I'll go upstairs to lie down for a bit.'

'Good idea,' Ella said. 'Don't you want to drink your coffee first?'

'Oh yes.' Lucille sipped the hot brew, looking at Ella over the rim of the cup. 'I'll be thinking about the house and the boys and what you said. I'm beginning to see how strange I've been acting. But it was because… Well, you know. Do you think they'll forgive me?'

'I'm sure they will,' Ella said.

'Martin might. But Rory will be angry. Do you think… Could you talk to him? He seems to like you.'

'But we always argue,' Ella protested.

'He does that for fun. And so do you,' Lucille said, with a glint of laughter in her eyes.

'Do I?' Ella said airily. 'I'm not so sure about that.'

'Absolutely,' Lucille declared. 'Please, Ella, could you talk to him? Explain everything so that he understands my motives. That would be such a help.'

Ella softened. 'It should really be coming from you. But okay, I'll talk to him. We're meeting for a drink tomorrow night anyway.'

'Thank you,' Lucille said, slowly getting up from her chair. 'And I'll call Martin and tell him, which will be easier. And now I'll have that little snooze and a think. And then we'll sort it all out eventually, won't we?'

'Of course you will.' Ella got up and gave Lucille a warm hug. 'I do love you, you mad thing. You helped me so much this summer.'

Lucille hugged her back. 'And you have helped me. More than you know.'

*

When she was alone, Ella stayed on the terrace enjoying the sunshine and the light over the endless ocean, feeling more positive about Lucille. She had been so frantic when she arrived, trying to create a safe environment because she had never truly felt at home in the family house. But now things would be a lot better. Lucille could sort things out with her sons and let them have the house while she settled into village life here at Sandy Cove. Ella felt dart of happiness about having Lucille living so close. It felt a little like having a mother again, someone to care for and who would care for her.

Ella knew that telling Rory would demand some diplomacy. He'd be hurt that Lucille had shared neither her fears with him, nor what had happened at that funeral and what she had overheard. Lucille's sons probably never knew how hurt she had been about Johnny's family's opinions of her.

And then there were the feelings Ella was beginning to have for Rory that she couldn't deny, even to herself. She knew she was being pulled into something with him and that she should step away. In that case why was so she afraid to tell him the truth about Lucille's house? The fact that she had been pretending not to know about it would probably drive him away, which would be a good thing, her head told her.

But what her heart said was a different matter…

Chapter Twenty

Butterflies whirled in Ella's stomach as she walked to the Harbour pub on Monday evening. It was one of those heavenly summer evenings that only Kerry could provide, with the sun bathing the mountains in a golden light, a soft breeze caressing Ella's skin, playing with her perfectly blow-dried hair. She stopped to look at the stunning views over the bay, gazing over the ocean and watching the birds gliding around over the still water.

She took a deep breath and continued, smoothing her white linen shirt as if trying at the same time to calm her heart that was beating like a hammer. The prospect of having to tell Rory about Lucille and watch him seethe with anger wasn't filling her with joy. She knew he'd be upset that his mother hadn't told him about her fears and that she hadn't trusted her sons to give her the support she needed. She also knew he would be unhappy to hear about his father's family and how they had treated his mother during all those years. That was the reason she was selling the house, and he had to be told. What would Rory think of her, and the secrets she'd been keeping from him on Lucille's behalf?

Ella sighed. Oh, how she wished this was just a straightforward drink with a friend and not an evening that would be fraught with conflict and upsets. Maybe she could just forget about talking to Rory about his mother? Just for tonight? But she had promised Lucille and she was committed to that promise. If Lucille was to sort out her situation with her sons, they had to know the facts. But being the messenger was not an easy part to play, especially with someone as volatile as Rory.

As she rounded the corner of the last house of the main street and walked down the hill towards the harbour, she spotted Rory waiting for her outside the pub. He waved as he saw her and she waved back, checking her hair at the same time.

'It's perfect,' Rory said as she approached. 'Your hair, I mean. All of you, actually. Nice to see you in something other than black.' He leaned forward and placed a light kiss on her cheek. 'Thank you for coming. You smell wonderful. What is it?'

'Shalimar by Guerlain,' Ella said, pulling away, but not before she had been made slightly dizzy by the touch of his lips on her cheek.

'Delicious. You French girls know about perfume. And it's just a hint, not like you used the whole bottle.'

'I'm too stingy for that,' Ella remarked. 'It's a very expensive perfume.' She looked up at him and took in his thick black hair flopping into his dark eyes and his cheeky grin, feeling a little overwhelmed by him. Then she pulled herself together and reminded herself of her task. This would not be the fun date he seemed to have imagined; it would a be an evening of discussions and even heated arguments. But first, she needed a drink.

As if reading her thoughts, Rory gestured at a table just outside the back door of the pub. 'I thought we'd sit outside as it's so warm. In any case the place is packed and you can't hear yourself think.'

'Great idea,' Ella said and approached the table, surprised when Rory pulled out her chair. 'Thank you,' she said and sat down glancing at the beautiful view of the harbour and the little fishing boats at anchor. She breathed in the salty tang that floated in on the breeze and let out a contented sigh. The surroundings would help to keep things calm and fairly pleasant, she told herself.

'I ordered a glass of Pinot Grigio for you,' Rory said, cutting into Ella's thoughts.

'And a pint of Guinness for yourself, I bet,' she replied with a teasing smile.

'But of course.' Rory laughed. 'Are you psychic?'

'No, I just know Irish men very well,' Ella replied. 'And you know what? I would have preferred a glass of Pinot Noir.'

Rory looked suddenly annoyed. 'A polite person would have just said thank you and drunk it.'

'And a man who thinks women can make their own decisions wouldn't have…' Ella stopped. 'Oh God, here we go again. Arguing. Okay, I'll drink the Pinot Grigio. It's really not an issue. It's just that every time I see you I have this irresistible urge to annoy you.'

Rory sighed and sat down opposite her. 'Yes, me too. What is that, do you think?'

'You bring out the twelve-year-old in me, I think. I want to stick out my tongue at you and go, "Nah-nah-nah."'

'And I want to pull your hair and run away laughing.'

'What can we do about it?' Ella said and took a swig of the glass of white wine that had just been served.

'Maybe we need therapy?' Rory suggested, drinking from his pint and wiping his mouth.

'Probably. But not together.' Ella took another sip and pulled herself together.

'No, then the therapist would need therapy after dealing with us.'

Ella laughed and then pulled herself together. 'Never mind all that. I have something to tell you.'

'Yes? About what?'

'Lucille. Something happened yesterday and we had a long talk.'

Rory nodded. 'Okay. So tell me. I sense there's something going on.'

'Yes. Lots of things.' Ella paused and then launched into a long explanation of what Lucille had overheard after the funeral and how it had ripped open some old wounds.

'So that's why she's moving here?' Rory asked. 'To get back at some old bag that said nasty things in the ladies' loo?'

'Not just because of that. But because of all the things she had to put up with through the years,' Ella countered. 'That kind of trauma has stayed with Lucille all her life.'

'Trauma?' Rory said. 'Isn't that a little OTT?' He drained his pint and waved at a waiter. 'I think I need another drink after this. How about you?'

Ella looked at her empty glass. 'Eh, yes, but…'

'Another pint, please,' Rory said to the waiter who had just appeared at their table. Then he looked at Ella. 'How about you?'

'I'd love a glass of Pinot Noir, please,' Ella said to the waiter, who nodded and walked away with their empty glasses. 'That wasn't too hard, was it?' she said to Rory. 'Letting a woman make up her own mind, I mean.'

Rory smiled. 'You French girls are so assertive.'

'Probably because we have to be,' Ella said with a pang of guilt at keeping up the French act with him. Maybe it was time to come clean before anything happened between them. 'I'm not really,' she started.

Rory laughed. 'Yes, you are. Assertive in that French way. I have to say I like that. Maybe that's what makes me want to argue with you all the time. The French assertiveness is such a challenge. And also quite sexy.' He paused, looking awkward. 'But back to Mum and her trauma and the snooty old ladies. Can we do anything about it to make her feel better? And maybe convince her to go back home and not buy this house?'

'Possibly,' Ella said, deciding to leave the subject of her nationality alone for a while. She needed to smooth his ruffled feathers about his mother and the house first. 'She said she was going to talk to Martin. And she asked me to talk to you. But now that you know everything, do you think you could calm down and listen to her? Maybe tell her how you feel and why the house is so important to you?'

'I'm perfectly calm,' Rory said, looking annoyed. 'But there is one thing left to sort out and that is why on earth my mother disappeared suddenly last week. Do you know anything about that?'

'No,' Ella said. She'd been wondering the same thing – nothing Lucille had said yesterday explained her recent absences, the letters or the phone calls.

'Are you sure?'

'Of course I'm sure,' Ella replied, feeling that irritation rising again. 'Do you think I'm lying?'

'No, not really. I thought perhaps Mum had sworn you to secrecy about whatever it is she's involved with.'

'She refuses to talk about it. But I can tell you that Thomas, my neighbour, spotted her at the RTE television studios in Dublin last week when he was there for an audition.'

'Television studios?' Rory stared at Ella. 'Why would she be there?'

'I have absolutely no idea,' Ella replied. 'She says there is going to be a big surprise soon and there are four bottles of champagne in my fridge for some kind of celebration. That's all I know right now.'

'Oh God, this is getting really weird.'

'I know but…' Ella leaned forward and looked into Rory's eyes. 'This time, why not just trust her? Maybe it's something fun, it's something she's proud of that she's been doing all by herself. I have a feeling it has to do with that phone call from Australia.'

'You think?' Rory looked thoughtful as the waiter arrived at their table with their drinks. 'Do you want anything else?' he asked. 'I never thought to ask if you've had dinner.'

'I did,' Ella replied, smiling at the waiter. 'Lucille cooked a delicious Indian curry, so I'm stuffed.'

'I can imagine,' Rory said, as he paid the waiter. 'Mum's curry is famous. She is a good cook.'

'Wonderful when she's in the mood to cook,' Ella said, raising her glass. 'Cheers, Rory. To better days and a happy ending.'

'And peace between the two of us,' Rory said, clinking his glass to Ella's. 'I have decided to bury the hatchet and forget about all the sniping and nasty little digs. Do you think you could do that too?'

'I'll try,' Ella promised. 'But isn't it going to be boring withou
our sparring?'

'We could try to think of other ways to have fun,' Rory said with
a flirtatious glint in his eyes. He suddenly reached across the table
and took her hand. 'I know it's been hard for you to cope with Mum
and all her mood swings and secrets. You've been so supportive and
made her feel more secure. I do understand why she wants to live
here now… Not just what you've told me today but just spending
time in Sandy Cove myself. I'll do everything to help her. In fact,'
he continued, 'I could see myself coming to visit Mum once she's
settled in her new house.'

'That'll make her very happy,' Ella said, touched by the look
in Rory's eyes. 'But it'll take time before all the work on that little
house is done. Until then she'll be staying with me.'

Rory let go of Ella's hand. 'But she could go back to Tipperary
while the building work is done.'

'And be all alone through the winter? I think she'd be happier
here with me.'

'It could be more than six months before the house is ready,'
Rory argued. 'Are you sure you can put up with her for so long?'

'Of course I can,' Ella declared. 'We get on really well.'

'Good.' Rory paused to drink from his pint. Then he looked at
Ella for a while. 'Can we talk about something else now? It's such
a lovely evening. Too nice to sit here and talk about my mother
don't you think?'

Ella laughed. 'Yes, maybe you're right. Let's talk about something
else,' she said, relieved that he wanted to leave the subject of his
mother alone for now. She had to tell him about the house going on

the market at some point, but right now she didn't feel like ruining the atmosphere that seemed to have brightened considerably. 'What have you been up to today?' she asked, smiling at him.

'I took a drive around the Dingle peninsula. Thought I'd see another part of Kerry. There is so much to see there. The Gallarus Oratory, for example. I think it's from the eighth century. The most amazing place I've ever visited.'

'Yes, it's incredible,' Ella agreed. 'Eerie. When you're in there it's as if you hear the voices of a thousand people, even though it's so silent. The voices and prayers of those that worshipped there in early Christian times seem to speak to you.'

'Beautiful,' Rory said. 'Exactly the feeling I had. And there is that presence of God… or a higher power or something.'

'Like the Pantheon in Rome,' Ella said. 'Have you ever been there? I have always felt that despite all the people, the beam of light through that hole in the domed ceiling is the eye of God looking down on us right there.' She shook herself and smiled. 'Now you'll think I'm really mad.'

'No,' Rory said, looking serious. 'I know exactly what you mean. And what you feel,' he added.

'I love visiting those old places,' Ella said. 'They're all so alive somehow even though they are so silent.'

'The silence is full of spirits, maybe?' Rory said.

'Could be,' Ella said while they looked into each other's eyes and she felt a new, deeper understanding growing between them.

As the sky darkened and the sun disappeared behind the headland, they started to talk in earnest about their interests and passions. Ella told him about other places in Kerry to visit and Rory shared his favourite places in Dublin. As the evening wore on, they went on to talk about other things, their favourite music, books and movies, and found to their astonishment that they had a lot in common despite their differences.

Later on, when it was getting too dark to see each other, they got up from the table and wandered slowly back to Starlight Cottages, Ella with Rory's cashmere sweater around her shoulders as the breeze turned chilly. It seemed so natural for them to walk and talk like this, and when Rory took Ella's hand, she didn't protest or pull away. His grip was warm and strong and she felt a warm glow inside as she listened to his deep voice telling her about his student years and the small bedsit he had lived in then.

'That's when I was at École des Beaux-Arts in Paris,' Ella said. 'Just as broke and living in a tiny studio flat with...' She stopped as the memory of those days hit her.

'With?' Rory asked.

'With the first man I fell in love with,' Ella said softly. 'He was Spanish and studied at Sorbonne. We were together for three years. Lovely, exciting, but stormy. It ended in tears and a lot of shouting.'

'I can imagine,' Rory said with a laugh. They had come to the end of the main street and the path that was lined with a low stone wall from where they could see the water of the bay glinting in the moonlight.

'What a beautiful night,' Ella said, looking up at the star-studded sky. 'I can see the Milky Way.'

'Fantastic,' Rory said. 'Let's sit here for a while. It's heavenly.'

Ella sat down on the wall and swung her legs to the other side so she faced the ocean. Rory joined her and they sat together looking out over the starlit bay.

'Tell me more,' he said. 'About you and your life.'

'My life?' Ella said with a little laugh. 'Up to now? That'll take a while. All night maybe.'

'Just some highlights, then,' he suggested. 'The things that brought you here to this beautiful spot.'

'Oh…' Ella hesitated. 'Lots of things. But mainly my failed marriage.'

'What happened?' he asked. 'I don't mean to pry, but if you want to talk, I'll listen.'

Ella suddenly felt it would be good to talk to Rory, who, despite all their arguing, felt like someone who'd understand. 'Well,' she started, 'it was all going so well. Jean-Paul and I were like this ideal couple, so in love and so committed to having a family. We had this lovely flat in a very nice part of Paris and we had started to do up one of the rooms as a nursery. I was pregnant very soon after our marriage and we were so excited. But then I lost the baby. It was early on in the pregnancy and my doctor said it didn't mean we couldn't try again. So we did. That time, I miscarried at six months and it was like losing a real child, somehow.'

'Oh,' Rory said and took her hand. 'I'm so sorry, Ella. That must have been terrible for you both.'

'Yes.' Ella was quiet for a while. 'It was. Jean-Paul was devastated. He couldn't talk about it. I felt so alone. We waited a year or so and then we decided to try again. I had no problem getting pregnant, but I lost yet another baby. My doctor didn't know why, he said it could have something to do with hormones or something. He wanted to do a big investigation, but I was so fed up with doctors and hospitals at that stage that I didn't want to go through with it.

Jean-Paul tried to help, but in the long run, we drifted apart, not being able to support each other the way we should have. In any case, I was heading into my forties, so I felt it was too late to either keep up the pretence that we could patch things up and stay married or try again. I felt he wanted to break up with me so he could marry someone else who could give him children when I couldn't. It was quite bitter at the end.'

'How horrible it must have been for you.'

'Yes.' Ella sighed, feeling suddenly tired after having gone through all those emotions again. 'Sorry to pile all this sorrow on top of you on such a beautiful evening,' she said apologetically.

'I don't mind,' Rory said and put his arm around her. 'Just to keep warm,' he whispered, his lips nearly touching her hair.

'Yes,' she said. 'That's all.' She moved closer and put her head on his shoulder. 'Just to have a little rest,' she mumbled, breathing in the clean smell of soap from his skin. 'So that's my story and the reason I felt such a huge comfort when I came here to this little village.

He pulled her closer. 'Thank you for telling me.'

'Thank you for listening,' she whispered back, the strong arm around her a huge comfort while she tried to push away all the sad thoughts. She had seen a new side to him tonight, a strong, solid, understanding side. So different to Jean-Paul, who would never have sat down and just listened.

They sat like that for a while, as if neither of them dared move or speak while the stars glimmered and twinkled above them. Then a streak of light crossed the sky. 'A shooting star,' Rory said. 'Doesn't that mean you can make a wish?'

'I think so. But it'll be your wish. You saw it first.'

Rory laughed. 'Thank you.' He turned his head and looked down at her. 'Then my wish is to kiss you. Would that be allowed?'

She sat up, slightly alarmed. But when, without waiting for an answer, he gently took her face in his hands, all her resolve to resist him deserted her. Their lips slowly met and Ella felt herself melt into his arms as she kissed him back and all her locked-in feelings surged to the surface. She put her arms around his neck as his lips lingered on hers and pressed herself against his strong body. They kissed again, long and hard, and then Rory pulled back. She could see his teeth gleam in the dim light of the moon as he smiled tenderly at her.

Ella pulled away and tried to catch her breath. 'Oh God,' she whispered. 'That wasn't supposed to happen.'

'No. But it did,' Rory said, stroking her cheek.

She caught his hand. 'I've been fighting with myself for weeks to stop myself feeling the way I do right now.'

'Me too,' he said. 'I keep telling myself that getting involved with you would be disastrous for me. I thought I needed someone calm who would always agree with me and let me take the lead. But here I am, falling in love with someone who has been annoying me ever since the first time we met over five years ago.'

Ella giggled. 'I know. Remember that first time when Mum had just moved in with Lucille and they had a dinner with us all to celebrate? I thought Martin was fine but a bit stiff. You, however, annoyed me even before we had said more than "hello". You looked at me from a height and said some snooty things about artists and how most of us are just pretending to have any talent. Most of it is about marketing and fooling people, you said.'

'Did I?' Rory said. 'How rude and horrible. I think I might just have said that to get a rise out of you. But I don't remember you taking the bait. I recall that you just smiled sweetly and said something bland.'

'While I was seething inside,' Ella filled in. 'My mother gave me that look that told me not to reply and to behave myself. In any case I wanted her to be happy living with Lucille, so I swallowed the snappy retort and kept my cool. I didn't want to make trouble for Mum.'

'Good for you. The two of them had some good years together. I had no problem with Rose moving in with my mother at all. I was just having fun watching you getting annoyed. It had nothing to do with your mother. I thought she was terrific.'

'Why wouldn't you? She was a star,' Ella said with a wistful sigh. 'I miss her so much.'

Rory held her tight. 'Of course you do. Just as much as I miss my father. That never goes away, does it?'

'No,' Ella replied.

They were quiet and sat there looking out across the moonlit bay, each in their own thoughts, until Ella shivered. 'It's getting cold. And you gave me your sweater. I think it's time to go home and get some sleep.'

'I could sit here forever with you and look at the stars,' Rory said. 'I don't want to break the spell.'

'Or wake up from this dream,' Ella filled in. 'That's how it feels right now. But it's real and truly amazing.'

Rory kissed her lightly on the lips. 'Are you sure? Maybe it is a dream? I feel a little sheepish right now, I must admit. I mean… This came on so suddenly, I'm quite overwhelmed by all these feelings.

'I could pinch you,' Ella offered.

He laughed. 'No thanks.' He kissed her again. 'I prefer this.'

'What do we do now?' Ella asked, touching his face. 'Where do we go from here? Except off this wall that's beginning to feel really uncomfortable.'

'I have no idea.' Rory slowly pulled away and stood up. 'But you're right. I'm getting stiff and cold. We're not twenty-one any more.'

'Reality rears its ugly head,' Ella said with a laugh as she got up from the wall. 'I only have a few yards to walk to my house. You have to find your car and get back to your lodgings.'

'Oh? And I thought you'd invite me in to stay the night.'

Ella smiled at him and shook her head. Would his teasing ever stop? 'Let's see what the future will bring. Tonight something magical happened. But who knows how we'll feel tomorrow?'

'I suppose you're right. But I know what I want to do next. I'd love you to come to Tipperary. I know you've been to the house, but I want to show you everything I loved there when I was growing up. And the house has so many hidden nooks and crannies I'm sure you never knew about.'

Ella stood there for a while, breathing in the mild night air, wondering what to say. It was so sweet of him to want to show her around the place where he had grown up. But that wasn't possible. She had nearly forgotten what she had promised Lucille to tell him during all the magic that had happened between them. But now she knew he had to be told before he started to make plans. 'Rory,' she said, taking his hand. 'I have something to tell you before you go. It's about the house in Tipperary.'

He froze for a moment. 'What about it?'

'It's going on the market next week.'

'What?' he exclaimed. 'How do you mean? Going on the market She's actually doing it? Selling our house?'

'Yes.'

He pulled his hand away. 'Did you know this all along?' he asked, his voice hoarse with emotion. 'All the time when we started to become friends, and then now, tonight, when we—'

'Lucille made me promise not to tell you,' Ella interrupted, startled by the anger in his voice. 'She was afraid you'd try to stop her.

'Damn right I would.' He stepped away from her and she could see the whites of his eyes gleaming for a moment. 'I can't believe you kept this from me. That you'd be… That we'd be doing what we were doing just now, having this sweet moment that meant so much to me, and all this time you knew.'

'I couldn't bear to tell you,' Ella whispered, feeling her heart contract. Here she was again, dealing with an angry man and facing into what would develop into a violent argument. 'But then I thought I would before you saw the ad somewhere. In any case Lucille asked me to break the news to you.'

'I see,' he mumbled. 'In fact, I'm beginning to see a lot of things. Mostly about you.'

Ella bristled. 'Yeah, and all of it bad, I bet.' She started to walk away. 'I'm not staying here to be shouted at for trying my best to help everyone. I've been put in a very difficult situation in the middle of a family row that is not at all my fault.' She paused. 'What happened between us was truly wonderful and I thought for a split second you were different. But I see that you're not, so we'll end this – whatever it was – right now.'

'I don't know what to say,' Rory muttered.

'Well, I do. Good night, Rory.' She turned on her heel and started to walk home, stumbling on the path as tears and the darkness blurred her vision. *You stupid eejit*, she thought, *why on earth did you imagine he would be any different? He's just as difficult and angry as all the rest of them.*

Ella glanced over her shoulder and saw his shadowy form disappear as she headed home, while she relived every moment of the past hour, before she told him about the house. She had been responding to Rory without thinking, letting her emotions take over, but so had he. And then it had all ended before it even started, because he was so angry with her for keeping her promise to Lucille.

It had surprised and delighted her that Rory had also had misgivings about her and tried to push away his feelings for her because he was afraid of the eventual outcome. *And then we had both been right,* she thought bitterly. Maybe it was better to have ended it before she got in a lot deeper and started a relationship that was doomed to fail. *Yes, much better*, she decided. She would forget all about him and avoid him as much as she could.

But as Ella reached the house and looked up at the stars, she knew he had already found a way into her heart.

Chapter Twenty-One

Lucille was on the sofa in the living room talking to someone on her phone when Ella came home. She quickly hung up and beamed a smile at Ella. 'Hello there. You're very late. I thought you were just having a drink with Rory. Did you go on somewhere?'

'Eh, no,' Ella said. 'We went for a walk as it's such a beautiful evening.'

'In the dark?' Lucille asked, raising one eyebrow. She leaned forward and studied Ella for a moment. 'Did you have an argument? You look a little strange.'

'Yes, we did,' Ella said, her face hot. 'It started in quite a... civilised way. But then I told him you were putting the house on the market. He got really upset.'

'And he lost his temper and shouted at you?'

'No. He said nothing but I could tell he was furious. Then walked away before he had a chance to start shouting.' Ella sank down beside Lucille, trying her best to hold back her tears.

'You're upset,' Lucille said, looking concerned.

'Yes. Because we were beginning to…' She stopped. 'Never mind. I'm trying not to think about it. How did your talk with Martin go? You said you were going to call him.'

'It went quite well,' Lucille said. 'At least he didn't blow up. He's coming here so we can have a family conference. I've realised that it's not their fault that Johnny's family treated me the way they did. Martin said the best revenge is for me to be happy. I didn't realise that until now. I thought I could get back at them by selling the house so it would be lost to the family. But why should I cut off my nose to spite my face and hurt my own children?' She sighed, looking sad. 'I've been a stupid old woman, haven't I?'

Ella patted Lucille's hand. 'Not at all. I think you're wonderful. It's been so hard for you. Rory will be so happy to hear you're not selling after all. It will be good for you to move here. Everyone in the village loves you already.'

'Thank you, darling,' Lucille said and kissed Ella on the cheek. Then she stood up. 'I'm going to bed. But before I go, I have something else to tell you.' She paused for a moment while Ella remained on the sofa. 'Something big is going to happen, which involves this house and this village. It's going to be a big reveal and I want to invite a few people here to celebrate.'

'What do you mean?' Ella asked, mystified. 'I thought we were celebrating something like you moving here. What's this big reveal about?'

'If I tell you it won't be a reveal,' Lucille replied.

'Please don't tell me any more secrets I have to keep to myself,' Ella begged. 'It always lands me in a lot of trouble.'

'I'm not going to tell you anything,' Lucille declared. 'You only need to say yes to a bit of a gathering here. Just champagne and a few nibbles with friends. I want to invite everyone in Starlight Cottages and Rory and Martin. And a surprise guest.'

'More surprises?' Ella said, alarmed. 'When is this going to happen?'

'Wednesday night at seven o'clock.'

'Wednesday night? This week?'

'Yes.'

'Oh, eh…' Ella tried to take in this latest bit of news. Lucille galloped ahead so fast sometimes that it was hard to keep up. 'Is it someone's birthday?' she asked.

'No. But a very special occasion,' Lucille stated. 'Something very exciting. Could we organise some food, do you think?'

Ella shook her head, trying to clear her mind, which was immediately going to all those letters and phone calls. Would this be the link to Australia? 'Okay. I'll get the two Marys to prepare the nibbles for the surprise party.'

'Not a party. The big reveal,' Lucille corrected.

'Who's the surprise guest?'

Lucille winked. 'If I told you, it won't be a surprise.'

'I suppose you're not going to tell me what the occasion is either,' Ella said with a resigned sigh.

'Of course not. Just wait till you find out what it is. It'll blow your mind.'

'Oh God, will it?' Ella said, trying not to laugh.

'Totally,' Lucille said. 'Time for bed,' she added. 'I need a lot of beauty sleep before Wednesday. Good night, pet,' Lucille said and with that, she turned on her heel and left the room.

Ella heard the stairlift go up, and sat there wondering what on earth Lucille had cooked up this time. As she got up to follow Lucille she realised she was still wearing Rory's sweater over her shoulder. She took it off and buried her nose in the soft cashmere, breathing n his scent, closing her eyes as the memory of his kiss floated into er mind. Had it really happened? Was she falling in love with him lespite her struggle with her feelings for the past weeks? But it was mpossible after his reaction to what she had told him. His seething nger said everything. Starting a relationship with him would be foolish thing to do and it could only end in tears. But oh how weet it was to think about all the things they had shared during his magical evening. Maybe, maybe, this time it would work... If •nly they could make peace again.

Ella padded up the stairs, knowing she'd go to sleep dreaming bout him, sending a wish to the stars and the moon as she opened he window in her bedroom. 'Please make it all right again,' she vhispered into the night. 'He has to understand that I couldn't •reak my promise.'

In bed, she hugged the sweater, her tears soaking into the soft ashmere, until she fell asleep.

ucille's elder son, Martin, arrived the next morning with Rory for he family conference. A tall, stern-looking man with fair hair and ucille's blue eyes, he was the complete opposite to Rory's darkling ooks and lively manner. Ella had always found it strange that the ivacious Lucille had such a staid and dour son. But maybe he was throwback to some stern-faced Victorian in Johnny's family, she ad often wondered.

After serving tea and scones, Ella left them to their meeting o go and place the order for the party nibbles at The Two Marys' nd do some other errands in the village. She had avoided Rory's eyes on her as she didn't want Lucille to suspect that anything was going on, even though she was dying to talk to him and ask him to understand why she had lied. But that had to wait until their issues with the house were resolved and the family was back on better terms with each other. Once he found out the house wasn't to be sold, perhaps he'd be less angry. She hoped it would go well and Lucille would come out of it smiling.

Ella returned an hour later to find the two men gone and Lucille sitting on the sofa looking over some notes on a piece of paper. 'All done and dusted,' she said to Ella as she came into the living room. 'I'll be selling the house to my boys for a very good price. Enough to buy the little house in the village, do all the rebuilding and still have a tidy sum left over. They get the house to share equally and all the headaches with upkeep and taxes as well. They will also pay for my medical insurance so I can go into the best private hospital if I should come down with anything nasty.' Lucille smiled. 'Now we have to concentrate on the little get-together tomorrow. Did you order the food?'

'I did,' Ella replied. 'They promised to pull out all the stops when I said it was for you.'

'Wonderful. Everything is falling into place,' Lucille said happily. 'My new house and the boys happy. And now the project I have been doing will be broadcast tomorrow on TV.'

'TV?' Ella said, shocked. 'What do you mean?'

Lucille patted her hair. 'It has to do with my little research project. I've been working on it for months but I got nowhere until recently when…' She stopped and put her hand to her mouth. 'Oops. I didn't mean to blab like this. But I'll say no more.'

'Why not?' Ella asked, disappointed. 'Can't you tell me?'

'Absolutely not,' Lucille stated. 'You have to wait till tomorrow like everyone else.'

'You're such a tease,' Ella said.

Lucille laughed. 'Yes, and it's fun to watch you trying to figure it out. What I can say, though, is that this will be the real revenge on those old biddies. I wish I could see their faces when they find out.'

'Find out what?' Ella asked even though she knew it was no use. 'You're driving me crazy with all this mystery.'

'I know,' Lucille said, looking pleased. 'That's half the fun. I've booked an appointment for this afternoon at the Wellness Centre for a massage and facial with those lovely natural products they do. And tomorrow morning we're both going to have our hair done at Susie's hairdressing salon. Then we need to tidy up the house and prepare for the evening, dress and put on make-up.'

'Sounds exhausting,' Ella said.

'It won't be if we pace ourselves.' Lucille looked through her notes. 'My guest will be arriving at six thirty, and I've asked Martin and Rory to be here then too. The rest of the guests are invited for seven fifteen and then we'll turn on the TV at seven thirty. Then the TV crew will arrive…'

'TV crew?' Ella exclaimed. 'What are you talking about? Are we all going to be on TV?'

'Yes, we are. And it'll be live so we can't rehearse. But don't worry, you only have a minor part. It'll only be a few minutes for the late-evening news, that's all.'

'That's all?' Ella asked, staring at Lucille. 'What on earth is this about? If there's going to be a TV crew at my house, don't I have the right to know why?' she asked.

Lucille looked thoughtfully back at Ella. Then she nodded. 'I suppose you do. But if I tell you, you have to promise to keep it to yourself.'

Ella folded her arms, glaring at Lucille. 'Oh, please. Don't tell me.'

'But I thought you wanted to know,' Lucille insisted.

'I've changed my mind. I don't want to know. It has to be something big, but I prefer to wait. The last time I had to keep quiet it ruined something that could have been amazing.' Ella stifled a sob as the memory of Rory's anger hit her. 'I'm sorry, but I'm not feeling very well right now.'

Lucille's eyes softened. 'Oh, my darling girl. Come and sit here beside me. I think we need to talk.'

'Okay.' Ella went to sit beside Lucille. 'What do you want to talk about?'

'Me. And you. And Rory,' Lucille said, looking suddenly grief stricken. 'I put you in a very difficult situation when I made you swear to keep the sale of the house a secret. But I didn't know you and Rory would become so close.' Lucille twisted her hands in her lap. 'I had a feeling something was up when he asked about you today. But now you're both miserable and hating each other even more than before.'

'Well, I…' Ella started. 'We were having a romantic moment last night on the way home. It was a beautiful, starry night and we had had a few drinks…' Ella's voice shook with emotion as she blinked away tears. 'He was so sweet and gentle and kind. And I thought we had changed and would become close from now on.'

'And then you felt brave enough to tell him about the house and he was being so sweet to you?' Lucille filled in.

'Yes,' Ella whispered.

'Did he shout at you?'

'No. He was very quiet and just stood there. It was dark, so I couldn't see his expression, but I could feel his anger in the air like hot steam. I just walked away then.'

'I see.' Lucille looked thoughtfully at Ella. 'I'm sure he was angry, but not with you. He was furious with me this morning and gave out to me about practically everything. But Martin managed to calm him down so we could discuss things. We sorted everything out quite calmly but Rory still looked miserable when he left, I have to admit. And it's all my fault.'

'Miserable?' Ella asked, her spirits lifting. 'Are you sure?'

'Oh yes. I'd say he was devastated, actually.' Lucille put her hand on Ella's shoulder. 'I think you should talk to him.'

'Me?' Ella exclaimed, shaking off Lucille's hand. 'Why should I be the one to take the first step?'

'I suppose he should,' Lucille said. 'Or I should talk to him and apologise for making trouble between you. Tell him how loyal you were to me.' She shook her head. 'How selfish I've been, only thinking of myself and my troubles. And dragging you into this mess.'

'I did feel a little like the meat in the sandwich,' Ella confessed. 'But maybe I overreacted with Rory. I should have stayed and had it out with him. But I was fed up with all the arguing. I couldn't take any more.'

'You were right.' Lucille sighed. 'Honestly, I don't know what to do. Maybe just leave things alone for a bit? Let it rest and wait for him to see things differently?'

Ella nodded. 'Yes. That sounds like a good plan. And we need t get organised for this… this thing you're going to surprise us with

Lucille sat up straighter. 'Yes, we do. Can you forget about a this for now, do you think?' She put her hand on Ella's arm. 'An forgive me?'

Ella felt her heart soften as she looked into Lucille's earnest blu eyes. 'Yes. Of course I forgive you,' she said, hugging Lucille tigh 'Nothing much to forgive, anyway. I completely understand ho you were feeling. And besides, I agreed to lie for you; I have to tak responsibility for my own choices.'

'Oh,' Lucille said, her eyes full of happy tears. 'Well, I am gla you aren't mad at me. You have no idea how happy that makes me

Ella jumped up from the sofa. 'Great. Now let's roll up ou sleeves and get to work.'

Lucille clapped her hands. 'That's my girl. I think tomorrow wi be a landmark day. For me as much as for everyone else.'

Ella looked at Lucille, tempted to ask her to reveal her secre But then she changed her mind. It would be like opening presen before Christmas. Better to wait, and better still to get stuck in an try to push Rory and their botched attempt at romance out of he mind. Even if it would take her a long time to get it out of her hear

Chapter Twenty-Two

The following day flew by so fast Ella didn't have time to think. Lucille, fresh-faced after a good night's sleep and the massage and facial at the Wellness Centre, kept everything moving at breakneck speed and at six o'clock, they were both groomed to perfection, dressed to kill and ready for the evening ahead. Lucille looked elegant in a turquoise ensemble and Ella wore her little black dress with her best sparkly earrings and killer heels, her hair gleaming after the wash and blow-dry at Susie's salon. The champagne and the food were laid out on the dining table in the living room and the sofa and chairs lined up in front of the TV.

'So, here we are,' Ella said, looking around. 'All ready for the show to start.'

'It all looks fabulous,' Lucille said happily.

The doorbell interrupted her and she checked her hair in the mirror over the fireplace before she ran to the door, Ella following behind.

Lucille opened the door and smiled at the tall, deeply tanned, silver-haired man. 'Liam Brosnan?' she said.

'That's me,' he said and held out a hand. 'Nice to meet you at last, cousin Lucille.'

Lucille giggled. 'Must be tenth cousin or something,' she said grabbing his hand and shaking it. 'And this is my friend Ella, who owns this house.'

'Hello, Ella,' Liam Brosnan said, shaking her hand. 'I'm the long-lost relative from Australia,' he continued in his broad accent.

'Lovely to meet you,' Ella said, shocked, wondering if this was the surprise Lucille had planned. 'But please, come in. We're just about to open the champagne and the other guests will arrive shortly.'

'Thank you.' Liam stepped inside. 'So nice to be here at last. Is this place where the story began, so to speak.'

Story? Ella thought. What on earth did he mean? 'Must be incredible for you,' she said. 'Even though I have no idea what you're talking about...'

'You will very soon,' Lucille said, leading the way into the house.

'Is this the house?' Liam asked as they entered the living room. 'The place where he lived?'

'We don't really know which house it was,' Lucille said. 'It was one of the houses in this row, anyway.'

'I see. How amazing to be here.' Liam looked at the paintings on the walls. 'Wonderful artwork. Is this yours?'

'Yes,' Ella said proudly. 'All my own work. I'm glad you like them.'

They were interrupted by the doorbell and then there was no more opportunity to talk as everyone seemed to arrive at once. Martin and Rory, who gave Ella a long, brooding look that she tried to ignore; Jason and Lydia, looking tanned and happy after their holiday in Boston. Then Saskia swished in wearing a wonderful red taffeta skirt and rows and rows of bracelets jangling on her arms, and nally Thomas and Mandy, who rushed into Ella's arms, covering er face in kisses.

They opened the champagne and handed out the nibbles that vere more like a full-on buffet dinner, with sausage rolls, scampi, iny meatballs, chicken pieces on skewers, spring rolls and mini vraps stuffed with all kinds of meats and salads. 'Dinner on sticks!' Mandy declared and stuffed everything she could get her hands on nto her mouth, while they all laughed.

Then Lucille clapped her hands and asked for silence.

'Dear friends and neighbours,' she began proudly. 'You might not know why we're here today drinking champagne and eating ovely food, but all will soon be clear when you see what's on TV n just a moment. Please take your glasses and plates and gather round the TV. The show is about to begin…'

They all looked at each other and laughed, and then went to it or stand in front of the big flat-screen TV on the wall while Lucille turned it on with the remote. The commercials ended and he music started and they stared at the text that said: THE LOST ONS OF IRELAND.

There was complete silence as an old photo of the coastguard tation came into view, and the voiceover read the script:

'*This is the coastguard station in Sandy Cove, County Kerry, where his particular story begins. But what happened here was not unique to his village – it happened all over Ireland and indeed Britain at around he same time and all through the rest of the nineteenth century. It's the ong-forgotten story of the convict ships and who was on them all those ears ago. Many young men and women were sent on ships to Australia*

having been found guilty of minor crimes and misdemeanours, ofte
dying during the horrible journey.

'*But the hero of this story survived the passage and lived to carr*
out an amazing life in the new world. His name was Joseph Brosnan
He had been working as a coastguard in Sandy Cove for only two yea
while the famine raged in Ireland. His mother and siblings lived in
little cottage nearby, just above a little bay known as Wild Rose Bay,
beautiful, windswept place where life was harsh.

'*When the crops failed, they had nothing to eat and Joseph move*
them to live with him in the cottage of the coastguard station. The
his mother fell ill. Joseph knew his mother needed a doctor, whic
he couldn't afford. In those desperate circumstances, it didn't see
such a sin to pilfer a little money from a rich man who happened
stay at the local inn, where Joseph called in to buy a glass of porte
It was easy to slip his hand into the pocket of the man while h
was enjoying a pint of ale and take the coins that Joseph had hear
jingling there. The rich man wouldn't notice the few shillings gon
Joseph thought, and his mother's life could be saved. But he wa
caught and prosecuted and then sentenced to penal transport to
prison colony in Australia.'

Everyone stopped eating and drinking as the documentar
continued, describing life in Australia for convicts, mapping ou
Joseph Brosnan's continued existence at the prison settlement an
then later on as a free man. They all kept stealing glances at Liar
as he stood with Lucille, the two of them looking emotional.

The voiceover explained that once Joseph had finished his ser
tence, he married a young Irish woman called Kathleen and foun

work in Sydney where he later started his own business. As time went on, his grandchildren and great-grandchildren continued his work and many of them became important men in the community. Indeed, the Brosnan family became one of the most influential families both in business and politics, as one of Joseph Brosnan's descendants was prime minister of Australia in the 1950s.

'Wow,' Rory mumbled. 'I had no idea.'

'Incredible,' Ella whispered, her hand to her mouth. 'What an amazing story.'

Rory glanced at her. 'You didn't know?'

'Just that Liam is some kind of cousin ten times removed. Which I only found out when he arrived.' Ella looked back at him, her heart beating a little faster. 'The rest is a complete surprise,' she said. 'This time I truly hadn't a clue. Lucille tried to tell me, but I blocked my ears. I've had enough of secrets.'

There was a flicker of a smile in his eyes. 'I'd say you have,' he said before he turned his attention back to the screen.

When the documentary ended and the credits rolled, Martin pointed at the screen. '*Script and research – Lucille Kennedy*,' he exclaimed, turning to his mother. 'Is that you?'

'Indeed it is,' Lucille said with pretend modesty. 'I should have used my maiden name, of course, but I like my married name too much.'

'Mum!' Rory exclaimed, hugging Lucille so tight she groaned and pushed him away. 'Is this the project you've been so busy with all this time? Why on earth didn't you say anything?'

'I didn't want to be distracted,' Lucille said. 'I needed peace and quiet to work on it. I even told Ella a fib.'

'That's right,' Ella said, laughing.

'This is amazing,' Thomas interrupted. 'I'm sure it'll be watche over and over again by all those people whose families were affecte by this.'

'Like mine,' Liam Brosnan said.

'Exactly,' Lucille agreed. 'And it was Liam who got me starte He contacted me about six months ago when he was doing researc into his family tree. My great-great-great – whatever – was Josep Brosnan's brother, you see. Liam was doing some research on tha ancestry site and found my family. He managed to get my ema address through my Facebook profile and then sent me a lon message telling me what he had found. And it was that email tha made me realise that my ancestors came from this very spot. An in a way it was partly why I wanted to stay with Ella right here i this house.'

'How wonderful,' Lydia said. 'You have to develop this into book or something.'

'I'm working on it,' Lucille said. 'But that will be a while befor it's finished.'

'You're going to be famous,' Saskia said. 'How extraordinary.'

The doorbell rang just as everyone gathered around Lucille t congratulate her and ask questions. Ella ran to the door to let i a man with a camera on his shoulder and a young woman with microphone. 'RTE news,' she said. 'We're here to interview Lucill Kennedy and to film all the occupants of this beautiful coastguar station. It's in connection with—'

'We know,' Ella said and held open the door. 'Lucille is insid with the occupants. Do you want to film us inside or outside?'

'Outside,' the woman said. 'We just want a few minutes to show the coastguard station the way it is now.'

It took a while to call everyone to order and get Lydia, Jason, Saskia and Ella to line up outside on the path in front of the row of houses. They were filmed and photographed, and then the RTE team said goodbye and left as the party continued on the terrace. Saskia rushed next door to fetch a big chocolate cake she had made as a surprise and Ella went inside to open the last bottle of champagne.

Rory caught up with her in the kitchen. He took the bottle she had just taken from the fridge and put it on the table. 'Just a moment. I want to say something to you in private.'

'What?' Ella said. 'I thought you weren't talking to me.' She looked at him, trying to decipher his expression. 'I know I should have told you everything,' she said. 'But I just couldn't do that to Lucille. Of course, you'll think differently. So to avoid another fight, I'll just say I'm sorry.'

'No more fighting,' Rory ordered and put his arms around her. 'Now that Mum's problems have been sorted and her big secret has been revealed, I want to say that I know how hard it was for you.'

'You do?' Ella said, suddenly dizzy with joy at his gentle tone and his arms around her.

'Of course I do.' He put his hand under her chin and made her look into his eyes. 'I was angry when I found out you had kept the truth from me. But then, when you walked away, I realised that by being angry I was throwing away something really wonderful. But I was so confused. I needed to think, to sort out my feelings. That night I turned and twisted everything around in my head so many times and always came back to the same conclusion.'

'What conclusion was that?' she whispered, even though h
eyes told her everything.

'I think you know. Could we go back to where we were the oth
night? Before you told me about the house?'

'Okay, Mr Bear,' Ella said, smiling into his dark eyes that were n
longer sad or angry. 'That would be a very happy place to go back to

'The best.' He placed a gentle kiss on her mouth. 'That's fo
being so sweet to my mother. And for being my darling French girl

'Oh,' Ella said, pulling back. 'I have something to tell you. I'r
not French, you see.'

'Of course you aren't,' Rory replied with a laugh. 'I knew tha
But I always thought of you as French.'

'You knew?' Ella asked, astonished at this revelation.

'Yes. Of course I did. You're no more French than I am. But yo
still have a way about you that's so alluring and very French to m
And you have a bit of a French accent sometimes.'

Ella laughed. 'I know. I lived so long in France and was marrie
to a Frenchman that it became second nature. And then, when m
paintings started to sell in France, my agent thought I should stic
with that French image. It was good marketing, he said. I kept m
French husband's name after the divorce as I had been known b
that name. It went so well with the brand I had created as an artist
She drew breath and looked lovingly at him, relieved that it wa
more like an amusing little detail and not a huge deal to him. '
doesn't matter, does it?'

'Of course not.' Rory pulled her close to him. 'I don't care abou
your image or marketing or whatever. You could tell people you'r
from Mars for all I care. I love you for a lot more than that. You

kind heart, your sense of humour, your feisty, independent spirit, your courage and talent and much more.' He stopped and smiled into her eyes.

'You love me?' Ella whispered.

'Yes, I do. All that passion behind our arguments, the amount of times I came to your cottage to spar with you… What else could it have been? God help me.'

Ella stood on tiptoe and kissed him. 'Me too. You, I mean. I tried and tried not to, thinking you'd be bad for me, that the way we were always arguing meant you were wrong for me. But I've come to realise that I couldn't possibly be with anyone who doesn't have strong opinions and who doesn't want to discuss things, even if it ends in a heated argument – even a row. I don't mind a good old fight if it's with someone I love and trust. That's actually quite fun.' She looked at him, realising that she couldn't possibly be with someone who wasn't ready to respond to her ideas, or was afraid to show his feelings. That was healthy and honest but not in the slightest way negative, the way it had been with Jean-Paul, who had shut her out and never wanted to share his true feelings with her. It had taken her a long time to understand this but now she did and it filled her with joy.

'That's very true,' Rory said, nodding in agreement. 'So you trust me?'

'Yes, I do now. And something Lucille said yesterday made me realise that we're very alike, actually.' Ella drew breath and laughed. 'Long speech, but that's how I feel.'

He held her close. 'The best speech I have ever heard.' He let go of her. 'Sorry. I didn't mean to squeeze you so tight.'

Ella closed her eyes and leaned against him. 'No, please squeez
me even tighter. It makes me feel that all the broken pieces insid
me come together and heal.'

'Like this?' he said, hugging her.

'Exactly,' she whispered in his ear.

They sprang apart as the door opened and Mandy entered.

'What are you doing?' she asked, staring at them.

'We're making friends,' Ella said.

'Very good friends, as you can see,' Rory agreed.

'You did it,' Mandy said and pointed at Rory.

'Did what?' Ella asked.

'You tamed the bear!' Mandy exclaimed.

Rory enveloped Ella in his arms again, beaming at Mandy. 'Yes
he said. 'She did.'

Epilogue

A year and two months later, Ella found herself on top of a ladder again. A solid, steady ladder with a solid, steady man holding it at the bottom. Her knees shook as she slowly made her way higher up, a small bucket of paint with a brush hanging from her wrist. She looked down, and felt slightly dizzy for a moment.

'Don't look down,' Rory ordered. 'I have a good grip here.'

'Okay,' Ella called back, her voice shaking. Then she looked up at the design and the cloud and sky that she had nearly finished painting before that horrible fall the year before last. She had felt she needed to go up again to rid herself of the trauma and face her fears. Rory hadn't wanted her to do it, but when he realised how important it was for her, he offered to go with her.

Ella had arrived at the point where she could easily reach the top of the painting. She dipped the brush in the paint and slowly painted the other wing of the seagull and filled in the outline. It was just a matter of a few brush strokes but it was important to do it, otherwise there would only be half a seagull and that would look weird, she had explained. One more sweep of the brush and it was done.

'There,' she called to Rory. 'I've done it.'

'Fantastic,' he called back. 'How do you feel?'

'Happy,' she said, feeling a surge of pride and satisfaction a having finished the mural and managed to go up the ladder despi being frightened to death of falling again. But now as she slow made her way down, she knew the circle was closed and she coul move on. The ladder moved slightly as she reached the last rur and she wobbled and lost her footing.

But Rory caught her in time and held her in his arms, laughin 'Whoops,' he said, squeezing her tight. 'You don't want to do th again, do you?'

Ella closed her eyes and pressed her face into his chest. 'I wor fall now that you're here to catch me.' She looked up at him an smiled. 'You have no idea how good that makes me feel.'

'Me too,' he said and carefully put her down. 'Are you okay?'

'Fine,' she said. 'Except I got some paint on me. Lucky I wa wearing my overalls.' She looked up at the mural and the new painted seagull. 'Finished at last. I thought I'd never manage it.'

'But you did,' Rory declared. 'And so much more besides. He get out of those overalls and go and change. We have a lunch dat remember?'

'Where are you taking me?'

'It's a surprise.'

'But I don't have clothes for a fancy place,' Ella protested. 'I wa going to change into my jeans and shirt in the ladies'. You didn't say..

'Stop complaining,' Rory laughed. 'It's not fancy, just lovely. little roadside café on the way back home.'

'Oh. Good.'

'So go and change and then I'll see if I can get someone to take
way the ladder and the sheet and clean up the paint you spilled.'

'Okay, boss,' Ella said. 'I'll report back in plenty of time for
inch.' She shot him a teasing grin and went to the fancy ladies'
estroom where she had left her clothes before pulling on her overalls.

As she peeled them off, she looked at herself in the large mirror,
hinking about the past year and everything that had happened since
hen. It was like a colourful kaleidoscope in her head as all kinds of
ifferent scenes went through her mind, starting with that evening
hen Lucille's project had been shown on TV and the subsequent
iterviews and newspaper articles. Then Lucille had finished her
ook and had a launch at the library in Sandy Cove to which nearly
veryone in the village had been invited. Then Ella's own children's
ook had been published, which resulted in nearly as much media
overage for Ella and the author, with the cartoon strip appearing
a the *Sunday Independent* every week. It was hard work to produce,
ut Ella soon worked out a schedule that allowed her to also get
ack to painting.

Ella had been surprised at how happy she was to see Thomas
nd Maura start dating. The fleeting attraction she had felt for
homas had turned into a close friendship which included Maura.
lla and Rory even volunteered to mind the three children so they
ould go out to dinner on their own. Those evenings were hectic
nd tiring, but fun. It made her realise that even if she would never
ave her own children, she could still have them around her in this
ay. Mandy had bonded with Ella in a delightful way and that was
omething she would always cherish.

Lucille's new house had taken all winter to finish, but in Ap
she could finally move into the beautifully restored house and sta
the landscaping of the garden. And now, in late summer, she was
organised with a beautiful garden, a henhouse at the back and her d
and cat newly installed. It was lovely to see her so happy, Ella thoug

And then Rory… Ella smiled as she thought of him and ho
he had decided to stay in Sandy Cove and establish himself as
solicitor in a small office just off the main street.

Being his own boss suited him to perfection. And then he ha
moved in with her at Starlight Cottages, which felt so natural
their relationship grew into something she knew would last. The
were surprisingly well-matched and it seemed to Ella that as the
were so alike, they understood each other in a strange way – ev
though both were hot-tempered, they often clashed and had heate
arguments where neither of them wanted to give in.

Despite his stubbornness, Rory wasn't anything like the me
she had lived with before. He had a deep sense of fairness and h
temper tantrums died down as fast as they started. Like a summ
storm, Ella thought. Sometimes their arguments were just for t
sake of it, each trying to win in some kind of virtual wrestling mat
they both enjoyed because of the mental stimulation.

As she brushed her hair and refreshed her lipstick, Ella thought
how different life was for her compared to when she had been stru
gling to recover from her accident. Then, she had been depende
on the kindness of friends and neighbours for practically everythin
But now, more than a year later, she had Rory and Lucille, wh
despite not being relatives by blood, were still a family to her.
family of the heart.

*

n hour later, Rory pulled up at a roadside café on the edge of a cliff
ith glorious views of the ocean. The expanse of blue sky above made
lla feel as if she was hovering in the air as the soft breeze played
ith her hair and cooled her hot cheeks. 'This is an amazing spot.'

'The best views in Ireland.' Rory pulled out a chair at a table near
he low wall at the edge of the terrace. 'I think this is the best table.'

Ella looked around the deserted terrace as she sat down. 'There's
obody here.'

'I hired the whole restaurant so we could be alone.'

'No you didn't,' Ella said, laughing. 'I saw a packed tourist bus
rive away as we arrived.'

'Okay, so we're just lucky,' Rory confessed. 'I'll go in and order.
Vhat would Madam like for her luncheon?'

'If they have any kind of shrimp or crab, that's what I'd like.'

'Great. I think they do crab sandwiches.' Rory disappeared to
lace the order in the café and came back only minutes later with
loaded tray. 'I ordered before we left,' he said.

'But you asked me what I wanted.'

Rory put the tray on the table. 'I knew you love fresh crab, so
took a chance. But, of course, I had to ask you just to make you
el like the independent woman you are. I have learned a few
ings since last year.'

Ella laughed and laid out the plates of crab on soda bread, two
nall glasses of white wine and two cupcakes with pink icing. She
ughed and pointed at them. 'What's this? Looks like a very girly
essert.'

'We had to celebrate with something,' Rory said, still standin
beside her.

'Celebrate what?' Ella asked, intrigued.

Rory didn't reply but went down on one knee beside Ella. 'I wai
to ask you something. I was wondering if you might…'

Dizzy with joy, Ella laughed and threw her arms around hin
'The answer is yes! I do want to marry you. I know I've been marrie
before and it was a complete disaster, but with you, it'll be…'

'What are you talking about?' Rory asked. 'How do you kno
what I was going to ask?'

'You said you wanted to celebrate with two pink cupcakes an
you're down on one knee saying you want to ask me somethir
important. What else could it be?'

'I was tying my shoelace.'

Ella blinked, feeling stupid. 'Oh. God. You must think…'

He took her hand. 'I'm joking. Of course that's what I wante
to ask, sweetheart.'

Ella hit him on the chest with her napkin. 'You eejit. Get u
before I push you over the edge of the cliff.' Her heart soared
Rory got up and sat opposite her, taking her hand and covering
in kisses.

Rory's eyes were full of laughter. 'You said yes. Then I'll die happy

'Stop it.' Ella sighed happily. 'So are we engaged then?'

'Yes, except for one thing. I didn't buy a ring. Didn't dare. V
have to choose it together.'

'Good idea. We can go back to Killarney later and pick on
Would that be okay?' Ella asked, her eyes welling up with happy tea

'Absolutely perfect,' Rory agreed, picking up his knife and fork. 'So let's enjoy this amazing sandwich and then head back to Killarney. And then, my sweet, we're going home to tell everyone. I want the whole world to know that I've won your heart.'

Ella let out a little sob, looking lovingly at him. 'You did that a long time ago.'

She closed her eyes briefly and opened them again, looking at Rory's dear face and the stunning views behind him, knowing she would remember this moment for the rest of her life.

A Letter from Susanne

I want to say a huge thank you for choosing to read *The Lost Secret of Ireland*. If you did enjoy it, and want to keep up to date with all my latest releases, just sign up at the following link. Your email address will never be shared and you can unsubscribe at any time.

www.bookouture.com/susanne-oleary

I love returning to Sandy Cove while I write the stories about the women who are swept away by the beauty of Kerry and the wonderful people who live there, just as I am, time and time again. I often write in our little cottage only minutes from a beautiful beach and feel so blessed to be able to come here and enjoy it all. You can imagine how inspiring it is to gaze over the ocean and to meet friends and neighbours who have been so welcoming ever since we started to spend our holidays here. I think all this spills over into my writing and hope that you, the reader, feel as if you're here in your imagination.

I hope you loved *The Lost Secret of Ireland* and if you did I would be very grateful if you could write a review. I'd love to hear what you think, and it makes such a difference helping new readers to discover one of my books for the first time.

I love hearing from my readers – you can get in touch on my Facebook page, through Twitter, Goodreads or my website.

Thanks,
Susanne

authoroleary

@susl

837027.Susanne_O-Leary

www.susanne-oleary.co.uk

@susanne.olearyauthor

Acknowledgements

Huge thanks as always to my fabulous editor, Jennifer Hunt, ar all at Bookouture! You continue to be the best ever publishers work with.

I also want to thank my friends and neighbours in Kerry for th support and enthusiasm and for reading my books. I hope I ha managed to capture your wonderful county in all its beauty ar fantastic atmosphere.

And many, many thanks to all my readers for the lovely messag and emails you send me. I haven't had time to answer them a so I take this opportunity to tell you how much I appreciate yo getting in touch.

Made in the USA
Columbia, SC
04 February 2023